Praise for Tim Hemlin's first Neil Marshall mystery, *If Wishes Were Horses* . . .

"Tim Hemlin is a welcome new voice in the mystery field."

—EARL EMERSON

"A very promising, quite smart, launch to a new series . . . a Southern-fried tale blessed by an unconventional cast of characters."

—*Publishers Weekly*

"Tim Hemlin is a thoroughbred among mystery authors. This debut novel serves up down-home characters and a delicious, fast-paced plot that readers will want to devour in a single sitting."

—DEBORAH ADAMS

"What a debut! . . . Gourmet cooking and spirited horseflesh combine to make this premier mystery first at the post!"

—*Meritorious Mysteries*

"Tim Hemlin's *If Wishes Were Horses* . . . is one of the most entertaining first mysteries I've read in several years, and aspiring writer Neil Marshall is the most engaging amateur sleuth to come along since Jeff Abbott's Jordan Poteet. This novel is so good I'd like it even if it weren't set in Texas."

—BILL CRIDER

By Tim Hemlin
Published by Ballantine Books:

(in chronological order)
IF WISHES WERE HORSES . . .
A WHISPER OF RAGE
PEOPLE IN GLASS HOUSES

PEOPLE IN GLASS HOUSES

Tim Hemlin

To Don,

Best wishes!

Tim D. Hemlin

10/20/9?

BALLANTINE BOOKS • NEW YORK

Copyright © 1997 by Tim Hemlin

All rights reserved under International and Pan-American Copyright Conventions. Published in the United States by Ballantine Books, a division of Random House, Inc., New York, and simultaneously in Canada by Random House of Canada Limited, Toronto.

http://randomhouse.com

Library of Congress Catalog Card Number: 97-93914

ISBN 0-345-40902-7

Manufactured in the United States of America

First Edition: October 1997

10   9   8   7   6   5   4   3   2   1

To David Hemlin, Nancy Hemlin, and Dale Pinkerton—
with much appreciation for your love and support.

Acknowledgments

Once again a special thanks to my editor, Joe Blades, for his infinite patience and tremendous encouragement. Also, my wife, Valerie, for her editorial help in whipping this book into shape. Many thanks to the Houston Writers' League for their enthusiastic support, and to the Houston Police Department's Citizens' Academy for making their rich resources available. Finally, I'm much obliged to Sergeant C. E. Elliot of the Houston Police Department for enduring my countless questions and for giving me a tour of HPD offices and interrogation rooms.

1

Mattie Johnson's wide-eyed look of terror told me that we were in for more than just a long night of work.

I followed the direction of her gaze and caught the stony visage of the thick-armed guard who stood at the servants' entrance. He was a newcomer around Chip Gunn's antebellum. Usually Cracker or Jimmy, a couple of gold-medal bone crushers, tended the fort.

"Neil Marshall," I said, catching my reflection in his dark glasses. "With Perry Stevens Catering. Mr. Gunn's expecting us."

The rest of the staff waited behind Mattie and me—food, serving pieces, and liquor in hand.

His nod sent Mattie scurrying across the brick-tile kitchen floor like a grasshopper heading for high grass.

"Appreciate it," I said.

"So do I."

Oh God, I thought as little warning bells tangled in the back of my mind, what were we walking into? I stepped by him, noticing we were about the same height, but he had a physique cast of iron and was seasoned a deep ebony.

"Is Mr. Gunn around?" I asked, removed my glasses, and wiped a thin film of sweat off my forehead with a handkerchief. After sundown the heat would slacken. Not cool, by any means, but slacken. The staff began toting in our equipment.

"He'll be down later," the big man said in a gravelly voice. "He said you knew what to do—told me to get you anything you need."

Though he spoke to me, his attention was focused toward Mattie.

"I have everything I need." I hooked my glasses back around my ears.

"Then that makes one of us."

Mattie wasn't the only person spooked by this guy. The vibes in the room were strong enough to electrocute an elephant.

"I've been a patient man," he added, strangely, and closed the kitchen door after the last of our equipment made it inside.

"Excuse me?"

" 'Course, you can't expect it to last. Nobody's perfect." He took a step toward Mattie.

"Except maybe Mr. Gunn," I tossed out, trying to break the tension.

"That man's only good at snapping fingers, and I don't jump to snapping fingers."

So much for tension breaking. We went from the skillet to the fire.

"Then you're in the wrong business." I unpacked my chef's knives on the butcher-block table. "You also don't know Mr. Gunn very well," I added.

"Know him as well as I need to." He folded his arms. "But there's someone else I best soon be acquainted with."

The staff paused, including Mattie, whose eyes had been down since entering the large kitchen.

"Listen, buddy—"

"Name's Lamar. Lamar Fowler."

"Fine, Lamar," I said, and lined my knives up according to length. "I've got work to do. Whatever's going on here—"

"Ain't your business," Lamar stated emphatically.

"When one of my functions is disrupted," I said sternly, "it becomes my business." My racing heart screamed *fool* to my brain. Was I out to get myself killed? And right before payday.

"This is between me and Mattie," he said. "Come on, girl. Let's take it outside."

Mattie's hand flashed to her mouth, and she madly shook her head.

Lamar unwound his arms.

"Your discussion will have to wait," I told him.

He turned his full presence to me.

I stood my ground, hoping the blood he left on my starched white chef's coat would pass as beef-tenderloin stains and not as my own.

Then the dining-room door swung open and in strolled the dapper Chip Gunn and his original muscle, Jimmy, who was even bigger than Lamar.

"Been waiting five years," Lamar whispered to Mattie. "Don't figure five hours will matter none."

"Neil, so good to see you again," Chip Gunn said, extending a hand.

Lamar faded back by the servants' door.

"Thank you, Congressman." I met his grip. We hadn't been in touch with each other since Jason Keys's funeral.

"Not congressman yet," he said, chuckled, and slapped my back.

"After tonight's fund-raiser, you never know," I replied.

"And that is precisely why I requested the most exemplary chef from Houston's most exemplary catering company."

"I wondered why my number came up."

"Yes." The smile on his face was as stiff as his over-sprayed hair. He adjusted the lapel of his maroon smoking jacket. "Yes," he repeated. "Young man, it is imperative this night be resplendent. Is there anything you require?"

"As a matter of fact, Mr. Gunn"—I turned to Lamar—"you can ask Mr. Fowler to leave us to our duties."

The request caught Gunn off guard. Even big Jimmy stirred behind him.

"Take the sunglasses off in the house," Gunn ordered Lamar.

Lamar hesitated, then lifted the shades so they rested on his flattop.

Gunn jerked his head and Lamar left the room, followed by Jimmy. I heard the swish of the door. So much for Lamar's big talk against snapping fingers. The staff's rustling began to pick up. Gunn addressed me in a soft voice. "I don't know what happened, Neil, but watch your step around that one. I'm still not certain I'll retain him."

"I think you need to retrain before you retain," I muttered.

"I beg your pardon?"

"Why'd you take him on?" I asked.

"A favor." A smile reappeared. "I expect a superfluous performance," he announced, and spread his arms around the room.

The trim man came up to my shoulder. I could've patted him on the head. "I'm confident we won't let you down," I responded for us all.

Gunn nodded. Before he left, however, he took my elbow between his forefinger and thumb and led me into the dining room. "Neil," he began, voice low, "I appreciate your confidence about my election to Congress. However, I need to be perfectly clear on a certain point."

"Jason Keys was my best friend," I told him, anticipating the direction of this little conference. "His memory, and all the action that surrounded it, will remain that—a memory."

A practiced deadpan overtook his face as he examined me. Then the smile returned. "Very well," he declared, and went about his business.

This was the strangest beginning to any assignment I'd ever had in all my years at Perry Stevens Catering. I could almost write about this evening and read the truth as fiction at my next creative-writing class at the university.

I took a deep breath. "Let's get busy, people," I called. I talked to Booker Atwell, who was filling in as beverage and floor manager tonight. We coordinated the timing of the hors d'oeuvres, the buffet, and the desserts—chocolate-mousse tortes and fresh raspberries.

The house hadn't changed much since the last time I'd entertained Mr. Chip Gunn. The flavor was classic Southern, the furniture Victorian, the floors wooden, and the ceilings high. A huge oil painting of Gunn, in Napoleonic mode, loomed over the living-room fireplace. From the grand hall, crisp piano notes echoed throughout the chambers.

I tried to talk privately to Mattie, but in the beginning it was impossible. After I conferred with Booker, Dean Shriver approached me. Dean was one of my impoverished writing friends who'd cajoled me into hiring him part-time. He claimed to have waiting experience, but after suggesting he tuck the tail of his tux shirt in, use gold buttons instead of a paper clip to hold his steward's jacket closed, and even to comb his lengthy black hair out of his eyes, I had my doubts. I decided to give him the role of bar back. This job entailed keeping the bartenders in supply of ice, water, mixers, and clean glasses. Thus the boy would be busy, not in direct contact with the guests, and out of sight as much as possible.

"Hey, dude, what do you want me to do?" he asked, standing beside me. A fishing pole cast more of a shadow than Dean did.

I executed my bar-back plan.

"No problem." He perused the huge kitchen with all of its state-of-the-art appliances. "So this is how the conservative materialistic pigs live, huh?"

"Keep Kerouac, Burroughs, and Ginsberg under wraps tonight, my beatnik friend," I told him. Dean was forty years out of step, and both Professor Keely Cohen and I agreed he wrote some strange stuff, but I could forgive him for that. Ten years ago I worshiped the expatriate writers of 1920s Paris and fancied a style that was nothing more than pseudo-Hemingway.

"Loosen your tie, man," Dean assured me. "I'll be as square as Beaver Cleaver."

God help us, I thought as he headed for the bar.

The hour rolled around for the beautiful people to arrive, and on this typically humid, late-summer evening the guests' drone crescendoed until it drowned out the whine of cicadas outside the kitchen window.

Finally, I caught Mattie in between mushroom strudel and the shrimp brochettes. "Rumor has it that Bush might make an appearance," I said. There was really no truth to that rumor, as I was the person who'd made it up. The fact that the ex-president had taken up residence not too far away, though, gave the statement an air of credibility.

Mattie, however, was impressed only to the point of shrugging her narrow shoulders.

"Maybe Barbara will show with her dog," I continued. "You know, the fur ball she wrote that book about."

Another shrug as she dried her hands on a kitchen towel.

"What's the matter with you?" I asked. I spoke low so I wouldn't parade Mattie's business in front of Gunn's Mexican maid, though her grasp of English was, to say the least, limited. The maid, already up to her elbows in soapsuds and dirty dishes, paid little attention to us, anyway.

"Nothing." Even though Mattie had just popped the brochettes into the oven, she flicked on the light, cracked the door, and checked them.

"How do you know Lamar Fowler?" I pushed.

"I don't."

I could barely hear her.

"Mattie—"

A deep voice behind me growled, "She don't want to ever admit she was my woman."

I faced Lamar, feigning coolness at his having surprised me. Muscles rippled even in his face.

"Doesn't look like she does," I agreed.

" 'Cept she's got something that belongs to me, including my only son."

Mattie had a child? I thought. Young Mattie, skittish as a doe at the beginning of hunting season? I opened my mouth but nothing came out.

"Heard you killed a man," he suddenly said.

"What I heard, too," I replied calmly. This could well be one situation when the inaccuracies about my homicide charge came in handy. Gunn must have fed Lamar the information.

"You don't look like the type," he continued. "Even with the scar."

I stroked my blond beard, which partially concealed the long wound from the knife cut. The mark was a result of coming to the aid of private investigator C. J. McDaniels after he'd been shot. The attackers had thought I could identify them.

The *type*? "I'm not," I responded.

Lamar straightened, projecting himself from big to humongous. "I've done time for less."

"For the record, the victim was about to saw me in half with a shotgun."

"Don't matter."

"Did to me. My sight ended where those double barrels began."

"You just been lucky. You ain't tough enough to be dangerous. I've been at the mercy of the world."

I noticed Dean hesitate behind Lamar. Willowy as Dean was, he wasn't much shorter than the big black man.

"I've been knocked down a few times," I said, "and managed to pull myself to my feet. So far."

"My bootstraps broke a long time ago. I don't go down no more."

I understood his twisted logic, and there was some truth to what he said. Lamar was a hard man made harder by the world. And I had been lucky in many instances. I also realized that Lamar's anger was directed more at Mattie, for whatever reason, than toward me—it was simply my luck to be in the line of fire.

"Damn judge won't even let me see Joseph," he said, and glared at Mattie.

"His name's Joey," she said, voice shaking. "He likes J.J."

"My boy."

"You'd probably give the kid nightmares," Dean piped up.

"Watch your mouth or I'll snap you in two like a dried twig."

"I don't scare easy," Dean replied. A crazed look in his eyes made me believe him.

"Definitely a character fault."

"All right," I said quickly. "Back to the bar, Dean."

"I need some water," he stated, and under Lamar's burning stare, he filled his pitchers at the sink.

Suddenly another heavy voice resounded in the kitchen. "Mr. Gunn told you to keep your ass at the front door," big Jimmy asserted.

Mattie jumped and dropped the pan of shrimp brochettes. The Mexican maid fumbled and broke a glass.

Lamar rocked from foot to foot a second, then exited the kitchen. Jimmy set his flat eyes on me.

"Meet the former Mrs. Fowler," I said, pointing at Mattie.

"I was never married to him," the girl declared as she scooped the hot brochettes from the tile.

Jimmy scrutinized both of us as if we were a couple of chickens about to have their necks wrung, then he left.

"Such a stimulating atmosphere," I muttered. "And Candace bitched because I wouldn't let her work this function." Candace Littlefield was my adopted baby sister, and though she didn't live with me, she was to a large degree my responsibility. I was executor of the estate the late Jason Keys had left her—namely the stables. These days I was providing her work at the catering company to help with her first-semester college expenses.

Mattie stood, tears forming at her eyes.

"God, what did this guy do to you?" I asked.

"I ain't worried about what he's done." She dropped the shrimp and pan into the sink—much to the chagrin of the Mexican maid—then lifted her white apron and wiped the now streaming tears.

"Mattie?"

She leaned into me and sobbed.

"Easy, girl, we have a job."

"It's what he'll do," she choked out. "He won't stop until he gets Joey. Or he's dead. Or I am. Maybe all of that."

I noticed that Dean was still hovering, two pitchers of water in hand.

"Get to work!" I snapped.

"Yes, sir, man." And he drifted out.

"Lamar's not going to do anything tonight," I tried to comfort, counting on Jimmy. Crises make strange bedfellows.

The door was pushed open and in glided the short, tidy Booker Atwell. "We need more hors—" On seeing us, he cut himself off.

"Technical difficulties of the old-lover kind," I explained.

Mattie broke from me, wiped her eyes again on the apron, and mumbled, "More shrimp coming up."

Booker's eyebrows furrowed.

"Like the lady said, 'coming up.' " I patted him on the back. "Pray for this party," I added.

"Did you know the mayor was going to be here?" Booker whispered.

"No." An active mayor's almost as good as a retired president, I thought. I wasn't too far off the mark.

"I know it's not like when you cooked for Kissinger or Reagan, but Mayor Taylor ain't exactly chopped liver."

"That explains why Gunn has the extra muscle tonight," I said.

"Doesn't he use Houston cops?"

"Not Gunn. But I reckon a couple of officers will come and go with the mayor." He nodded. I switched gears. "We've got to get this function on track," I said. Claudia, Perry Stevens's official kitchen manager, would be furious at my apparent lack of control. Too much like Perry himself, she'd say.

"Everything's fine out on the floor," Booker stated. He picked a piece of lint off his lapel and flashed me his boyish grin.

"Maybe the anxiety's just back here, then. But you

make sure every waiter has a silver tray and is either passing food, serving drinks, or busing glasses."

"Yes, sir."

"Good beverage man." I gave Booker an encouraging smile and he cruised off.

The evening progressed. Early on, Chip Gunn was introduced by the mayor and proceeded to deliver an inspired speech. Though Gunn was basically a mobster, he was a sophisticated, educated mobster. After his calculated rhetoric, he invited all his friends to enjoy the exquisite buffet. Instead of the conventional beef entrée, we served what animal-rights activists scream about—veal. Rolled with feta cheese and sun-dried tomatoes, sautéed gently in garlic butter, and topped with a creamy rosemary sauce and green capers, the main course was inhumane, perhaps, but delicious. And finally, as I accepted accolades from a number of guests, I began to relax.

It didn't last. I was in the dimly lit dining room checking on the buffet when I noticed a visibly shaken Chip Gunn.

Booker was helping serve drinks, but I grabbed hold of Dean as he headed for the kitchen with a trayful of dirty dishes.

"Any idea what's going on?" I asked, nodding at Gunn.

"None."

"The mayor seems happy. The food is perfect, service good. Maybe he's not getting the money he expected."

"Well," Dean said slowly, "I suppose you'll hear anyway. Mr. Gunn asked me how things were going, and I told him straight out they'd be fine if he wasn't running for Congress. I said that people didn't need another fascist in the government."

My hand slowly cupped my forehead as my demeanor sank. Helping friends, old or new, was dangerous. "Get back to the bar and stay there," I ordered. Gunn would chew my ass later. Or have his thugs pound Dean's.

After consideration, though, I realized Dean's comments wouldn't shake up Chip Gunn, only piss him off. Then Lamar entered the scene, and I watched as Gunn had the big thug escort a short, bald man through the house and into the kitchen.

Dessert, in all its chocolate decadence, was placed on the mahogany buffet table. I quickly instructed the serving procedure to a couple of the waitresses, then made for the kitchen myself.

"Did your favorite ex march through here?" I asked.

"With some old, fat guy," Mattie said. "Didn't give me a second look."

"How strange."

"Mind if I take a cigarette break?" she asked.

"You smoke? I'm sorry—I mean, no, I don't mind." Damn, I'd learned more about Mattie in the last few hours than in the past eight months, which was about as long as I'd been off cigarettes.

Booker poked his head in the kitchen. "The mayor's leaving," he explained.

"Is Gunn still upset?"

"Upset? When was he upset?"

"Never mind," I said, and waved him off. "I'll explain later."

Mattie slipped out the kitchen door to the side of the house. I felt a twinge at my heart. Not long ago I snuck a similar break, and it was the last time I saw Jason Keys alive.

I released a heavy sigh and followed Booker onto the floor, my stomach twisting like a pigeon-toed bronc. All the pretty people fawned over the lanky old mayor and his classy wife. Mozart was suddenly switched to "Hail to the Chief," which drew laughs, whistles, and cheers. The mayor flashed his toothy smile, gestured at Gunn, then waved as if he were about to board *Air Force One* before disappearing into the night. I noticed that Jimmy minded the front door and the stoic Cracker hung near Gunn. I had no idea where Lamar Fowler was.

That pigeon-toed bronc spun from stomach to the nape of my neck and chilled its way down my spine. I eased out of the foyer and into the dining room. Dean bumped my shoulder. He was sweaty and disheveled.

"Christ, the bartenders are working your ass," I mumbled.

He flashed me the thumbs-up sign and was about to speak when we heard the scream. It came from the kitchen.

I hit the swinging door first. Gunn's maid was nowhere in sight. Mattie stood alone, by the back door, my chef's knife in her hand. The blade was covered in blood.

"He's dead!" she cried. "Lord Almighty, he's dead."

"Mattie, what?" I bolted to her.

"Lamar. He's lying by the bushes near the catering van." She sank to her knees. I knelt down and carefully relieved her of the knife that, even in my line of my work, had never been so crimson.

"Put this on the counter," I told Dean, handing the razor-sharp instrument to him with two fingers. He clumsily grabbed the hilt and set it on the butcher-block table.

Then I ran outside, followed by my young beatnik friend.

But the brick driveway on the side of the house was empty. Empty of everything except the white van and a bright maroon trail of blood.

Mattie staggered at the door. "He was there," she garbled.

I jogged the course of blood, which wound down the drive and into the street. There the macabre drops vanished. I glanced at Dean, who was puffing beside me.

"Man," Dean said, "what the hell's going on?"

"I've got a better question. Where the hell is Lamar Fowler?"

2

When I turned, I came face-to-face with Cracker. He was a tidy mass of curly black hair fitted suavely in his dark blue Cardin suit, but he wasn't a big man, or even muscular. What he lacked physically, though, he made up for in meanness.

"What the hell's going on, Marshall?" he demanded.

"Someone took his aggressions out on Lamar with my chef's knife," I replied. "And then took Lamar."

"Cut the shit."

"Cut the shit," I repeated. "Poor choice of words, Cracker." I ran a hand through my hair that was longer than it'd been in years. I couldn't tell if the moisture between my fingers was from the heat of the night or good old-fashioned nerves.

Cracker set one of his compact arms against my shoulder and gave me a solid shove toward the house. "Come on. We ain't going to stand here and attract a crowd."

My temper flared, but I bit it back. "A simple 'let's go inside' would do."

"Shut up or I'll slice your balls off and cram them down your throat."

"Is everyone knife-happy tonight?" I asked, and glanced at Dean. The radical brashness had ebbed. He stood trembling beside me. And then he heaved.

"Jesus Christ!" Cracker snapped. "What's his problem?"

"Just another sensitive poet," I replied.

"Well, haul his sensitive ass around back so the money people don't see him barf."

13

Dean straightened himself. "No, I'm okay." He ran a hand across his forehead, a sleeve over his mouth.

"Let's go talk to the boss," Cracker stated. His voice put a chill in the humid air.

"He'll have all the answers," I said.

"Shut up."

"Never have forgotten my knocking you on your ass last year, have you, Cracker?"

"Or forgiven," he said.

Dean and I walked up the brick driveway as if Cracker had a gun to our backs. His hands were empty, but the sensation was as real as the traces of blood on the ground. Here and there a few guests were leaving, but they paid no mind to us. Nor did it appear that Mattie's scream had created any uproar. Perhaps her cry had seemed loud to me because I was only a swinging door away. Or perhaps rich folks were used to ignoring cries for help. Now, Neil, I scolded myself, can the cynicism.

When we reached the hard light of the kitchen, we found Mattie sitting on a stool near the butcher-block table, trying hard to swallow back her quiet sobs. Standing at the sink was Chip Gunn. They were the only ones in the kitchen. Gunn had the water on so hot that steam billowed into the air-conditioned room like chaotic smoke signals. And, using a long-handled brush, he was scrubbing the blood off my chef's knife.

Cracker closed the door behind us as we entered the Twilight Zone.

"Mr. Marshall," Gunn said through clenched teeth, "this is not my idea of resplendent."

"What are you doing?" I asked, even though his actions were quite obvious. My question simply sprang from the realm of disbelief.

"My campaign can ill afford the negative publicity this domestic squabble might raise."

"A man's been murdered," I said.

"How do you know that?" Gunn retorted, whacking my knife against the side of the sink. "Show me the body."

"Mattie said—"

"She doesn't know if she killed Lamar or not."

"I didn't cut anybody," Mattie said, barely audible.

"What do you want me to do, boss?" Cracker asked.

Gunn rinsed the stainless-steel blade, then held it up to the light and examined it. Satisfied, he placed the knife in the dishwasher.

"First," Gunn ordered his man, "mind the front door. Jimmy's keeping vigil outside the kitchen to make certain no one enters. Thank God the mayor and his officers are gone. If anyone inquires about the scream, say that a large tree roach flew in through the open door and startled the girl. I'd prefer people to think I have a problem with tree roaches in the kitchen than bodies in the closets."

"Yes, sir."

"And Cracker. After everyone leaves I want you and Jimmy to wash down the driveway. Then find what's left of Lamar."

Cracker gave a short nod and left.

Gunn picked up a piece of steel wool and scoured the butcher block where the knife had rested, then he sopped up a couple of spots on the floor.

"I don't believe this," I said. Dean's mouth hung open, too.

"I didn't cut anyone," Mattie repeated. "Lamar was just lying there, blood on his clothes, on the ground, on the knife."

"My dear," Gunn stated, "I really don't give a rat's ass if you and your man carve each other up for Thanksgiving. However, such intimate pleasures should be restricted to one's own home."

"Jesus, Chip, you're an asshole," I blurted.

"Don't push me, Neil."

"What's to keep Lamar, saying he's even alive—"

"Oh, I'm positive he's alive," Gunn broke in.

"Then you must know more than you're letting on. Come to think of it, Cracker was at the end of the driveway pretty damn quick. And what about that man Lamar escorted out the kitchen door?"

"Mr. Marshall, I strongly advise you to control your imagination. This incident was a domestic altercation pure and simple. It just should never have happened on these premises."

"Wouldn't Mattie have blood on her if she was, in fact, the one who committed the atrocity?" I asked straightforwardly. Gunn understood, and was sometimes receptive to, grace under pressure.

"Not necessarily. But I assure you, we shall locate Mr. Lamar Fowler and clear this up."

"What's to clear up? The man was knifed. Fatally, for all I know. And as I started to say, what's to keep him from going to the police? Or a hospital? Even a doctor is obliged to contact the authorities."

"I can guarantee that Lamar would not take that chance," Gunn replied.

"Priorities appear mighty different when you're on death's bed."

"How philosophical." Gunn put his suit coat back on, then walked over to Mattie. "Young lady, you should be grateful. Had I been forced to summon the police, you would've found yourself in an inordinate amount of trouble."

"What a guy," I quipped. "You've got my vote."

Gunn grinned broadly. In the lapse of conversation, the refrigeration units kicked on, adding an eerie hum to the eerie silence. I met Gunn's stare.

Finally he spoke. "I never doubted I had your vote, Mr. Marshall. After all, you are an acquitted killer yourself." He turned to Dean Shriver. "Now, what was that remark you made about America not needing another fascist in the government?"

Dean shrugged weakly. I read his gesture as an attempt to cop a so-what attitude. Instead he was more like a dog cowering beneath a raised hand.

"I thought so. You look vaguely familiar. What's your name?"

"Dean Shriver."

"Shriver? Yes. Any relation to MacArthur Shriver?"

"He was my father."

Gunn's eyes narrowed. I followed his gaze at Dean's long, dark hair, scruffy goatee, and angular features.

"Of course," Gunn said. "Following in the old man's footsteps, I see. Well, Mac was a decent man. He supplied a quality crop, but the poor creature didn't have a lick of business sense."

"He didn't have much of a chance," Dean stated.

"We all create our own destiny, boy. Your father was no different."

"Destiny is a fool's belief."

The tension was so thick I believed I could pare slivers of it off the air.

"Have a long talk with Mr. Marshall, Mr. Shriver," Gunn told him. "Refresh your memory concerning my methods. If you have any questions, Mr. Marshall is quite capable of providing answers. Now, let's bring this function to a close. My coffers are overflowing, and despite this unsavory incident, the evening has been successful. Thank you one and all." He patted Mattie on the cheek, then lifted her chin so their eyes met. "It's always the young, pretty ones who take up with the biggest jerks." He half smiled, then marched out of the room.

For a moment we were left with the swooshing noise of the door. Then I turned to Dean.

"You know Chip Gunn?" I asked.

"I saw him a few times when I was a kid, that's all."

"This is incredible. What kind of business did your father have?"

"Produce."

"Produce!" I responded. "Fresh produce? That doesn't sound like Gunn's style." Although, I thought, when I first met Gunn he was into horses.

"Guess every capitalist pig has to start somewhere," Dean replied.

"Oh, stuff the radical rhetoric."

"Mostly, though, my dad dealt with his brother," Dean added.

"Gunn has a brother?" I asked.

"Yeah, man. You notice the short, chubby, bald dude Lamar walked out the back door?"

"That was Gunn's brother?"

"It's been a while since I last saw him, but I'm pretty sure," he replied.

I shook my head. "Jesus Christ, what else could happen?"

"That son of a bitch could be elected to Congress."

"Distinct possibility," I said, "and he wants it bad. So listen to his not-so-veiled threats carefully. Charity is not a plank on his platform."

"I'll listen to whoever I want," Dean said, and started to leave.

I grabbed his shoulder and turned him around. "The man has too many smoking guns—"

"Funny."

Pun unintended, and I was growing frustrated. "Man, you know what I mean. You're into karma. It'll come around to get him."

"And maybe I'm supposed to be part of that process."

"Dean—"

"And how can you stand there after this man has decided to cover up a crime, maybe a murder—"

"That I would be accused of," Mattie spoke up. She stood.

"Shit, you didn't knife that man," Dean said. "We know that. Right, Neil?"

He was right. I didn't believe Mattie had attacked Lamar, but a nagging little voice told me not to hasten to judgment.

"Let's say the jury's still out," I said as I caught Mattie's eye and forced a smile. She began sobbing again and darted out the kitchen door.

"That was a shitty thing to do," Dean snapped.

"Yes, it was. But I'd be fooling myself not to think anything's possible."

Dean shook and his face turned red. For a minute I thought he might take a poke at me.

Booker entered the room. Dean swung around, faced him a moment, then stormed out.

"Keep your eye on him," I told Booker.

"The party's history."

"Organize the breakdown," I said. "I've got something that needs tending."

"What the hell is going on?"

"Not now."

"This is one trippy catering company," Booker commented, and almost collided with the incoming wait staff and their dirty glasses and plates.

The maid reappeared, confused and quivering. How much had she seen? I wondered. I stepped out into the hot night, searching for Mattie.

The young woman was by the van in an uncontrollable crying fit. I kept my distance, leaned against the front bumper. And waited. Now, instead of the guests, the cicadas serenaded us with their high trill. This was their death call, attracting mates to propagate the species.

When Mattie finally slowed, I grabbed the opportunity to talk.

"I don't believe you had anything to do with whatever happened to Lamar," I said. "I'm sorry. But if Dean goes off half-cocked, he's going to run straight into Chip Gunn's so-called political machine. And that mechanism will chew him up and spit him out like he's compost under a mulcher."

"It's not right."

"No, it's not. But what if we call the police? And I know a damn good lieutenant who's dying to get the rap on Gunn. But Mattie, there's no body, no weapon, and soon, no evidence on the driveway. Not to mention the prime suspect would be . . ." My voice trailed off.

"Me," Mattie finished. "You can say it. You're protecting me as much as anything."

"I am." I moved closer. "You've got to believe that Gunn will get his due sooner or later."

"You think Gunn's behind the knifing?" She was steadying herself. I pulled out a handkerchief and handed it to her.

"At his own fund-raiser?" I asked. "Even Gunn wouldn't take a chance like that. I believe he's guilty of covering up what happened. But I'd like to hear what Gunn's brother knows."

"You think Mr. Gunn is covering for his brother?" she asked.

"Why attack Lamar? It doesn't make sense. But what from this night does make sense?"

"Maybe someone was trying to kidnap him," Mattie said.

"Lamar was attacked with my knife. Whatever happened originated from inside this house."

"So what do I do?" she asked.

"Be patient," I told her. "Pick up Joseph—"

"Joey," Mattie corrected. "Only his . . . father . . . calls him Joseph."

"Okay. Easy, now. Pick up Joey and stay with a relative or friend. Don't hang around your apartment."

"My sister . . . moved . . . to Dallas, and Lamar . . . knows my friends."

"All of them?"

"Except you."

"Well . . ." I said, my surprise evident in my hesitation. After a few seconds I continued: "I have a small place, but you're quite welcome." And then I recalled Mama, family friend of C. J. McDaniels. She was a wonderful lady who tended me after I'd been attacked by two knife-wielding thugs. She would take in Mattie for a while. Mattie and her son could stay with me a couple of days, until she calmed down; then, if need be, I'd drive her out to Mama's.

The door opened and our merry group began to reload

the van. Mattie shot up, caught my eye. "Thanks," she said warmly, then headed into the kitchen to help. I didn't.

Instead, I stood in the shadows of the house. A thin film of sweat covered me. I noticed Cracker close by, smoking a cigarette, waiting for us to vacate the kitchen so he and Jimmy could erase the last bit of evidence that any trouble had seeped under the feet of candidate Gunn.

Oh, the American way.

I wanted a smoke.

Or a drink.

And a peaceful night's sleep that once again would be out of my reach.

3

"Wow, this place is real small," Joey Johnson said as I flicked on the switch for the standing lamp. We entered my apartment, and I locked the door behind us.

"Hush, J.J.," Mattie told her son.

"He's right," I replied. "Two rooms, a kitchenette, and a bath isn't a castle. But it keeps me humble."

Mattie rolled her eyes and tried to laugh, but there was a shiver that streaked her narrow shoulders.

"God, I can't believe I still have this thing on," she said softly as she removed her white apron. Though I'd encouraged Mattie to change at her apartment, in her haste she'd refused. We both still wore our black-and-whites from the catering job.

"You go by J.J.?" I asked the boy. He was a muscular, curly-haired character who reached a head above my knees. "How many names do you have?"

"Joey Johnson's a dumb name, but J.J.'s tight."

"Tight, huh? How old are you?"

"Five."

"Going on twenty-five," Mattie added. She flashed a warm, albeit nervous smile, and ran a hand through her long black hair.

My eyebrows furrowed. "It's none of my business, but how old are *you*?" I asked.

"Twenty-three. I had J.J. when I was eighteen."

"I didn't figure you were much over nineteen," I said, and opened the door to my bedroom.

"Most people don't, and that's just fine with me,"

22

Mattie replied. "I may have a five-year-old baby, but I'm still young and I'm going to be young for a long time."

"No doubt." I began rearranging piles of laundry. "I don't think there's anything growing in here, so you two can have my room. I'll take the couch."

"No, Neil—"

"Please, I prefer it. I usually stay up late writing or studying. J.J. will have an easier time sleeping, and I won't feel like I'm bothering y'all." I looked at the little big man. "I even have a television," I added. "Small, of course."

"It's too late tonight," Mattie spoke up. She opened an overnight bag and pulled out some bedclothes for J.J.

"Holler if you need anything," I said. As I closed the bedroom door I heard the boy tell his mother, "I like your new boyfriend. He's nice."

"J.J., Neil's not my boyfriend. He's just a friend."

"Then why we staying here?"

"He's helping me with a problem."

"Well, he's still nice."

I quietly closed the door. Good judge of character, I thought, and I checked the messages on my answering machine.

Candace Littlefield announced that she was entered in a barrel race at the end of the month and told me to write the date in big letters on my calendar. Linda Garcia's message was of longer duration because it took a while for her to get to the point; essentially she wondered if she and I could get together for a drink sometime. (Linda was PI C. J. McDaniels's daughter and formerly an intimate of mine. We'd met shortly after my divorce, sent rockets red glaring, then fizzled. Still, the friend part of our relationship remained.)

The final message was from Dean. He left word that he had to talk to me in the morning. His voice, a half octave higher than usual, reawakened the turmoil of the evening.

I glanced at the clock. One-eleven. Hell, I wasn't going to wait until morning. I found my address book on the kitchen counter beneath an empty Taco Bell bag. Before calling, I made myself a light margarita on the rocks, in a beer mug, with lime and salt.

Dean's answering machine picked up on the first ring. "Talk to me, Ginsberg. Why'd you call? Dean, get your lazy butt out of bed—"

There was a clattering, a squeal, and then his voice. "Dude, I said I'd rap with you when the sun mooned us from the horizon."

"You been smoking cheap pot again?"

"A man's got to do what a man's got to do."

"What's going on in that weed-infested brain of yours?" I asked.

" 'Morning, dude."

"It's morning enough."

"No, man, I mean that as a salutation. Morning's a state of mind. And in the state I'm in, this is all the morning I'll be seeing till the day after tomorrow." And he hung up.

Act stupid, I thought as I replaced the receiver and gulped my drink. I didn't care. Though I knew Dean fairly well. Once he came down from that high mountain, whatever grandiose scheme he'd concocted would be nothing more than a whisper of smoke.

From my compact-disc player Jerry Jeff Walker groaned about the virtues of sangria. The volume of the music was only a hair above a whisper, and still the Texan's coarse voice squeezed the night's silence into a little ball.

I sipped my drink and wandered to the small window that looked down on the driveway. Mattie's car was snug to the garage door below me. My old VW Bug was behind it. Both vehicles were screened by the house where my landlord, Jerry Jacoma, lived. Anyone searching for Mattie would have to know exactly where my apartment was and that the driveway wound behind the house. Apparently, all was well.

The drink was soon history, and I pulled a grungy shade down to the windowsill. Of course, someone would have to stand on Jerry's porch roof and use binoculars to have half a chance of seeing inside my apartment.

I resisted another drink, rinsed out the mug, and set it in the freezer. With a couple of tricky jerks, I opened the old cedar dresser I'd inherited from Jason Keys and pulled out a quilt my grandmother had made. Using another blanket as a pillow, I curled up on the couch and lay in the darkness for a good hour.

I would've gone for a run if I hadn't been afraid of leaving Mattie and her kid alone. Instead, I checked the .38 on the coffee table. With a kid around, I realized I didn't want to leave a gun there, so I slipped it under the couch.

In the morning I'd tuck the .38 into the cedar chest with the quilt. I had a .45 stashed in the kitchen and determined to put the handgun in the chest, also. Had I brought the 30-30 from the stables, Jason's old place and now Candace's haven, I'd have possessed a regular arsenal. I could defend this little apartment like Travis held the Alamo. Now, was that being a good Texan, or the result of high anxiety?

I closed my eyes. Spirits were on the warpath tonight. Particularly one. Chip Gunn hovered like the devil trying to possess my vote as if it were my soul. In his hand was the chef's knife. Mattie cowered in a corner. Dean lay across the butcher-block table, high as a kite. I felt Lamar was near, but I couldn't see him. Only Jimmy and Cracker grinning, tipping their hats, overcoats hiding their sawed-off shotguns. Then Booker popped in, asking for more hors d'oeuvres. "Neil," he said, "Neil! Wake up, Neil, I'm hungry. Neil—"

My eyes sprang open. Someone shook me. Morning light creased the apartment with its inviting beckon. And staring me in the face was Joey Johnson.

"I'm hungry, Neil." He crawled on top of me.

"Can I have some of your energy to keep my eyelids open?" I mumbled.

"You got some Sugar Pops?"

"What time is it?"

"I don't know."

"Go look at the numbers on the stove clock."

He wriggled down and ran into the kitchen.

"Seven, two, three," he called.

My eyes burned. "How old are you again?"

"Five," he answered proudly.

"Want to live to be six?" I muttered.

He didn't hear me. "You got some Sugar Pops, Neil?" he repeated.

"J.J., just what in God's name are you doing?" Mattie asked from the doorway. "You get in here and leave Neil alone."

"No, no," I said. "I think I woke him up. I was dreaming about Sugar Pops." I swung my legs over the couch and ran my hands through my hair. "Think I'll go for a run, then buy a box of those culinary morsels on my way back."

"Neil, I'm sorry."

"Don't be ridiculous. Hey, kid," I called. "See if I have any milk in the fridge. Oh, no wait! Don't check. Last time I had milk here was before the divorce. If there is a carton of cow juice, it'll pull you in with it. I'll pick up a half gallon with the cereal."

"Neil, you don't have to—" Mattie began.

"I said I had a hankering for Sugar Pops. Now if you'll slip back into the other room and allow me to change into my sweats, I'll be on my way." I tossed aside the quilt and put the guns away with the comforter.

Mattie hesitated. "Are all white guys like you?"

"Only the nice ones. With scars."

She corralled J.J. and closed the door.

I was out into the bright morning in my sweat shorts and Rockets tank top without another word. These days I stuck to the neighborhood and avoided Allen Parkway. It was at that wonderful jogging path by the bayou that I came across a gunned-down C. J. McDaniels. This near-fatal crime led to my meeting Linda Garcia. With such an inauspicious beginning, it was no wonder Linda and I didn't last.

Within half a minute I was drenched in sweat. Actually, it felt good. The air was thick, as was my groggy mind, but with exertion the evils from the night before began to lose their strength. In about a mile, and a healthy stretch of the legs, I was awake. I decided to jog three miles and plotted my return route so I could pick up J.J.'s sustenance at a nearby market. It was probably a good thing he'd awakened me. As late as it was when I'd fallen asleep, and not thinking to set an alarm out in the living room, I'd have dozed past my writing class, taught by Keely Cohen. And I really needed to talk to her about last night.

By the time I reached the market, I'd had enough of this aerobics crap. I purchased the breakfast essentials and walked the last stretch to my apartment, wishing I still smoked—I was a smoker on hiatus and only jogged to curb the sensation. I approached my humble abode carefully. No sign of any problem. Jerry Jacoma's truck was gone. He worked as a technical writer for one of the big oil companies—I could never remember if it was the corporation that spilled all that oil in the Alaskan waters or if it was the one that was screwing up off the coast of South America.

I hiked up the narrow stairs and unlocked my door. J.J. immediately jumped and pointed to the paper bag I held.

"Go get a bowl, sport," I said, shaking the cereal at him. "I know I have clean bowls at least."

I glanced at the couch and noticed that Mattie had folded the quilt and blanket. She'd also sorted my laundry into appropriate piles. I appreciated the effort, but began to feel uncomfortable.

In the kitchen, I poured the big little guy a bowl of Pops, then doused it with milk. Mattie appeared at the entrance.

"Take it into the bedroom and watch cartoons or whatever it is you watch at this ungodly hour," I said.

"Neil, it's almost nine," Mattie said.

"Go on," I told the boy.

He peered at his mother for approval.

"If Neil says it's okay, then I guess you can," she called after him. "This time."

Not too much milk sloshed to the floor.

"I know it's almost nine," I told Mattie. "I don't have to be in to work until this afternoon. I have a class this morning."

"You're a sweet man," she said.

I cleared my throat. "Thank you," I said. "Think I'll put the coffee on." I stepped to my small Braun coffee-maker and discovered a full pot.

"You'll make somebody a good wife someday," I said, and filled a Houston Rockets mug.

I signaled to Mattie with the pot; she nodded, and I topped off her cup.

"I take my coffee black, but there's fresh milk, if you like," I said. "Don't know if I have any sugar, though." I yanked open a couple of drawers, looking for a misbegotten McDonald's packet I might have saved.

"I already tried to be a good wife," she replied, and sat at the kitchen table.

"Just a minute. Here's some Sweet'n Low." I flashed the pink packet. Then I registered what she'd said.

"Thanks." Mattie accepted the sweetener and stirred the contents into her cup. She crossed her arms and drew her white bathrobe in tight.

"I thought you said the two of you were never married. I mean, J.J. doesn't even go by his father's last name."

"Lamar acted like we were and, for a while, I went along. But when I quit him I wanted to put Joey as far from that man as I could."

I sat across from her. "I'm not the best person to talk to about relationships. I made a mess of my marriage. As if that wasn't bad enough, I jumped immediately into another affair, got scared, and jumped right back out." I stopped there, with reference to Linda Garcia. It was no small wonder, I thought, that I was attracted to Keely Cohen—lovely, intelligent, and safely married.

"I'm not looking to discuss relationships."

Good, I told myself. I didn't like to dig into anyone's business I didn't have to—too many sordid details.

"But I'll say this," she continued. "After I got pregnant, I tried hard to make Lamar happy."

Her insistence was once again proof that I didn't have to dig—people naturally unburdened themselves to me. I looked at it philosophically. God had to have a sense of humor to bless anyone short of a priest with this talent. I listened.

"He was just impossible to live with," Mattie said. "Lamar wanted his family and his fun, too. Finally, I couldn't take it. I ran away."

I noticed the time and realized I needed to hit the road. Being late to anything ran against my nature, especially a class I loved. Mattie, however, wasn't finished.

"Of course Lamar wouldn't have no woman of his running off," she said, and absently stirred her coffee. "And he would've found me long ago if he hadn't had a run-in with the law. Seems he was posing as a repo man when he was really stealing cars."

"Probably pilfering them for Chip Gunn," I muttered.

"What?"

"There is a certain risk in that line of work."

"Risk, huh! Lamar was incarcerated."

"And you were free."

Mattie nodded. "Now he's back."

"Is he?"

"I hope Lamar's dead," she suddenly spat. "Lord forgive me, but I hope he's dead."

The vehement outburst caught me off guard. Her tone had been reflective and confessional until this deep-seated anger surfaced with all the subtlety of a triggered land mine.

"I'm afraid to think it," Mattie added. "Not because I'll go to hell, but because I'm afraid it's not true. In my heart I know Lamar is alive. I can feel him out there. Sooner or later he'll show up, and you'll bear his fury. Me and J.J. got to leave." She began to rise. What was going on? I wondered. I touched her shoulder and eased her down.

"Let's think this out. You came over last night because of Lamar. Unless something's happened I don't know about, then he may still be around, meaning you and J.J. remain in potential danger. Now, I suggest you hold off on any impetuous action."

"Maybe I do have a friend I can go to," she said.

"I may have a better friend," I said quietly. "Her name's Mama. She's family to a private investigator I know. I recuperated at her house after I received this scar." I stroked my beard.

"Listen," I continued when Mattie failed to say anything, "I know you have J.J. foremost in your mind. Keep your situation in perspective, too. I can help, and I'm not afraid to help."

"You don't understand Lamar."

"Don't underestimate me."

My coffee had cooled to the point of it not being very good, but at the moment I didn't want to leave Mattie. So we sat in silence, the sound of cartoons emanating from my bedroom. What eventually broke the trance was the phone ringing.

I jumped up.

"Hey, dude," the voice howled.

"Dean?"

"Told you I'd call once morning wore a respectable face."

"What's up?" I asked nervously.

"Those Gunn brothers ain't going to run the show forever."

"Dean?"

"I'm going to the press," he told me. "I'm going to spill my guts, and Chip Gunn ain't going to be elected dogcatcher."

"Dean, there's no evidence at Gunn's house. Not now."

"I can cause a lot of problems, man."

"So can they. Take it from experience. We can land those fish another way."

"My turn, dude."

"Why you telling me this?" I asked.

"Should my bludgeoned body appear in the bayou, you'll know the story."

"What story?"

"After I sing to the media, I'm going into hiding," he said, and hung up.

The sound of a dial tone, I thought.

Hell waiting to connect.

4

After a quick shower and change of clothes, I packed my notebook and copies of my latest poem, then chugged off to class in my old VW. Dean's words injected a near overdose of fear into my veins, though I'd played it down to Mattie. The last thing she needed this morning was to worry about a myopic radical carrying her case to the public.

On the positive side, I gathered that Dean had a romantic image of justice—the underground underdog fighting for truth then "going into hiding," as he'd said. His actions, though, also smacked of ego. As the avenger, Dean not only righted wrongs; he gloried in the attention he received as well. Maybe he wasn't diving naively into the fray, after all. Maybe Dean was grooming an image. Instead of being a political phoenix within the system, he was revving his engine in a renegade fashion. I shook my head. God, I made him sound like a tenth-rate actor plunging into a low-budget remake of *Easy Rider*. Of course, any publicity would certainly provide a nice jump start to his literary career.

There you go again, Neil, I chided. The rising cynic. Perhaps. But there was one thing I was well aware of— Chip Gunn would be quite displeased.

And the rub was that he'd accuse me of being a party to whatever trick Dean pulled.

Cruising through town, I questioned who in the world would listen to Dean. The way the young poet acted, he'd surely be dismissed as a flake. There was no evidence to back him up. And with his hipster's cadenced vocabulary, credibility wouldn't be his strong point to begin with. Still, he was walking—no, prancing—in some sort of righteous style across a bed of hot coals. I put a hand on my stomach, swallowed hard, and kept my eyes on the road ahead.

What to do? Chip Gunn's antics couldn't go unnoticed. Confronting him on Dean's level, though, wasn't the way. That was how George McMichael, the arrogant motorcycle-driving son of a bitch, met his end. He'd been a hothead who'd pushed the wrong buttons—in this case it had been an associate of Gunn's—and ended up floating facedown in the bayou. People like Gunn had to be outfoxed, not outmuscled.

However, that didn't mean running to the police. The dignified Lieutenant Paul Gardner at HPD was itching to get his hands on Chip Gunn, but he'd need more to go on than the words of a Kerouac wannabe and an acquitted killer. I'd bet the ranch that the third witness, Mattie Johnson, wouldn't talk as long as her crazed ex-boyfriend was unaccounted for.

As usual, I was in limbo. And I knew this was one situation that wasn't going to fade away.

By sheer luck, I found a parking place in the student lot not too far from the English building. The day was muggy and bright, the sky blue as a damp denim shirt, and the walkways were bustling with activity. The academic year had just begun. Freshmen looked younger than ever. I had more than ten years on the entering class, and with my scarred face and beard I looked as if I'd been ridden hard and put up wet. And that was precisely how I felt.

In Texas there were no colorful leaves to anticipate. The big live oaks lined the campus and were green with humidity. And when the change came, they would simply turn brown and stark as old telephone poles.

Pines were predominant, though, keeping a camouflage green hugging the landscape year-round. The fountains spewed like zealous whales. My pace picked up as I thought of meeting with Keely Cohen.

I hit the classroom door a couple minutes after Keely had distributed the weekly package of student poems to be critiqued.

"Late again," I announced. "Sorry."

Keely flashed a wink and gave me the poems.

We met downstairs in a room full of light and sat around a large conference table. It was nice to have a seat that wasn't bolted to the floor, as were the desks in many of the other rooms. A chill from the murmuring air conditioner—a retarded unit that only had two options, cold and off—forced most of us to wear sweaters or long-sleeved shirts. It didn't matter the temperature was ninety degrees outside. After setting down my notebook, I slipped on the dark-patterned brush popper that I'd been carrying. Though a contrast of styles, the Western shirt matched my navy Tommy Hilfiger quite well.

Eleven of us were present, the obvious absentee being Dean Shriver. I sat next to Sondra Anderson, my old friend and the unofficial foster parent of Candace. After the death of Candace's grandfather, Sondra and her husband, John, volunteered to let the girl stay with them, a gesture for which I would be forever grateful.

She patted my hand, then whispered in her Virginian lilt, "I need a few minutes of your time after class."

I hesitated, tilted my head back, and sneezed. Damn chalk, I thought. Whoever used this room before us was obsessed with the stuff. A small dusting attacked my nose, and I swore I could taste the chalk, too. "Is Candace okay?" I finally managed to ask.

She nodded, put a finger to her lips.

Keely cleared her throat. "Neil, since you seem to be in a talkative mood, why don't you go first."

I smirked. "Thanks." I shuffled through the papers until I found the short unrhymed sonnet I'd turned in a week earlier. It was a love poem. I read the words clearly, and slowly, knowing it was sensual but with any personal message buried beneath a touch of melodrama. The poem ended:

> With church bells sounding
> like the chimes of an ice-cream man,
> and my hand cupping the small of your back,
> we lay in thick, melancholy light.
> Night is over. Still
> speak to me of love.

Lingering silence rivaled the chalk in the air. Not an unusual aftermath, but I was anxious to receive a reaction. A love sonnet was a definite departure from the divorce and death poems I'd written the last year or so. It was Keely's response I craved most, though I'd have to wait. Traditionally she spoke last. For now, she sat at the head of class, preparing to mediate.

Finally Sondra looked at me. "Whatever provoked this surge of passion, my dear, keep it up. I find it very, uh—"

"Stimulating, Sondra?" John Carlyle spoke up, which set off a round of laughter. He scratched his ear with a fake Mont Blanc pen.

"Well, yes," Sondra said. "Quite sensual."

"But does the ice-cream image work?" I heard someone ask.

"Good point," Keely pointed out. "Does it?"

"I'm not so sure," said Tyron Goodard, the youngest but certainly not the shyest in the group. "I mean, those chimes sound more like carnival music than church bells."

"True," piped in John. "But I like the contrast. The calm of ice cream on a Sunday mixed with the bells of worship. Of course, if there were ever carnival bells, it would be—".

"Please!" snapped Tyron.

I supressed a laugh. John was baiting the young Baptist.

"Let's stay on task," Keely interjected.

"I agree with John," someone spoke up.

"On which point?" he asked. Again, laughter.

"I like the poem in general, in particular the ice-cream-man image," Anne Brian explained. She was a mother of two and worked hard at developing her art in spite of her husband's lack of support. "It works," she plainly stated.

Thank you, I thought. So far a sweep with the women, a split among the men. Wonder what Dean would say? Cut it, Neil, I told myself. At the moment I didn't want to think about Dean's absence.

I was fortunate to be in a good writers' group. By no means were we a back-pat coterie, but there was the element of support and desire to turn out some damn good writing. Egos and insecurity, undeniably present, did not reign supreme. This was all for the best as those two bitter ingredients made the creative cake fall. And I'd been part of a writers' group that had collapsed on itself. Not a pretty sight.

The buzz died, and Keely brought the evaluation to a close. "Sondra used the best word," she said. "Passion. Passion has always been in your work, Neil, but not like this. Strong images. A nifty metaphor, I think, with the ice-cream man. You usually don't relate to church bells in that sort of positive, almost innocent manner. At least not on the heels of an obviously passionate night. Innocent interlude complete with the sadness." She paused.

I waited, elated at my mentor's reaction.

"Any other comments?" Keely asked, planting a large smile on her face. "Okay, then, let's move on to John's."

We rustled through the sheets of poems, then John began reading. At one point I glanced at Keely, but she was tuned in to John's narrative on poverty. Lovely woman, I thought, then I refocused my attention on the piece before me. Poverty.

A much more approachable subject than love. Easier to fix, too. The remedy for the poor was to provide access to money. I half smiled at Keely. And sneezed. Lovers were damned.

The procedure continued through John, then Sondra,

and on until the classtime was quickly spent. We broke up—a little tired, though quite rejuvenated. At its best, the class was a spiritual service unto itself, and I looked at my colleagues with a hell of a lot of respect. I strove to be as good as Sondra Anderson and John Carlyle, the two most gifted writers in our group.

Outside the classroom, Sondra touched my arm. "Lovely poem, my dear. If only I were twenty years younger."

"And not married," I said. "Now, what is Candace up to?"

"She wants to move out," Sondra whispered so it wouldn't echo in the large hallway.

"Oh? And how does she think she can afford to live on campus?"

"She doesn't. Candace wants to move into Jason's old trailer. Now that she's a college girl, and earning money at the place you work—which, I might add, is a fortune compared to what she earned at DQ. Well, the girl's got the notion in her head it's time to be on her own."

I shrugged. "The trailer's hers."

"You're still executor of the estate."

"It's a long drive from the stables to class—and work," I said. "She doesn't realize that."

Keely approached us.

"But she's a tough cookie," I continued. "I say let her go. If it doesn't work, she hasn't burned any bridges."

"I was afraid that would be your approach. I've taken such a shine to her. Like one of my own moving out again."

"Why hasn't she said anything to me?" I asked.

"Because, darling," Sondra said, and wrinkled her nose, "you're a hard man to pin down." She gave Keely a gentle hug. "Got to run, kids."

"How about a beer at The Ale House Thursday night?" I asked. When she hesitated, I followed with, "You say we never invite you to after-hours."

Sondra dipped her head and peered at me over her

glasses. "All right, Neil. Thursday night." And she hurried off.

"Your poem got to her," Keely said.

"Parlez-moi d'amour," I said, the words rolling against my tongue like a fine Cabernet.

"Which means?" she asked, a spark of interest in her eyes.

"Basically, speak to me of love. It's a line from a song in a great offbeat flick called *The Moderns.* Check it out sometime."

"I will. Do you speak French?"

"Enough to get into trouble," I replied. "Made a fool of myself in Paris, once."

"Paris? I envy you. I've been dying to get to France."

"Envy me not. I'm talking about Paris, Texas. Got drunk in a redneck bar and started singing 'All My Ex's Live in Texas' in the language of love. Taught it to my friends, in fact. Loudly. We were asked to leave in no uncertain terms."

"You worry me, Neil."

We began to walk. She wore blue jeans, a white shirt, and a brown, fringed vest that gathered tight at her narrow waist. Her brown boots, pulled over her jeans as opposed to hidden under, clicked in the hall.

"I had a weird experience last night," I said, switching gears. "Can we talk?"

"Sure. Buy you a coffee."

"Deal."

We walked out of the building together, and I fought the urge to put my arm around her. A short hike away was the student center, but it was late morning and the place was packed. I knew of a little ice-cream shop downstairs and bought a couple of frozen yogurts. Considering the climate, the cool treats were a much wiser choice than hot coffee. In spite of the heat, Keely and I opted for a bench outside. I took off my brush popper.

"You're the only person I know who wears redneck clothes over preppie," Keely said.

"Designed especially for the Renaissance Texan."

"Sounds like identity-crisis material to me. Bet you wear dress shirts with sweatpants, too."

"So?"

A short, congenial laugh escaped her. "Tell me about your weird experience," Keely said, and spooned in some frozen yogurt. "I have to drive Mark over to get his car pretty quick. The Acura needs to be inspected before his trip to Austin."

Mark was her husband. And damn it if he wasn't a nice guy, too. "Mark doing okay?" I asked cordially.

"Working himself ragged, but otherwise fine. Thank you. Now, talk to me. I promised your mother I'd keep an eye on you." She pointed at me with her plastic utensil in big-sisterly fashion. How nice.

Keely had met my mother a few months ago when I'd spent a fuzzy day or two in the hospital. After that unfortunate encounter, my mother's parting words were, "Too bad that girl's married. You could've had yourself a keeper."

A keeper, I thought. Friend. Confidante. Speak to me of love. Instead, though, I spoke of the events at Chip Gunn's the night before. And of my phone conversations with Dean.

"Dean's blowing smoke," Keely said. "He's too young to do much else."

I was closer in age to Keely than to Dean and would almost have agreed with her had I not detected the frenetic spark when he talked to Gunn, heard the arsonist's determination in his voice.

"He's looking for trouble," I said. "And he's playing with a man who dislikes trouble so much he'll eliminate it any way he has to. You know that."

"The guy's running for Congress!" she exclaimed.

"Oh, Keely. There really are politicians who do bad things to get elected—and worse once they're in office."

I knew her comment wasn't derived from naïveté but rather from a code of high standards she held people to, and I probably shouldn't have responded flippantly. With Keely, if you were a writer, you'd damn well better sweat over every word. And if you were a politician, you'd at least better not have a criminal record. Or intents.

"Mock me not, Neil Marshall. This is really pissing me off."

"I know. I'm sorry. Just don't you go running half-crazed after Gunn, too."

"Well, what are *you* going to do?"

I finished my frozen yogurt. "Go to work."

Her narrow frame trembled.

"And what I want you to do is sit tight. If Dean Shriver's up to something, he'll contact one of us. Probably you, Keely. You convince him that being a fugitive from hard muscle grows old fast. And *he* won't."

"Won't what?"

"Grow old."

"I see," she said. Keely spread her thin fingers and rubbed them across her thighs.

I took her empty container and tossed it into a trash can with mine.

"I have to get to work."

"Yes," Keely said, eyebrows furrowed and mouth drawn tight, "I suppose it's time." She strapped her purse around her shoulder and rose. As she proceeded to step to the sidewalk, however, she caught the heel of her boot on the end of the bench and stumbled into me.

I caught Keely by the shoulders and allowed her petite frame to roll into my chest instead of to the ground. She smelled delicious—fresh and sweet. I welcomed her perfumed scent into my lungs and felt my spirits rise. The softness of her body pressed hard against me. I could have held her all day. Instead, I helped her regain her footing, gave her a gentle hug, and as quickly as she'd fallen into my arms, she was out.

"Well, damn!" she exclaimed. "That was graceful." Her delicate brown eyes landed softly on mine.

"Are you all right?"

"Yeah, just a little embarrassed."

"Must have been the frozen yogurt," I quipped.

"No kidding. Next time I'll have ice cream." Keely ran a hand through her short dark hair and pulled a few strands from her face. "Thanks," she said.

"For what?"

"For catching me."

"Oh, Keely—"

"And for the yogurt."

"You're quite welcome."

"But mostly," she added, her voice shifting to sultry, "thanks for the lovely poem."

I pushed back the silly grin and eyed Keely cautiously. She seemed grateful without appearing threatened. What was her assessment of the poem in class? *Innocent interlude complete with the sadness,* I thought. Nailed that hide to the wall.

"My pleasure," I finally replied. She winked. And in the thick, melancholy midday sun, we leisurely made our way back across campus.

5

Shortly after eleven I coasted to a stop in front of the renovated ranch house popularly known as The Kitchen. It was within these walls that Perry Stevens designed creations that turned clients into drooling ATM machines. This little hole in the Heights, just down the road from the Farmers' Market, was also where I'd recently sweated myself below one hundred and ninety-five pounds for the first time in years. I felt great physically, but I didn't think I could make money by selling a culinary-sweatshop weight-loss program. Contrary to myth, not all chefs looked like a double shot of the Pillsbury Doughboy.

The baby magnolia tree in the front yard was already dropping large brown leaves. On the right side of the driveway, by the Cyclone fence, the commercial trash bin was topped to its limit. Big-bellied flies buzzed around the partially cracked lids. Close to The Kitchen's French doors the van sat half-loaded. As I opened the door I came face-to-face with Robbie Persons. His pale gray eyes widened when we met.

"About time," he said, and set a case of Jack Daniel's in the van. He stood almost as tall as me, and glanced around.

"Where's Mattie?"

"What do you mean?" I asked cautiously.

"Heard you had a problem last night and that she was with you. Figured you'd both show up to work together."

"Who'd you collect that info from?"

"Booker, of course."

Good, I thought. At least Dean hadn't called here. No telling what he'd say.

"It was no big deal," I offered.

"Then why isn't Mattie with you? And why did she stay at your apartment last night?"

"What did Booker tell you?"

"Neil, talk to me. You haven't acted this evasive since Jason died."

Robbie was an old friend, cowboy hard and lean, and as honest as a Texas summer day. But I wasn't going to put him in a vulnerable position with the likes of Gunn and Lamar if I didn't have to. Talking to Keely was different. Mattie had nothing to do with the university, so it was unlikely anyone would scour that area for information. She did, however, have strong ties to the catering company.

"Does Perry know?" I asked, keeping the conversation vague.

"That Mattie's old lover was there? Hell, no. And neither does Claudia."

I appreciated Robbie's candor about last night, and I was thankful the news hadn't drifted Claudia's way. I could imagine how our beloved kitchen manager would rail on Mattie concerning the trials of love and its fallout. Claudia had all the finesse of a mule kicking down a barn door.

"Mattie needs to collect herself," I offered. "I expect she'll be up to snuff in a day or two."

"If you don't want to let me in on what's going on, that's your business. But don't insult my intelligence with weak explanations."

"I'm not insulting you, Robbie."

"I'm willing to help."

"Let's give Mattie some time."

Robbie hesitated.

"I'm probably going to take her to Mama's."

"Last time you were this tight-lipped you about died."

"If there's anything you can do, I'll let you know," I said. "Hell, it's a well-known fact you take in fugitives."

His was yet another place I'd once crashed at when I was down and out.

He studied me carefully. "All right, Neil. I hope you know what you're doing."

"Don't I always?"

"No."

He pushed open the front door, and I followed. Air-conditioned bliss hit me, then the strong smell of garlic and onions sautéing.

"Is Perry here?" I asked.

"He's out meeting Senator Beauchamp's wife," Robbie replied. "With election time so close, she wants the dinner party perfect."

"I'm sick of politics."

"It pays our bills, child."

"Somewhere beneath that statement lies a great irony," I told him.

Robbie shrugged. I knew he'd rather drink recycled beer than talk politics. Despites his reticence, though, Robbie did consistently participate in a way a few million other Americans refused to—he voted.

"Alan Shepard's going to be at the senator's," he added.

"The astronaut? Really?"

"But you ain't working that job," Claudia announced from behind me.

I turned. It seemed the only times we saw eye to eye was when we faced each other. Claudia was a big, tall woman.

"Fine," I replied. "I've served Alan Shepard before, anyway. At the English consul general's house." I wanted to stick my tongue out at her. What held me back, though, was not any incredible sense of maturity but the fear that she'd grab hold and rip it out of my head.

"Get your sassy, late self back there," Claudia ordered. "We got the doctor's lunch to fix."

"Yes, ma'am." I wrapped a clean white apron around my waist.

Robbie disappeared into the front office to answer the

phone. I checked the boneless chicken breasts that were in a stainless-steel bowl in the vegetable sink. Cold water ran over them. The chicken was a little stiff, but thawed enough to work with. I turned off the faucet.

"And where's that girl?" Claudia demanded.

"Who?"

"You know damn good and well who!" She put her hands on her hips and leaned toward me.

"Mattie had personal business to tend to," I stated. "I think it's something to do with her son. So I told her she could take the day off."

"*You* told her!"

"I only did what I thought you would do."

"You don't have no business trying to think like me." The imposing woman picked up a rolling pin and proceeded to pound it against the stainless-steel worktable. She hit the stress points of her following words perfectly. "And—it—ain't—your—place—to—be—giving—nobody—time—off!"

"Jesus, Claudia, calm down. I'm sorry." I truly believed in the axiom that it was easier to ask for forgiveness than to ask for permission. Until I met Claudia. Asking her for anything could prove to be fatal.

"Yes, you is sorry."

I drained the water off the chicken breasts. "I didn't think it'd be such a big deal," I explained. "We're not exactly swamped today."

"That ain't the point," she said, and whopped the table so hard she dimpled its surface. Conrad, the dishwasher, ducked out of fear. I guessed he was worried that Claudia was fixing to throw it like a tomahawk. I didn't know why he flinched, however. If she was going to bury the rolling pin into anyone, I was the likely target.

Robbie darted from the office. "My God, what the hell's going on back here?"

"Culinary disagreement," I replied.

The veins in Claudia's neck were big as nightcrawlers. She took off her apron and tossed it by the large mixer.

"I'm going to the bank," she proclaimed. "You take care of them lunches. I'll be back later."

"Yes, ma'am," I responded.

"And don't you never give nobody time off without asking me first," she added.

"Yes, ma'am."

I waited for the front door to slam before telling Robbie. "I took the rap for Mattie not coming in."

"I figured. But you've got to stop riling Claudia up. She's an old woman."

"You're right. Someday she'll pop a gasket and keel over right before our eyes. Hopefully she'll still be on the rolling-pin level and not have graduated to throwing knives."

"Neil, I'm serious. This power struggle has to end."

"Claudia and I are not having a power struggle," I said for the thousandth time this year. "I don't want Claudia's job." I grinned. "I want to write and teach—I want Keely's job."

"Face it," Robbie said, "you'd rather give the orders than receive them."

"Guess what we have here is a prime case of kitchen politics."

"And Perry hates politics as much as I do," Robbie interjected.

"Amazing how you can't get away from it."

"I'm not kidding."

"Neither am I." I began to pull the skin off the chicken breasts. There were twelve of them. "Believe me," I told Robbie, "I don't want to be the reason Claudia has an early appointment with Saint Peter."

"The possibility's stronger than you realize."

"What?"

"She's not going to the bank," he muttered.

"What's going on? Claudia sick or something?"

He lifted his eyebrows, widened his eyes.

"Oh, come on, Robbie. You know that no matter how I

explained Mattie's absence, Claudia would have flown off the handle."

He paused, taking in what I'd just said, then nodded. "You're probably right."

"I simply thought it might be easier for Mattie later if I diverted Claudia's anger toward me now."

"Your logic astounds me."

"Thank you," I shot back. "But you're not going to fill me in on Claudia, are you?"

"Nope."

"Tit for tat," I said.

"Yep. Listen, can you spare Conrad for a while? I want him to run to the warehouse with me so we can start gathering tonight's rental together."

"I don't know if I should make that decision."

"Ha. Ha. Ha!" He signaled for Conrad to join him. "Want me to lock you in?" he called from the front door.

"Don't worry about it," I said. "I'll secure the place when I deliver these lunches."

Robbie closed the door and suddenly I was left to the peaceful humming of appliances and the fragile notes of a Mozart piano concerto on the stereo. I had about an hour and a half to prepare the food and run it to their office. The doctors were a group of psychologists, old clients of Perry's, who met once a week. I often wondered what they discussed. Business at hand? New wonder drugs? The mental illness of the week? I also wondered if they made house, or rather, kitchen calls. This place was driving me crazy.

After skinning the chicken, I placed the breasts on the cutting board and gave them a couple of knocks with the tenderizing side of the hammer. Then I grabbed the big cast-iron skillet and melted a half-pound block of butter. This morning a dozen bunches of fresh tarragon came with the produce delivery, so I finely chopped one bunch and added a couple of large pinches to the melting butter. For good luck I tossed in some ground pepper, crushed garlic, and diced chives. When the concoction began to sizzle, I adjusted the gas burner so the butter wouldn't burn. The aroma bloomed into a symphonic bouquet. Four of the breasts laid flat fit perfectly in the skillet.

Dealing with the tarragon reminded me of Dean Shriver's father. The guy was into produce. Of all things, I hadn't picked that as Dean's background. Nor of Chip Gunn's. *Strange* was the word that flashed through my mind. *Strange.*

I flipped the chicken breasts, tender and moist. Just before they were done I doused them with bourbon, flamed the pan, then transferred them into a chafing pan. I cleaned the skillet and repeated this effort twice more. On the third set of breasts, I thoroughly deglazed the pan with bourbon and made a cream sauce. When I had finished, the sauce held a delicate smoky flavor to complement the tarragon and garlic. Delightful, I thought, remembering what Henry Kissinger had said about my food a few years back. *Delightful.*

Claudia had already prepared the brown and wild rice and Parker House rolls. I quickly sliced a mixture of fresh vegetables and steamed them. For dessert, the good doctors were going to have chocolate pecan pie.

I hoped Claudia was all right.

I spread out the Styrofoam to-go cartons and began to serve out rice with chicken breast, a ladle of bourbon sauce, scoop of veggies, roll, and pie. As quickly as I moved, it was still slow going. This was where I really missed Mattie.

The containers were full and I was snapping down the lids when I heard the front door open. The divider between the front and back of the kitchen blocked my view, but I was sure it was Perry breezing in. Fine timing, I thought. Always arriving when the grunt work was finished.

"Back here," I called.

And then I received today's shock.

Looming before me was big Jimmy, shadowed by Cracker. And gliding in between them was none other than the man himself, Mr. Chip Gunn.

6

I bit back my surprise as best I could, and continued to cover the lunches. "Well, Mr. Gunn," I said with exaggerated happiness, "you could've just mailed the bill. A personal visit wasn't necessary."

"Cut the bullshit, Marshall. Where is he?" Any tighter and Gunn's vocal cords would've snapped like a breaking neck. Mine.

"What?"

"Don't screw with me." Gunn snapped his fingers and Jimmy and Cracker approached.

"Why the hell do you think I know where Lamar Fowler is?" I asked quickly.

Cracker drove the palm of his hand into one of the lunch containers. On the other side of the table, Jimmy rested his arm down and prepared to sweep half of them onto the floor.

"Goddamn it!" I snapped. "Don't mess with the doctors' food. They may be psychologists, but on an empty stomach they're only as understanding as the next grouchy slob."

Gunn was about to come uncorked. He jabbed a finger toward me. "I'm not talking about Fowler, you idiot! Where the hell is Dean Shriver?"

"Who?" I asked, stunned.

Gunn looked to Jimmy.

"No," I pleaded, and grabbed the big ape's arm. Definitely not a smart move. He snared me by the scruff of my neck and lifted me up. "I have no idea where Shriver is," I squeaked. "He called me this morning with some

49

cockeyed idea, but I blew him off. He's always talking
trash when he's stoned." I'd tangled with these guys
before, but at least I'd had the chance to get the first lick
in before they beat the bejesus out of me.

"Stoned?" Gunn repeated, leaning back.

"Yeah, stoned," I reiterated. "You know: pot, wacky
weed, Mary Jane. Dean's major vice."

"Damn." He turned. Cracker was ready to pound lunch
into hash. For that matter, Jimmy was ready to do the
same to me. They waited for the sign.

"I don't know where he is," I said.

"Well, I can certainly apprise you of where he went."
Gunn snapped back around. "That little bastard ran to the
Chronicle to spill his guts about last night."

My insides fell so low I was about to tread on them.

"Like goddamn father like goddamn son," he growled.
"Fortunately, his words fell on the ears of an acquaintance
of mine. The story won't even make the back page."

Gunn gingerly touched his hair, then adjusted his tie and
collar. After a brisk nod, Jimmy released me; Cracker, a
look of disappointment on his face, gave the packaged
lunches their freedom.

"Mr. Marshall," he enunciated, "I believe you're not as
brazen as our young friend, or as foolishly ridiculous.
And you know I won't allow this incident to pass unno-
ticed—I will find him. However, should you hear from
Mr. Shriver first, I expect to be contacted immediately.
Understand?"

"No promises."

Jimmy and Cracker stirred like a couple of salivating
wild dogs. They rose the hackles on the back of my neck.

Gunn grinned, approached me, and softly slapped my
face a couple of times. "The stakes are too high to allow
a social deviant this much power."

"You know I just can't hand him to you, even if I do
locate him."

"Don't make the situation more difficult."

"I won't sign Dean's death certificate."

"As I once explained to you, Mr. Marshall, I am not a murderer."

"Unless you have to be," I added.

Gunn's smile bordered on a smirk.

I held my ground. "Why is Dean acting so aggressively?"

He jerked his thumb over his shoulder. Cracker and Jimmy headed for the door. "Best express those lunches to their hungry destinations," he said in a low voice. "They're getting cold." He poked the container that looked like a crushed top hat. "I'll be in touch," he added.

"Oh, joy."

And Gunn took his muscle out of the sanctity of The Kitchen.

"Shit," I whispered between my teeth. "Shit, shit, shit."

I stuck my finger through the broken Styrofoam.

And damn if Gunn wasn't right. Cold. Well, the good doctors were going to have to zap the lunches in their microwave if they wanted them piping hot. By the time I reheated the food it'd be ready for dinner.

I repacked the damaged lunch, grateful only the container had been mangled. A little more rice and a ladle of extra sauce made the meal as good as new. I had them trayed and was on my way out the door when Perry arrived. He glanced at his watch.

"Plenty of time," I responded to his gesture.

"Where is everyone?"

"For various reasons, out. Can I use your car? Robbie and Conrad have the van."

He stroked his red beard then dug a ten from his pocket as well as the keys. "I need gas. Get a receipt."

"No problem." And I hit the road.

Good timing, I thought. Delivering in a Lexus was slightly more impressive than puttering up in an old, un-air-conditioned VW. Perry's car had a phone, a CD player, and leather interior to boot. The only amenity my Bug possessed was the pine tree–shaped deodorizer dangling from the rearview mirror.

Speaking of rearview mirrors, though, about halfway

there I realized I was spending as much time looking at the traffic behind me as I was at the road ahead of me. Calm down, boy, I told myself. No one's trailing you. Unless someone wanted to jump me for a piece of bourbon chicken, there was no point in following me right now. Dean Shriver sure wasn't hiding at the doctors' office. And I'd lay odds that Lamar Fowler wasn't sheltered in the shadows of the museum district. Any moron would figure that out. Even one running for office.

I rolled around the idea of calling C. J. McDaniels, my private-investigator acquaintance. But what would I say? There was a crime with no evidence, and no available victim? A nutty poet was canvassing the town against a less-than-upstanding citizen—who just happened to be running for Congress? Perhaps C.J. would locate Dean for me, but I felt awkward approaching him after his daughter, Linda, and I had cooled our heels romantically. Besides, he'd probably want to be paid for his efforts, if one could imagine such a thing. And, as usual, I was broke.

The gravel driveway ground beneath the car's tires as I came to a stop at the doctors' compound, alone. Three redbrick buildings that resembled small libraries rather than psychiatric offices enclosed the drive. As usual, the area was silent.

Quickly, I hit the main building with the lunches, the jitters setting me in high gear. Occasionally I would run into a doctor or a secretary in the kitchen, but today it was quiet to the point of eeriness. I pushed through a swinging door to the conference room. Classical music softly filled the space. A large, well-polished oak table dominated the center of the room, and I positioned a meal at each place setting.

Sunlight illuminated the hardwood furniture and mounted diplomas. I glanced out the French doors to the small garden in back. And I almost dropped the tray I used to carry the lunches.

Sitting beneath an umbrella at a white wrought-iron

table and sipping on a glass of white wine was the short, balding man I'd seen the night before with Lamar Fowler. He wore a white suit and patted his forehead with a handkerchief. A dark cane was hooked around the arm of his chair. He appeared relaxed while the man with him was running his hands through his graying hair, opening his palms to the heavens, and generally gesturing in sharp, jerky motions.

Chip Gunn's brother must have sensed my presence because, in machinelike manner, he turned his attention to the French doors. And me. The man displayed no emotion, though I felt his pale blue eyes chisel my image into his mind. As casually as he'd noted me, he refocused on his animated tablemate.

I backed away, feeling exposed. If this was Gunn's brother, then they were as opposite as brothers came. Chip had a mean streak, but he was passionate about life. Flamboyant also came to mind. The man in the white suit was as warm as barbed wire.

And something told me I was about to become entwined in its mesh.

7

[faint text bleeding through from reverse side of page]

Cold bourbon chicken suddenly seemed the least of my worries. I sped out of the parking lot with shards of fear piercing my mind. There was no logical explanation—after all, it was only Chip Gunn's brother that I'd seen. And he hadn't said a word to me. No, the words were between the brother and the gray-haired man. It was the atmosphere that disturbed me. There was more warmth in the tail of a rattlesnake than in that man's eyes. I steadied myself, my father's voice echoing from childhood. "A man's only as good as his nerves," he'd said. Always thought he'd watched too much John Wayne.

Until now.

I zigzagged through neighborhoods and streets I didn't need to visit in order to assure myself I wasn't being followed. As best as I could tell, I wasn't. On the way back to The Kitchen, I decided to run by my apartment. Checking on Mattie and her son was the next step to keeping those nerves of mine in line.

Perry's car was delightfully cool, and I pushed in a Gypsy Kings CD. The raspy voices soothed my spirit and in no time I found myself in Jerry Jacoma's driveway, coasting to a gentle stop behind Mattie's white Geo at the base of my apartment.

As I eased out of the car, though, a large figure emerged from Jerry's back porch. Ever since I'd been knifed, I was acutely aware of whatever environment I was in. Even in my own driveway, I usually exercised caution. But I'd totally missed this character, and I felt stripped to raw fear. Perhaps

I was accustomed to Jerry's dog barking an advance warning. In this case, though, Samson the Doberman was at the man's heels, the dog's stubby tail wagging.

"Worthless watchdog," Lamar Fowler informed me.

Score one for Mattie's intuition, I thought. Rumors of Lamar's death were greatly exaggerated. He hobbled gingerly, a hand clutching his gut, though an air of don't-screw-with-me surrounded him.

I took a step back, glanced up at my apartment. No one was at the window. Good sign. A numbness thick as the humidity began to spread over me. Neither Mattie nor the child was down here, I forced myself to think. Maybe Lamar wasn't aware they were up there. Keep mouth shut, I ordered myself.

Lamar outwalked the Doberman's chain, and the dog came to an abrupt stop, its stupid tail still wagging.

"That dog's usually meaner than you are," I commented.

"Apparently not." He nodded at the back porch. "I could've walked right into your kitchen and made myself a sandwich."

So he thought Jerry's house was mine. No wonder he wasn't sitting up in my apartment having a nostalgic conversation with his ex-girlfriend and son. Now the trick was to keep it that way. And live to tell about it.

He leaned against the front of the car. It was obvious from his pallid complexion and lack of energy I had little to fear from a hands-on assault. However, I was certain he was packing a piece.

"What happened last night?" I asked.

Lamar fished a pack of cigarettes from the pocket of his nylon runner's jacket and lit one up. Sweat glistened on his forehead, and there was a tremble in the hand that held the smoke. The wind had picked up and clouds were dulling the afternoon. Lamar's breathing was heavy.

"Have you seen a doctor?" I asked.

"I been tended to."

"Mattie thought you were dead."

"I imagine she did, since she stuck the knife in me."

"What?" His words struck the air like the snap of a whip.

"I been over it and over it in my mind, and I keep remembering the bitch standing above me with the knife in her hand." He puffed weakly on the cigarette, then tossed it down.

"Mattie didn't stab you. She found you."

"If you think she's going to own up, then you're sorry white bread."

"How do you know it wasn't Gunn's brother?" I asked.

"Gunter?" he responded, and released a short laugh. "That Nazi pimp. I wanted to believe it was him so I could break his fat neck."

"Gunter?" I asked.

"He goes by the old name."

"And Gunn Americanized his," I said, completing the thought.

"Worst that Gunter did was push me out of his way to save his sorry ass."

"Let's stop the dance," I told him. "Tell me straight up what happened."

He studied me carefully, thumped out another cigarette, and fumbled with it from hand to mouth then back to hand.

"Might not be bad you should hear the circumstances surrounding my assassination attempt. That way if you is hiding Mattie, you is harboring a criminal."

Assassination attempt? I wondered. The man thought a lot of himself.

"It began with an argument I overheard. Gunn wants to be a congressman real bad, man."

"I know."

"His brother ain't exactly supportive."

"Why would that be?" I couldn't mask the surprise in my voice.

"Don't know," Lamar said, and finally lit the cancer stick. "But," he added through a cloud of smoke, "Gunter won't sell a piece of property Gunn wants to wash his hands of. The man's exact words were, 'That land is riddled with skeletons waving from the pasture.' " Lamar grinned. "Pretty picture. But Gunn don't see it that way and used some ten-dollar word instead."

Interesting, I thought, but I played it down. "So what's that got to do with anything?"

His laugh turned into a cough. "Shit, another dumb white boy."

"I prefer the word *naive*."

"I heard something I wasn't supposed to. They got a plot of bodies somewhere."

"News like that would surely hurt Gunn's chances of being elected," I muttered. But a plot of bodies?

"Get a man killed, too."

"What?" I said, and took another step back.

"You is jumpy." A weak laugh escaped him.

"As a strawberry roan," I shot back. "Glad it amuses you." Then I caught myself and took a deep breath. "But I guess I'm losing the thread here. If you were privy to secret information, what makes you think Mattie attacked you? Unless you're demented enough to believe they hired her to commit the so-called assassination attempt."

Suddenly he whipped the half-smoked cigarette to the ground. Amazingly enough, I didn't buck again. Instead, I froze.

"You done told me to stop dancing. Let me tell the story straight, then."

It wasn't hard to keep my mouth shut and watch. The sudden movement had slowed Lamar down, and he drew in a couple of thick breaths. Overhead, storm clouds were gathering.

"Gunn's face is bloodred he's so mad. Partly 'cause I walked in on them. He tells me to show his brother out. 'Yes, boss,' I say. But as we reach Gunter's car, someone comes at me from behind. It's dark and we in the shadow of the house, so I hear the bitch, but I don't really see nothing. The blade lands high on my back near the shoulder. Pain like you never felt in your life. But I don't scream. The bitch lets go of the knife and takes off.

When I close my eyes, I still hear the scraping of shoes on driveway. Then I fell onto Gunter, but the bastard shoved me to the ground and drove away.

"First thing that hit my brain," he continued, "was that Gunn set me up 'cause of what I heard. Not until my head cleared did I figure Gunn wouldn't attack me at his own party in front of a houseful of witnesses. Didn't think that then—I struggled to get my ass out of there fast as I could. I fell twice—second time near the back door."

"And that was when you saw Mattie."

"You's interrupting again." He pointed a large finger in my direction.

I held my tongue.

"I jerked the knife out my back before I blacked out," he told me. "Now, I don't know if my eyes popped open before or because that woman done screamed, but they did. And there's Mattie, big old knife in hand, my blood trailing off it. The look in her eyes told me all I needs to know. That blade was marked for my heart, man."

"Wanting to kill and killing are two very different things," I said slowly. "Everyone gets murderously angry at some point. I bet even Mother Teresa has fantasized about wringing someone's neck. Going through with murder is another whole ball game. You know that."

"She come back to finish the job. I seen the look in her eyes. She don't want to give up what she owes me."

"What she owes you! What are you talking about? She found you and freaked."

"Mattie's smart. Reads lots of books. I give her that. She got you fooled."

"If you're so convinced, then why don't you go to the police?"

"I handle my own problems."

"Which brings you to why you're here to see me," I pointed out, and met his fierce eyes.

"Maybe you not so dumb."

"High praise."

"Mattie ain't at her apartment," he stated.

"That so?"

"You knows where she is." Lamar edged off the car, balanced himself, and stood as straight as he could.

"Can't say as I do," I replied. "My advice to Mattie was that she stay with a relative or friend for a few days."

The sky brewed like strong coffee. The storm clouds' huddle grew tighter. Then Lamar pulled a 9mm from beneath his nylon jacket and even the tropical afternoon wind couldn't warm the cold prickles on the nape of my neck.

"We gots to play it the hard way," he said, and waved the gun at the Geo. "Whose car is that?"

"My roommate's girlfriend's," I quickly replied. "She leaves her car here when she has to go out of town."

"You has an answer for everything."

"I don't have an answer for that gun in your hand."

Lamar grinned broadly. "Yes, you do," he responded. "Where's Mattie?"

"Gunn's looking for you," I informed him.

"No shit." Lamar began to weave a little.

"But you still refuse to go to the police."

"You talking foolish again."

Foolish, hell. I was saying anything in order to buy some time. I glanced to my right. If I moved quickly, I could probably dive between the two cars and scurry to safety around the corner of the garage. Lamar was in no condition to chase me and, as unsteady as he was, barely in any condition to pop off a decent shot. I'd sure hate for Perry's Lexus to take a slug or two, though. Perry wasn't that understanding.

"And I see a foolish look in your eyes," Lamar spoke out. He pointed the gun at my chest. "Where's Mattie?"

As if the air could no longer stand the swell of humidity, the black clouds tore open and locust-sized rain began to pelt us. My glasses immediately streaked, cutting down my field of vision. Lamar showed no sign he was aware of the downpour. Not so much as a blink, though his jacket was soon soaked and clinging to his large frame.

I made my move, cut to the right. And slipped. Before I realized what had happened, I was on my side, glancing back at Lamar—anticipating a blast from his gun. Instead, thunder hammered down more tacks of rain. Gradually, a grin friendly as cactus spines reappeared on Lamar's face as he realized my mistake. I was his for the taking now, and I waited apprehensively for the gun to raise. As I began to scamper, however, I noticed something was wrong. Lamar suddenly seemed distant, frozen like a machine that had run out of gas. And the gun didn't rise. He simply laughed deeply, attempted a step, and collapsed.

The chaos of the afternoon and the suddenness of Lamar's breakdown caused me to wonder if he'd been shot by the mysterious assassin—a lone figure traversing the fringes of the storm, watching the scene play out until forced to strike down Lamar before he struck down me. But such a scenario was only in my swirling imagination. It appeared fatigue was the culprit. And loss of blood. Lamar's wet shirt seeped crimson near the shoulder, where he'd received the knife wound. I hesitated to approach. Instead I pulled myself up and bolted to my apartment.

My footsteps echoed up the narrow stairwell as I unlocked the door and charged into my living room. Mattie hopped from her chair at the kitchen table, where she'd been reading a magazine.

"What is it?" she asked, unnerved at my disheveled appearance.

"Nothing that a phone call can't remedy." I decided on an ambulance rather than the police. Undoubtedly the cops would soon be involved, but Lamar needed medical attention, and I could feign ignorance as to who he was.

I placed the call, and advised Mattie to keep J.J. glued to the television.

"It's Lamar, isn't it?" she whispered as I prepared to head back down to the driveway.

"Yes, but he's in no shape to do you any harm."

Her shoulders slumped. "Can't be that bad. He tracked me here."

"No," I said softly, "he doesn't realize you're in my apartment. He came to talk to me. Hold tight." I closed the door.

I eased my way down the stairs, fearing a last burst of energy from Lamar followed by a gun blast. The ferocious rain continued. As I glanced out the door, however, something was wrong.

I reentered the sweltering torrent of rain. The spot where Lamar had fallen was empty.

The son of a bitch had disappeared again.

8

Explaining to the paramedics that I'd lost the body was no picnic. After about five minutes they were ready to give me a Breathalyzer test. The pounding rain didn't help, washing away any traces of blood that could've corroborated my story. Finally the police arrived. First a blue, lights slicing through the rain, and then an unmarked car. A familiar unmarked car, which only added to the eccentricity of the day.

A tall, lean man approached me.

"I was, as they say, in the neighborhood," he stated, and flashed me a lazy half smile. "Hearing your address called out on the radio stirred too many memories for me to pass it by."

"Lieutenant Gardner," I replied, met his hand, and thought only the sight of C. J. McDaniels would've been more of a surprise. The fact was, though, that Gardner was often in the neighborhood. I ran into him frequently at The Flower, a Mexican restaurant a few blocks away, so I knew he usually ate a late lunch there. With the owner, a very beautiful woman.

Gardner's gentle attitude and Southern politeness were countered by piercing eyes and an intricately sharp mind. While I stood in the deluge getting soaked Gardner was protected by a fedora and a long lightweight raincoat.

"How is McDaniels?" Gardner asked.

"Don't know. Haven't seen him recently."

He nodded. "What's going on?"

"Billy Bob here called nine-one-one to report a bleeding

body in his driveway," one of the paramedics said of me, "but when we pulled up all we found was this guy standing in the pouring rain staring at his feet."

"His name's Neil Marshall," the lieutenant informed the paramedic. The fact that the detective knew me carried some weight with the paramedics, especially the one who'd been talking.

The latter looked sheepishly at me. "Excuse me, Mr. Marshall."

"Thank you," Gardner responded.

"There was a man here," I carried on. "He was injured and facedown on the driveway. Guess he stumbled in before the rain, then was awakened by the rain and stumbled out."

"I don't believe that bleeding people simply stumble in and out of your life, Mr. Marshall," Gardner stated. "What else can you tell me?"

"He's big. He's African American. Blood was seeping through the back of his shirt. And he was holding a gun."

The last bit of information grabbed their attention. They asked for a detailed description, and I gave it. Excluding name.

"Call for backup and comb the area," Gardner ordered one of the uniformed policemen. "And radio in to see if anyone's reported a robbery or attempted robbery," he added.

As they kicked into gear I eased under the protection of Jerry's back porch. I caught sight of Mattie staring out the apartment window and subtly signaled for her to back off and stay out of sight. If there were stories to be told, I'd rather they came from me. Besides, it'd be just my luck Mattie would take the opportunity to unburden herself, thus setting off a chain of events that would ultimately send Chip Gunn into an apoplectic fit. Or, worse for Mattie, land her in jail after Lamar swore—with Gunn's domestic-malice blessing—that she was the one who tried to kill him. Meanwhile Samson, ace guard dog, was barking like a fool at the good guys.

After the neighborhood was lit up with enough cop lights to illuminate an amusement park, Lieutenant Gardner turned his attention back to me.

"What's his name, Neil?" he asked.

"How in the name of sweet Jesus would I know that?"

He wasn't convinced. "New car?" he questioned, pointing at the Lexus.

"I wish. No, that's my boss's. I still drive the Bug."

"What were you doing here with his car?"

"I had to pick something up."

"What?"

"My wallet. And if I hadn't forgotten it I wouldn't be standing here now being grilled by you. Most likely you'd be listening sympathetically to one of my neighbors. And believing him."

"In all probability said neighbor would not be known for repeated involvements in well-publicized homicides," Gardner retorted.

A uniformed cop joined us. "No reports of any attempted robberies, assaults, break-ins, or anything recently," he said. "Could be domestic, though no reports on that end either."

"Could be gang-related," I offered.

Gardner eyed me hard. I should've kept my mouth shut.

"Why do you say that, Mr. Marshall?"

"Guess a lot of crimes these days seem to be . . . gang-related," I replied weakly.

"Are you aware of the manpower we have out here right now?" he asked.

"Quite aware." I was feeling incredibly guilty for not having played it straight with the lieutenant, and rather stupid for having backed myself into a corner. It was a sure bet that Lamar had hobbled to whatever means of transportation he'd arrived on and sped from the scene. Which meant the cops were wasting their time. Stupid, Neil.

Some people can threaten with a smile, turning a benevolent gesture into a weapon much the way a baseball bat can delight millions while in the hands of home-run hitter Jeff Bagwell but terrorize the person whose head is about to be bashed in by a maniac.

At this point my head was being bashed in.

"We will find this man," he said.

"I hope so."

Gardner paused, stepped to the edge of the porch, and drew in a deep breath. The air was as heavy as ever—rain in Houston never doused the city with coolness as it would in most places. On the contrary, it added to the thickness. And the downpour continued.

"Mr. Marshall," Gardner began, "I am talking to you now as a good neighbor."

"Good fences make good neighbors."

"The poet always, I see." He pointed a professorial finger in my direction. "But Mr. Frost's quote is precisely what I'm getting at. In this situation, fences are to be overcome. Without the fences, what would a good neighbor say about the injured—and armed—man?"

"He would say," I started slowly, "that the suspected victim is probably far away from here."

"And how would he know that?"

"He wouldn't."

"Then why would he say such a thing?"

"Call it a hunch," I said.

"I don't believe your neighbor would be any more help than you are."

"Perhaps there's nothing more to offer."

"Perhaps a trip downtown would fill the collection plate," he threatened.

"Fire and brimstone doesn't work on everyone."

Gardner was growing frustrated. He'd been on my tail ever since Jason's murder and my subsequent justifiable homicide. Gardner knew I hadn't done it, but could prove nothing without my testimony. Though, in a strange way, I think he also liked me. It was the poetry connection. He was a Wordsworthian at heart, although he once confessed that Shakespeare was his favorite. I knew the man.

And he also knew me.

"I'm glad my tooth doesn't have your nerve," Gardner finally said, then called, "Davis."

A uniformed cop jogged over.

"Tell Cruz and Shaw to cover the neighborhood. You check the local hospitals and clinics."

"Already have, sir. Nothing."

"Figures. Well, put an advisory out and send everybody else away."

"Yes, sir."

"Oh, and Davis?"

"Sir?"

"Whose white Geo is that?"

The uniformed policeman pulled out a small notepad. "Mattie Johnson. Lives on West Bellfort."

"Know her?" he asked me.

"I work with her. I could've told you that's Mattie's car." My mind was clicking fast, looking for a reason her car was here and a way to keep her out of the line of fire.

"Of course you could have, Neil," Gardner stated, adjusting his hat. "Let's just say I wanted official confirmation."

"I understand." I pointed to his head. "You know, Bear Bryant wore hats like that."

"Why is Ms. Johnson's car in your driveway?"

"It's been hesitating on her. Jerry Jacoma, my landlord, and I are going to work on it. I think it's the fuel pump."

"Doesn't that have electronic fuel injection?"

"Sounds like a lot of fun, huh?" I forced a smile. Cars, trucks, anything with engines were not my forte. But it was the best bluff I could think of given the time I had.

He glanced up at my apartment. "Forgot your wallet?" he asked.

"Absolutely."

Gardner stroked his chin. "And where might Ms. Johnson be at the moment?"

I made a show of checking my watch. "If I remember correctly, she was to take her little boy to the doctor's sometime this afternoon."

"When?"

"Not quite sure. Three-thirty, four o'clock."

"But if her car's here, how does she intend to get to the doctor's?"

"Mattie made some kind of arrangement with a friend," I stated, feigning exasperation. "I don't know what or with whom. I had offered the use of my VW, but for some reason she declined."

"I see." The smile returned. He had me on the run.

"Lieutenant Gardner, I really need to get back to work," I said. "Mr. Stevens is probably mad as a wet hornet by now."

"Of course. But first, Mr. Marshall, would you mind if I troubled you for a glass of water? I've just finished lunch and, well, you understand how salsa and jalapeños don't quit."

"A glass of water?"

"Please."

"Oh, you don't think—" I drew his attention from my apartment window.

"I'm very thirsty."

Then turn your face toward the heavens and open your mouth to the rain, I wanted to say, but didn't.

"Well, sure," I said.

"Thank you."

"I'll be right back."

"Oh, you don't have to wait on me. You spend enough of your time providing that service."

"I don't mind," I answered.

"In fact, I'd like to see an artist's flat. If it's all right with you, of course."

"It's not much of a flat," I told him. "Actually, my place is more of a pigsty."

He continued to follow me, through the rain and into the hallway. "Nonsense. It can't be worse than my office."

Again my mind raced, but this time I was wildly drawing blanks. We clomped up the steps, and when we reached the landing I knew I'd gone too far to suddenly deny him access without arousing a mountain of suspicion. The door was partly ajar from when I'd charged outside and so, carefully, I pushed it open.

"Anything wrong?" Gardner asked.

"Not at all." I held my breath.

We were greeted by silence. No television blaring. No bouncing J.J. No inquisitive, worried Mattie. Only a faint smell of cigarette veiled the air.

"You're too hard on yourself, Neil," Gardner said, taking in as much of the room as he could. "I'd hardly call this a pigsty."

"I have high standards."

He sniffed. "I thought you quit smoking."

"I have, more or less. Every once in a while I'll have a drag. Once a smoker always a smoker, I guess. It's only the length between puffs that changes. Here, let me get you that water."

Gardner poked his head casually into my bedroom. "Nice little place," he announced.

"Big enough for me." I rattled ice in the glass and filled it from the tap.

"Thank you," he said, accepting the water. As he drank, his eyes grew big. My heart sped.

He pointed to the cereal box. "Sugar Pops?"

"Don't tell anyone," I whispered.

He finished the water, ice clinking in the bottom of it as he did. "I feel much better," he stated.

"Good." So, I thought, do I.

"Could I trouble you for one more thing?" he asked.

"What?" Oh, God, what now?

"The use of your bathroom."

What was he saying about nerves and teeth? I wondered.

"Right here," I told him, opened the door, and flicked on the light.

As the door closed I was a little more than curious as to where Mattie and J.J. were. And wherever it was, if J.J. could remain quiet for another couple of minutes.

The door opened and Gardner reappeared.

"At the risk of being rude, Lieutenant, I really must be leaving."

"I'm sorry to have held you up, Mr. Marshall. But thanks for the water."

"I'll walk you out."

Back in the rain, Gardner thanked me again, then strode to his car. His driver let him in, hopped in himself, and they drove away. I went to Perry's car, unlocked it, and acted like I was going to do the same. Once they were out of sight, however, I shot upstairs.

I locked my apartment door from the inside and called out, "It's only me. I'm alone."

"Ouch!" I heard J.J. cry.

"Oh, hush," said Mattie.

I half expected them to come climbing up my fire ladder to the bedroom window. Instead they emerged from the tiny closet. Only a little kid and a woman who scarcely cast a shadow could fit in there.

"And to think we almost hid in the shower," Mattie said.

"He could check out the bathroom legitimately but not exactly snoop around and open doors."

"Looked to me like the man was pushing it, anyway."

"Best to ease his feelings and buy some time," I said.

Mattie patted her hair.

"Obviously you saw us coming," I said.

"And from your gestures, you didn't seem pleased."

"We hid from the bad man," J.J. told me.

"No, he's not a bad man," I gently corrected him.

"It's the only way I could keep him quiet," Mattie explained.

I knelt down. "J.J., you're too young to understand what's going on," I said. "Shoot, I hardly understand it. Just know that the lieutenant is a good man who helps people. But I don't want his help right now. I need some room to breathe."

He grabbed my shirt. "You're wet."

"I know."

"Maybe that's why you can't breathe."

"What?"

"You're catching cold, Neil."

A tired smile overtook me. It was becoming apparent I needed help and the only person outside the law I could turn to, despite my apprehensions, was C. J. McDaniels.

J.J. stared at me with his big eyes. "Neil," he repeated, patting me on the back, "you're catching cold."

"I'm afraid I'm going to end up catching more than that, J.J. A hel—er, heck of a lot more."

9

"Skeletons waving from the pasture?" C. J. McDaniels asked.

"Exact words," I replied. "And much too poetic to have originated from Lamar."

The young waitress arrived and we accepted our pints of beer. I had closed down The Kitchen for the day without too much of a tongue-lashing from Perry for being late, and now C.J. and I were at The Ale House, one of the best pubs in Houston. It was a rustic Tex-Brit-type place that served Newcastle Brown Ale on tap, among many others. Unfortunately, it was a little too close to the end of the traditional workday, so the place was full of young, up-and-coming professionals. After a couple of brews many of them made no bones about their impending importance. Only thing worse than arrogance was drunken arrogance.

"And you don't know where he is?" C.J. inquired, lighting a cigarette. My mouth salivated but I resisted, purposefully sniffing the secondhand smoke. The man was of the old, hard-living world. Drink and smoke as much as you want when you want because you only go around once. A red-meat man for whom stuff like tofu was the crud you picked from between your toes once a month. Like the original Marlboro man, C.J. would probably die of cancer.

"I don't know," I replied.

"It's a tough bastard that crawls off hurt. Twice."

"That's why I'd like Mattie and her son to spend a few days with Mama," I said.

"Reckon she'll go for it." C.J. snubbed out his smoke and ran his hand over his bald head. He leaned back against the bench and rested his beer on his ample belly. In deep thought, he was like a cannonball deciding whether or not to fire.

I'd told him the full story, including Lieutenant Gardner's visit. Since the situation was to the point where I needed help, I was calling in a favor for the bullet I'd taken from Del Westview that saved C.J.'s ass. And Linda's. Then again, if I was still dating Linda, I wouldn't have had to resort to calling in a favor, and he wouldn't be so contemplative.

"That all you want from me?" C.J. finally asked. "Let this girl stay with Mama a spell?"

I sighed, stared at my beer.

"Neil"—he spoke before I did—"just because you and Linda aren't cutting the dance floor anymore doesn't mean I'm not willing to lend you a hand."

"Thanks," I said, my anxiety easing. "Linda left a message on my machine yesterday, as a matter of fact. Offered to buy me a drink."

"It'll have to be after she gets back from Amarillo. Left sunup this morning."

I nodded.

Someone dropped money in the jukebox and a song I vaguely recognized by The Cranberries vibrated across the pub. From the contortions on C.J.'s face I feared he was about to brandish his gun and blow the music machine into eternity.

"Whatever happened to Luke the Drifter?" he grumbled. "And good old-fashioned heartbroke yodeling?"

"It's still around, if you listen real hard," I said. "Charley Pride held his own on 'Kaw-Liga.' "

C.J. glanced at me, surprised. "Might be right," he replied, but meaning, You ain't so dumb for a college boy. "Now what else do you want from me?"

"I guess I need to know what this field is all about," I

began. "There has to be a way to get Lamar off Mattie, and Gunn off Dean and me."

"Maybe you want me to find that hippie first."

"Dean Shriver?"

"Whatever his name is."

"He's a beatnik, not a hippie."

"A weirdo's a weirdo."

"Undoubtedly that's the way you see it. But Dean's harmless."

"I'm not concerned what he'll do. But if you favor him, be concerned about what Gunn will do to him."

"My gut feeling is that Dean will come to me, or Keely Cohen, our writing prof," I said.

C.J. nodded, lit another cigarette. "You know him best. But don't forget about Gunter."

"What about him?" His image still gave me a clammy feeling. I took a heavy slug of ale.

"He's bad medicine."

"You know him."

"Only by reputation. Mob connections like his brother, but worse. Drugs, prostitution, car theft—white slavery. For a long spell even old Chip didn't want anything to do with him."

"Did you say white slavery?"

"Testing your attention span."

"Is it true?"

"Rumor has it. Never busted, though. Remember that incident a few years back where two guys snatched a couple of girls and ended up in a high-speed chase to Intercontinental Airport?"

"Yes. For days that was the lead local news."

"Cops believe it was Gunter's men. Never went to trial."

"Somebody shot them on the way to court," I remembered.

"Be careful of him," C.J. warned.

I thought of seeing Gunter at the doctors' office when I'd dropped off the lunches. The gray-haired man talking to him was not a happy camper. "So how is it Gunter and

Chip are back together?" I asked, making a mental note to tell C.J. of the strange encounter.

"Wouldn't you like a congressman in your back pocket?"

"But Lamar indicated that Gunter wasn't exactly in Chip's corner."

"I think Lamar screwed up his facts." C.J. finished his beer and tried to signal for another. His latest cigarette had long since died in the ashtray.

"Lamar may not be an intellectual, but he knows his business." I finished my brew. C.J. caught the waitress's eye and flashed two fingers.

"Bet my flea-ridden dog that what Lamar picked up on was Chip Gunn resisting his brother's influence," C.J. said. "It comes down to their methods, and Chip's soft soap compared to Gunter, even if their end goal is pretty much the same."

"Which is?"

"Make money, gain a lot of power."

"So having a brother in the hallowed halls of government is very tempting, but they don't agree on how to use that power," I stated.

"Given an opening, Gunter would pressure Gunn too far beyond the edge of law."

The light clicked on. Knew there was a reason I'd called McDaniels. "I see."

"Could we have a bowl of peanuts, sweetheart?" C.J. asked as the waitress thumped down our ales.

"McDaniels, you ask for peanuts every time you come in here," Sweetheart retorted. "You know we don't have any."

"Figured maybe by now you'd have gotten the hint."

She grabbed the empties. "Want a menu?"

"Don't want nothing if I can't have peanuts," he griped.

"You big baby."

I'd like a menu, I thought. But she was gone.

C.J. winked at me and lit another cigarette. "So Gardner knows nothing?" he asked.

"Far as I can tell."

"Don't count on it."

"Well, nothing he can sink his teeth into, then," I said. After all, he'd missed finding Mattie even though he knew something was afoot. However, Gardner wasn't a man to let sleeping dogs lie.

"I'll check out the field for you, but it won't be easy," he stated.

"Thanks."

"Don't thank me. I owe you. Now we'll be even."

"I still appreciate it."

"You won't when we start stepping on Gunn's and Gunter's toes," he said.

"Then maybe I'll owe you."

C. J. McDaniels chugged a good portion of his ale. "Hell," he growled, "the way you stick your ass in the line of fire, you owing me won't be worth shit."

"I want a menu," I blurted. Looking up for the waitress, though, brought a different focus to the day. Strolling toward us was none other than Lieutenant Gardner.

C.J. puffed on his latest cigarette.

"Small world," I told Gardner.

"Isn't it?" Gardner said tersely.

"Paul," C.J. said, and nodded.

"Stay out of it, McDaniels," he replied.

"Out of what?" I asked, rolling my mind over the half-million possibilities. I scooted over. "Have a seat. Want an ale?"

"We found your mystery man," Gardner said.

I lowered my mug. "Where?"

"Mattie Johnson's apartment."

"What!"

"Your description was impeccable."

My stomach churned. "You serious?"

"As a homicide."

"Spit it out, Paul," C.J. said, eyeing him carefully.

"About an hour ago a blue checked out Mattie Johnson's apartment," Gardner stated. "The door was ajar. The officer investigated. A man identified as Lamar Fowler was found, hands bound behind his back. A knife wound near his shoulder. But that's not what apparently killed him. He was shot, execution style, in the back of the head."

I almost knocked my beer onto my lap.

Gardner leaned down to me. "Where's Mattie Johnson?"

"I don't know."

"Funny, we went back to your apartment to ask you this very question, and you know that white Geo with the bad fuel pump? Well, it was gone."

"Gone?" Damn, I thought, Mattie was supposed to wait until I talked to C.J. about her staying at Mama's.

"So how do you explain the arrival of Fowler's body in this woman's apartment between the time you called and when she was supposed to be taking her boy to the— what was it?" He pulled out a short notepad. "Ah, yes, the doctor's?"

I tried to speak but couldn't.

"The boy's powerful upset," C.J. spoke up.

"You stay out of it!"

"Don't reckon I can do that."

"You've been dancing free for too long now," Gardner said in my direction. "Time you paid the fiddler."

"For what?" I managed to squeak out.

"What do you know?"

"About what?"

"Where's Mattie Johnson?"

"I have no idea."

"She was at your apartment earlier." A statement, not a question.

"You were there," I responded. "Did you see her?"

"There is such a thing as being too clever."

"I wouldn't know."

The lieutenant's thin-lipped smile could've chilled a plate of sizzling fajitas. "Don't sell yourself short, my young friend. But let's continue this discussion down at the station."

"For crying out loud, Paul, parley with the boy here," C.J. piped up. "Atmosphere's a hell of a lot better."

"Don't interfere, McDaniels."

"As a matter of fact, I've grown quite fond of yuppie jocularity and electric guitars."

"I believe you've overindulged again," Gardner quipped.

"You have no reason to haul Neil downtown."

"Could be that I want to talk about the murder weapon," Gardner said. Another Cranberries song blasted on and I could tell that what was supposed to be a relaxing evening for C.J. was quickly growing into a major irritation.

"I'm waiting for the other shoe to drop," McDaniels finally barked.

I'm not, I thought, anticipating that Gardner had uncovered some evidence that linked Lamar Fowler to Chip Gunn.

"It was a .38," the lieutenant informed us, and bore his gaze down on me.

Oh, hell scrolled across my mind like a message on a screen saver.

"The very one you inherited from your late friend Jason Keys."

Hell, oh, hell, oh, hell.

Mattie, what have you done?

10

Downtown, Lieutenant Gardner hacked at me like I was a cord of wood to be split and stacked.

We weren't in his office, but sitting opposite each other at a table in a small interrogation room. The walls were a patchwork of black squares of lifted lines that alternately pointed horizontally or vertically. At first glance they looked like the cloth covering stereo speakers. I knew outside the closed door they could hear everything we said, but I doubted they had the candid camera rolling. Unless I came up with some juicy tidbit of information, the effort wasn't worth the videotape. Besides, this encounter was starting off more as a trip to the woodshed than anything.

Without realizing it, Gardner even quoted my mother when he said, "You can educate a fool, but you can't make him think." Mother was usually referring to Uncle Norman, who was highly schooled, but didn't possess a lick of common sense. The good lieutenant, however, was most pointedly slinging the insult my way.

I remained tight-lipped and stuck to a consistent, simple story. Truth was, I hadn't known my gun was missing until Gardner had informed me. Accounting for my afternoon was easy. After leaving Gardner and the paramedics outside my apartment earlier, I spent the remainder of the workday with Perry and Robbie at The Kitchen. From there I met C.J. at the pub. There was no window of time when I could have run across town to commit a tidy little murder. Though I never really felt the lieutenant was out to pin the crime on me, he used an accusatory approach to rattle my nerves. Then I realized why. After the formality of asking about the gun and an alibi, Gardner turned immediately to Mattie's activities and whereabouts.

"When's the last time Mattie Johnson was at your apartment?" he asked.

"Yesterday when she dropped off the car."

"Who picked the Geo up?"

"I don't know. I was at work."

"You didn't see anyone drive it from your apartment?"

"No."

"But I thought the vehicle wasn't operating properly," he said.

"Mattie said her car was hesitating, but she was still able to drive it out to me."

"And you were to fix the . . . ?"

"Fuel pump. I was going to ask my landlord if he could help me."

"What do you know about fuel pumps?"

"Not much," I admitted. "That's why I was going to solicit Jerry's help."

"You indicated you two had already planned to work on the car."

"Well, I hadn't enlisted my landlord yet, but he's usually pretty agreeable to stuff like that. Likes to show off his automotive knowledge, which is miles above mine."

"How do you explain the missing car?" Gardner asked.

"I don't."

"Why not?"

"As I said, Lieutenant, I was at work."

"But if it wasn't driving correctly?"

"I don't know. I was at work."

"And Ms. Johnson was at your apartment."

"Not that I was aware of," I stated.

"So initially she left your apartment after dropping off her car."

"Yes."

"How?"

"A friend gave her a ride."

"Who?"

"I don't know. We weren't introduced."

"Man or woman?"

"Woman."

"What time?"

I took a second to select my words. We'd had that job, which I wanted to avoid mentioning and put off any tie to Chip Gunn for as long as possible. Cautiously, I replied, "It was after the nightly news."

"Five, six, nine, or ten o'clock?"

"Ten."

"Why so late?"

"It was the only time we could connect."

"What was Mattie Johnson's relationship to the deceased?"

"I heard they once lived together," I replied cautiously.

"From who?"

"Mattie."

"What else did you hear?"

I raised my palms. "Taking into account my batting average with relationships, I shy away from involvement in anyone else's."

"Answer the question."

"Nothing. I heard nothing."

Back and forth we volleyed, and for better or worse, I kept to myself that Mattie had been at my apartment. I realized this left me open to accessory charges, before and/or after the fact. Or, at the very least, an obstruction-of-justice charge. But I had to talk to Mattie first, discover for myself what went down. And I needed to figure out how this unfortunate event was going to affect Chip Gunn and his happy marauders.

C. J. McDaniels finally sprung me from the downtown station, pushing Gardner to either charge me with something or let me go. Reluctantly, Gardner opted to set me free.

"You don't do nothing half-assed, do you?" C.J. said

in the parking lot. The rain clouds had dispersed and the late-summer sun was melting into dusk. A hot evening breeze lifted sand and shoved hollow Coke cans along the broken pavement.

"I don't know what the hell's going on. Mattie didn't kill him."

"I believe you believe that." On his third attempt, he lit a cigarette.

"Guess Mattie visiting Mama isn't such a good idea anymore."

"I suspect the police will track the girl down before we do," C.J. said. "If so, you better hope she doesn't say anything about spending the night at your apartment. Gardner will have your ass in chains if he finds out you lied."

"Don't think she will. Remember, she hid in the closet when Gardner came upstairs. She knows I made out that no one was with me."

"Listen, Neil," he added, smoke scattering in the wind like dust off an old bronze statue, "should you have the luck to catch up to Mattie first, don't call me. You best connect with Gardner. If the girl's innocent as you say, then her hiding won't work a spit in her favor."

"I hear you."

"I pray you do."

I hesitated—he cocked his head to the side.

"Think Gunn had anything to do with Lamar's death?" I asked.

"Wouldn't be surprised. Catching him's another thing. The bastard's slipperier than an eel in a barrelful of snot."

"Don't I know it. Except," I added, "Gunn still professes not to be a murderer."

"So he doesn't shoot 'em, he just casts the lucky bastards down the bayou in a cement canoe."

"Well, this one was shot."

"Put my money on Gunter."

"Why?"

"Besides it being his style," C.J. grumbled, "how the hell should I know?"

"Right."

"I'm going to check this field thing," he continued. "You watch your topknot."

"Ain't been no scalpings in Texas in nearly a hundred years," I drawled.

"Don't be so sure," he shot back.

And then we drove in separate directions into the sultry night.

Once alone, the reality of the past couple of days came thundering down on me. Lamar, first stabbed, now dead. By my gun. Mattie angry enough—and I had to face the possibility—to kill. The Chip Gunn political machine willing to crush anything, or anyone, in its path—including a misguided, radical poet out to stir up his own trouble. Talk of dysfunctional justice. Then I had C. J. McDaniels hunting for a mysterious field of waving skeletons—a prime piece of information that perhaps drove Lamar to his demise. And finally, if my scorecard was correct, somewhere on the periphery of this whole pseudo-Shakespearean mess was Karl Gunter, Gunn's icy-veined brother.

My head hurt. I wanted rest. Or at least peace. Peace of mind. Finding Mattie would help. Would she be waiting for me? Surely the police had my apartment staked out for just that likelihood. Mattie would know that. I was discovering that she was much more street-smart than her shy demeanor let on. Of course, if she did show up, that would lend to her innocence. Strolling right in the middle of a police trap was not the first thing a murderer would do. Unless that person was extremely savvy and had an airtight alibi.

My head ached like fury.

Since I'd been unable to eat at the pub, I ran by the market on the way back to my apartment and picked up a bunch of fresh basil, some Roma tomatoes, a few other vegetables, a package of fresh angel-hair pasta, a pound of crawfish tail meat, and a Cabernet Sauvignon from the Sainte Genevieve winery down the road in Fort Stockton.

I'd found over the last year that cooking was a great stress reliever. That and running, but I was too tired to lace up my Nikes. Kicking back with a good meal and a glass or two of wine held a much stronger appeal.

I thought about calling Robbie Persons to see if he wanted to join me for dinner. Keely Cohen was who I really wanted to invite, but I knew her husband, Mark, was in town and would likely frown on the last-minute idea. Not to mention it was getting late—I'd be lucky to eat by nine or ten. However, I did resolve to ask the two of them over sometime soon. Or better yet, I'd choose a night when The Kitchen was not in use and host them there. At least it was a way to spend time with Keely.

At any rate, I was feeling kind of lonely when the day's dying embers showed some flash. As I pulled into my driveway, preparing to back out was Candace Littlefield. I didn't know whose smile blossomed larger.

She hopped out of her truck. "I was beginning to think you were avoiding me."

"I am," I shot back.

Candace propped her hands on her hips. "Not funny, Neil."

I couldn't help but laugh as I climbed out of my Bug.

"And I'm not scheduled to work another job for a week," she added for good measure.

"You're low on the totem pole," I explained. "When business hits a lull you just have to ride it out."

Her sparkling green eyes eased my anxiety and put compassion back in the day.

"I'll talk to Robbie," I said, "and see what I can do."

"Thank you."

"Other than work, how you doing?"

"Fair to middlin'."

I grabbed the sacks of groceries. "You eaten?"

"No, and I'm starving."

"Come on, kid, and tell me how your classes are treating you."

"Better by the day," she replied, taking a bag from me. Her auburn hair glistened like a streak of setting sun, accentuating the freckles on her thin face. She spoke about her courses, all basic requirements that she was getting out of the way at U of H. I seldom ran into her on campus, though she knew Keely and Sondra and I were around to help and support her. I was as proud of Candace as if I were her natural brother, the way she'd persevered first through Jason Keys's death, then her grandfather's. She was out to become a veterinarian, and I had little doubt she'd eventually transfer to Texas A&M and work that goal into reality.

I kicked my car door shut and she followed me into the apartment. "So you're fixing to move to the trailer," I said as we hiked up the stairs.

"News travels fast."

"You here to get my blessings as well as work?" I unlocked the door and we entered my apartment. An uneasy feeling hit me as we stepped into the small living room.

"You don't think it's such a good idea, do you?"

"Oh, I don't know," I replied slowly, and set the bag on the kitchen table. I turned a full circle, straining my ears for any sound that would indicate we weren't alone.

"What's wrong?" the girl asked.

I shook my head, made my way into the bedroom. A stillness that masked a thousand feelings had a stranglehold on the room. I felt Candace behind me. Gently, I opened the closet door, unsure what to expect. But found nothing.

Candace continued to hold her tongue as I searched the bathroom and kitchen for good measure. Then I pulled out the bottle of tequila from the bottom kitchen cabinet and poured myself a shot. Double. Paranoia was working my nerves.

I needed a long trip to Disney World, or something.

"What is going on, Neil?" Candace asked.

I sighed, tossed down the shot—ground my teeth together and shivered—and proceeded to give Candace the *Reader's Digest* condensed version of Lamar's death, my episode with Gardner, and my missing gun.

"And I have to admit," I concluded as I rose to start dinner, "it doesn't look good for Mattie."

"Of course it doesn't look good for her," Candace snapped. "She killed her boyfriend."

"We don't know that."

"Shoot, Neil, it's me who needs to worry about you living alone, not you worrying about me. You let your emotions rule your common sense."

"Funny, that seems to be the general sentiment." I set a pot of water on for the angel hair and dumped the vegetables and herbs from the grocery bag onto the counter.

"Now, don't get your feelings hurt."

"Don't get your feelings hurt," I mocked.

"Most sensitive man I ever met," Candace muttered.

I cleared a space for a small cutting board and began to chop the Roma tomatoes, followed by a sweet Texas-grown 1015 onion, part of a Portobello mushroom, a yellow bell pepper, a small red chili pepper, a young zucchini squash, and two big cloves of garlic.

"Want a glass of wine?" I asked.

"Contributing to the delinquency of a minor?"

"Like giving a nickel to a presidential campaign."

"How rude!"

I grinned. "Want a glass of wine or not?"

"Yes, thank you. What are you making?"

"Angel-hair pasta with a fresh vegetable and crawfish sauce."

"I'll try to choke it down."

"Julia Child couldn't have given a more sophisticated critique of my food," I responded, and uncorked the Cabernet.

"You're welcome." She brushed a strand of her hair from her eyes and smiled like a kid in a candy store. I handed her a glass of wine.

I poured a little olive oil in the bottom of a cast-iron saucepan and lit a medium-low gas flame beneath it. As I minced fresh basil with a little Italian flat parsley, Candace asked, "You're not in any danger, are you?"

"Not at all," I replied too quickly.

Her smoldering emerald eyes caused my cheeks to flush.

I dropped the basil and garlic into the warming oil. "Really," I added, though I hardly convinced myself.

As the aroma of garlic and basil filled the apartment, I added the mushroom and gave the mixture a stir.

"Want me to bring the Winchester up from the trailer?" she finally asked.

I paused, then added a touch of Tony's seasoning and scraped in the onions. "Thought about it, but I still have the .45."

"Well, you're all set then if a grizzly bear charges you."

"Comforting, isn't it?" The pasta water was boiling, so I dumped a few tablespoons of oil in and some salt, then delicately separated the fresh strands of angel hair and slid them into the steaming water.

"You attract trouble like a horse's ass attracts flies," she said, and swallowed a mouthful of wine.

"That's the sweetest thing you've ever told me."

"And will be for a long time to come." Candace stood. "Where's your little television?"

"Bedroom." I tossed in the yellow bell pepper, the chili pepper, zucchini, and tomatoes. As the flavors melded I added a healthy splash of wine, a teaspoon of salt, and a couple of pinches of white pepper. The pasta cooked quickly, so I strained and rinsed it in cold water, then coated the fine strands with olive oil.

Candace carted the TV to the table so we could both see it. "I want to catch the early news on Fox, see if the Astros won."

"You don't follow baseball," I commented, and quickly added the crawfish tail meat, stirred the sauce, and turned the heat low. I didn't want the tomatoes to cook too long as I hadn't skinned them. The zucchini and peppers were also better if they held a firm texture. Half paying attention to

Candace as she tuned in the station, I grated a small block of Parmesan cheese onto a salad plate.

As I was completing the last step, tossing the pasta with the sauce, a political advertisement blurted from the television. It took a second for me to realize the candidate was Chip Gunn, preaching family values, reduced government intervention, and free trade—which caused me to wonder a minute on his definition of free trade.

Candace had to lift her chin off the floor. "I've been staying clear of that man," she said. "This is the first time I haven't turned a deaf ear to his bullcorn message. And it makes me sick. All I can think of is him standing there at the stables with his two goons waving guns in our faces like we knew where his stupid horse was. Idiot! Someone should make mincemeat out of him."

"Not a thought I want to dwell on since dinner's ready," I said. "Come on, shake it off."

Then the news came on, and we both lost our appetites.

"In southwest Houston today a twenty-three-year-old woman was arrested for the execution-style shooting of her former boyfriend. Mattie Johnson was charged with first-degree murder in the slaying of Lamar Fowler at her southwest apartment. Police caught up with Johnson . . ."

"Oh, my God," said Candace.

I couldn't say anything as I watched police lead Mattie away in handcuffs. It was one thing to argue her innocence because she was a friend—and in my heart I knew she didn't kill anyone—but it was quite another to observe events as they unfold across the airwaves. *Woman taken into custody. Hear the cold facts surrounding the circumstances. Pretty cut-and-dry, isn't it, viewer?*

It shook my confidence.

Distraught as Mattie appeared, though, I worried about one other person just as much.

Who was taking care of Mattie's precocious little boy, J.J.?

11

First thing in the morning I called defense attorney Alice Tarkenton. She was a tough old bird who drove a Harley and smoked like a stoked barbecue pit. I knew Alice because she had written Jason Keys's will and defended me during the grand-jury investigation over Old Man Littlefield's death.

"Neil Marshall, you old goat," she shouted. "How the hell are you?"

"Still kicking. I need a favor."

"Again?" Her voice was as subtle as a motorcycle changing gears.

"There's a young woman who's been arrested for a murder I don't think she committed."

"You talking about that Johnson girl the cops picked up last night?"

"Nothing escapes you."

"Heard that was a done deal."

"Well, maybe some things escape you."

"That ain't exactly the way to sweet-talk a lady into a favor. I'm guessing it's a favor because neither you nor Ms. Johnson has any money."

"I'm sorry," I said, feeling my face redden. "But Mattie really needs a friend right now."

"Sounds like she's got one."

"Trying to be."

There was a pause. Then: "I'll talk to her."

"Can I come?"

"Is she being arraigned?"

"I don't know," I replied, wondering why in the world she thought I would.

"Best move fast, then. Meet you at the Mykawa station around ten. We don't have long before they ship her down to the county jail."

"She's got a kid," I said before she could hang up. "Any idea where he'd be?"

"With a relative."

"Don't know if she's got anyone that close in town," I told her.

"At Juvenile, most likely. For the time being."

"I want to know if I can see him," I said.

"All it takes is the Johnson girl's permission and you can have him."

"Let's get her permission. Thanks, Alice."

"You owe me sex."

"What!"

She cackled. "If I were ten years younger, baby." Her smoker's hack erupted as she hung up.

I replaced the receiver and faced Candace. She'd spent the night as we had talked into the early hours of the morning and had put away a couple margaritas. After I'd convinced her to take my room, I'd fallen into a short, but heavy, snooze on the couch.

"I'm going to take Mattie's son to Mama's."

"What you should have done to begin with." Candace handed me a cup of coffee.

"Thanks."

"Black, right?"

"Absolutely." I was bone-weary, and the fresh coffee was welcome.

"You're into something deeper than you let on," she added, adjusting her robe as she sat on the couch.

"I told you what's what."

"What's what," she repeated like an insult. "You still think of me like a kid."

Two roads diverged, I thought. I'd given her the

Reader's Digest version, and she'd picked up on more. Now was the time to fill her in on the rest.

"So Chip Gunn actually washed the blood from the knife?" she asked incredulously.

"Yes."

"I'm going to barf the breakfast I can't eat!" she exclaimed. "Someone's got to do something."

Oh, no, I thought. Not another rabid Gunn hater. "Don't you go fanatical on me," I warned.

"Bite your tongue. That's a word for them liberals back east."

I smiled to myself. "Whatever you say, darling."

"Why are you laughing at me?" she demanded. "You think what Gunn's doing is funny?"

"No, ma'am," I replied as humbly as I could. I picked up the phone and punched in Perry's home number, then raised an index finger to hush Candace.

"I heard," Perry said, after he recognized my voice.

"You know it's a crock of shit."

"I would hope so."

"I've called Alice and I'm going to meet with her—and maybe Mattie—at ten. Thought I'd better let you know."

"If anyone can help her, it's Alice," he said.

"Be in touch as soon as possible." And we hung up.

Candace was fuming when I went in to take a shower. She was still steaming when I emerged wearing a pair of khaki Dockers, a short-sleeved red Izod, and my brown Tony Lama cowboy boots—preppie civility could carry me only so far.

"You going to Boys Town?" Candace asked.

I pulled up my pant leg and flashed my boots.

"Greenhorn," she muttered.

"Greenhorn? What do you mean?"

"Means you have no business dressing like an eastern college boy come west."

"You're in a pissy mood today."

"And you're not?"

"No," I said, my voice sinking. "I'm teetering between highly concerned and just plain scared."

Candace had her hair pulled back and was about to bind it into a ponytail when she realized I was serious. A sudden wave of affection swept across her face. She finished tying back her hair.

"Oh, blow that off," she said at last. "Just let yourself get hoppin' mad."

"Think that'll work?"

"Damn straight."

"Obviously you have it mastered."

"Getting there," Candace replied as she marched to the calendar in the kitchen. "Goddamn it, you don't have my barrel race marked down."

"Getting there? You *are* there."

"Well?"

"Who you riding?" I asked.

"Granger. Flying Dutchman's faster, but his timing's off. He keeps knocking over barrels."

"Well, I'll be there. I won't forget."

"Heard that before."

"Oh, shut up."

"Good, you're getting mad," she said, and we laughed.

Until someone cut us off by pounding on the door.

My first reaction was that Lamar had returned. As illogical as I knew that was, I still froze for a couple of seconds. Candace's deer-in-the-headlight look told me she was equally shocked.

"Think it's the cops?" she asked.

Cops. Gardner. Arrest Neil Marshall. Shit!

"Well, let's find out." I pried my feet from the floorboards.

Cops. Gardner. Arrest. I opened the door without bothering to ask who it was.

"Dude," Dean Shriver greeted.

A mix of relief, anxiety, and bewilderment stirred within me.

"You look dreadful," I said at his soiled, scrungier-than-usual appearance. Though he still wore his John Lennon–style sunglasses. "Where have you been?"

Dean stepped past me. I picked up the sweet scent of marijuana on his clothes. "Sleeping beneath a billboard that reads, 'Jesus set us free. Call Roy Bob Chambers, Bail Bondsman.' "

Candace shook her head as if to clear the room of this apparition.

"Jesus, Dean," I said, "you've become a street person."

"Close the door," he snapped, pointing at me with a large manila envelope. "They may be following me."

I humored him and shut the door, then eased to the window and peeked down at the driveway. Only saw my Bug. And Samson the wonder dog sleeping in the shade.

"Who may be following you?" I asked.

"Gunn and his thugs."

"How'd you get here?"

"My ten-speed." He grinned. "Got my little truck well hidden. They won't find me that way, dig?"

Why did I feel like I was being visited by the Unabomber?

"You're getting around Houston on a bicycle?" Candace spoke up. "Are you loco or trying to commit suicide?"

"A little of both," he replied. "Aren't we all?"

Candace looked horrified.

"Here down on dark earth before we all go to heaven," Dean quoted Kerouac. "Think about it—our stage the dark earth. I mean, lately I've become hip why the earth is dark—it is a reflection of the human heart. And it's that dark heart any sane man knows he must destroy. But in destroying the darkness, so goes the man. Is there any other possibility, I think not, Jack."

"What is he chawing about?" Candace asked me. She appeared ready to draw the .45.

"Life, sister," Dean continued.

"Sounds more like death, brother." Clearly, Candace was not amused.

"Life is the blues and death is the crowd we're all playing to," he said.

Somewhere in the distant past I heard the echo of fingers snapping.

"Writers are some weird people," Candace commented. "Makes me glad I'm going to deal with animals."

"Dean, what do you want?" I asked.

He lifted the dark glasses into his tangled hair and focused his bloodshot eyes on me.

"Huh?" he grunted.

"Are you looking for a place to stay?" I asked, trying not to sound too hospitable. "Are you hungry? Do you need money?"

"No, man. I'm cool."

"Is this a social visit, then?" I asked.

He popped his palm with the large envelope then handed it to me.

"It's not going to blow up, is it?"

"I'm out to rock the establishment any way I can, dude. That goes for the moldy university writing programs with all their barren words from infertile minds."

"Keely and I thank you for your vote of confidence," I said.

"Oh, man, not you or the sweet professor—there are exceptions. But too few, too few." He was rambling. "These are a batch of new poems I want you and the prof to peruse, dig? Highly explosive words to shake the powers that be."

"Why don't you just come to class?" I asked.

"And endanger my friends? Oh, selfish dude."

"Chip Gunn is not going to obliterate a classroom of poets in broad daylight."

"School is uncool. You can reach me through the classified section of the *Chronicle*. Put an ad in saying you have a rare Kerouac book for sale."

"And have every lunatic in Houston call me? No, thank you."

His countenance twisted. "You can say you're looking for a rare book."

"Looking, okay. Selling, no."

"That's what I said."

"Okay . . ." I hesitated and glanced at Candace. "So, Dean, if there's nothing else, I have to make tracks. Mattie needs our help."

"Mattie? What does she need help for?"

"She was arrested last night for Lamar's murder," I explained.

Dean began to shake. "How can that be?"

"Something's not right," I said. "I've got a lawyer meeting with her. She'll figure a way to spring Mattie."

"How can that be?" he repeated, not hearing a word I said.

"It'll be in this morning's paper."

"Can't trust the press anymore, man. Just another fucked-up establishment."

"Why don't you stay here for a while?" I surprised myself with the invitation. "Curl up on the couch and get some sleep. You'll feel better."

"The bastard!" he bellowed. "The bastard! He can't get away with this. He can't!"

Candace took a step back. "Who are you talking about?"

"The biggest bastard in the city," he growled.

I touched his shoulder. "Calm down. You're not thinking—"

He twisted away and glared at me, his eyes turning from hazed confusion to animosity.

"The bastard!" he shrieked one last time, then burst out the door and down the stairs. He was out in the sultry morning, on his bike, and halfway down the driveway before I even hit daylight.

"Dean," I hollered futilely. "Dean Shriver, you're acting the fool." *You can educate a fool, but you can't make him think,* I heard in my mind, a duo of Gardner and Mother.

"Dumb shit," I muttered.

"That was frightening," Candace said behind me.

"Not nearly as frightening as it'll get if he confronts who I think he's fixing to confront."

"Gunn?"

I nodded, ran a hand through my hair.

"Maybe it's about time someone did."

"I expect you're right. But half-stoned and armed only with crackpot jive isn't the way."

"So hard-hearted all of a sudden?"

"No. Just talking fact."

"And what is the way?" she asked.

"Hell if I know," I replied.

"But you're talking fact?"

"Why are you laying into me?"

"To relax you." The sparkle was returning to her eyes.

I couldn't help but raise a slight smile. "It's time to part ways," I said. "I don't want to miss Alice."

"Cool, hip, man, dude. Dig?"

If I wasn't so worried, I'd have laughed.

"I dig," I replied. "A hole that keeps getting deeper and deeper and deeper."

12

Alice Tarkenton wore a navy-blue suit and skirt, stood no taller than my shoulders, but I still felt as though I looked up to her.

"A real rat's nest," she said in a gravelly voice.

"Beg your pardon?" I asked as we entered the station. The Mykawa building was constructed of white and gray bricks with an Art Deco greenish trim. From the outside it looked like a renovated mini-mall. Inside, however, there was no doubt it was a police facility.

"The girl's caught in a real rat's nest," Alice repeated.

"That your legal opinion?"

"I was putting it in layman's terms." A smirk creased her weathered face.

"Appreciate the consideration.

We approached the front desk, which was behind a thick window with nerves of wire mesh running through it. And to my surprise, talking to the desk officer was Sergeant Victor Hernandez. He worked homicide with Gardner and was sweet on Linda Garcia, C. J. McDaniels's daughter. Though Hernandez had treated me cordially before, he was downright friendly now that Linda and I were no longer seeing each other.

"Neil Marshall," he said, pushing the button to release the lock on the side door so we could enter. "What the hell are you doing down here, amigo?"

"Lunching with the chief, of course."

"*Pendejo,*" he muttered, then caught Alice's eye. "Ms. Tarkenton," he added coolly with a nod.

"You two know each other?" I asked.

"Sergeant, we don't have time for male bonding," Alice snapped.

"No, ma'am. I know you've got scum to defend."

"How impartial of you, Sergeant." Alice was a veteran sparring partner.

"Mattie Johnson isn't scum," I said, feeling my blood pressure rise. Hernandez was a hard man, but he was also a fair-minded cop. His beef, I therefore figured, had more to do with Alice Tarkenton than the people he slandered.

"The Johnson girl," Hernandez said, his tone softening. "You got me there. She killed scum."

"I'm representing her," Alice told him.

Hernandez turned to me. "This has to be your doing. I can see that girl don't have no money."

"She's my friend," I replied.

"Which is probably why she's in trouble to begin with," he said only half-jokingly.

"What do you mean she killed scum?" Alice asked.

"Lamar Fowler had a rap sheet long enough to provide every stall in this building with toilet paper."

"How much time did he do?"

"Most recently? Three years, auto theft."

"I want to see her," Alice said.

"She has the right to counsel." Hernandez turned—and we followed him to an elevator and ascended to the second floor. A short way down the hall we entered a series of offices. He led us into a large room and past aisles of desks and finally to an interrogation room similar to the one in which I'd had the privilege to chat with Lieutenant Gardner. This one, too, was wired for video.

"Wait here," he said.

Alice pulled a chair on one side of the table. I stood quietly while she rummaged through her briefcase and extracted a notepad and pen.

"Well, how do you know Hernandez?" Alice finally blurted.

"He's a friend of C. J. McDaniels," I said.

"Oh, that's right. You know the old son of a bitch. McDaniels has done his share of work out of my office over the years."

I thought I should relate my previous conversations with C.J., my lies to Gardner, and my dealings with Mattie and Lamar—but I decided this wasn't the time. Or the place.

I opted for cute. "Bet you and Hernandez don't exchange Christmas cards."

"I've been a burr on his ass more than once," she replied. "Especially the Oakley case when Hernandez was working narcotics. Oakley was a poor bastard who thought he was driving produce to and from Mexico. Come to find out, behind those crates of onions and corn were bales and bales of marijuana. Well, Oakley gets nailed and spills his guts. But his contact, identified only as Big Mac, is nowhere to be found. So Oakley, who calls himself Little Fry, is hung in the sun to dry, and the DA says no deal. Turns out, the forces that be had the truck and a dummy company all in the poor simpleton's name, too." She stopped talking as she dug maniacally in her briefcase.

I watched her and silently counted one, two, three—and on four, Alice ceased her excavation and looked at me.

"I'm listening," I told her.

"Don't you want to know how I got Oakley off?"

"Of course, but shouldn't we be discussing Mattie's case?"

"There'll be plenty of time for that," she grumbled.

"Okay," I said, knowing what an appetite her ego had. "How did you get Mr. Oakley off?"

"I told you—Oakley was a simpleton. IQ wasn't higher than sixty-five. It was all he could do to drive the truck, never mind mastermind a complex dummy company for drug-running. DA wasn't aware of that. Jury didn't take ten minutes to agree with me. Hernandez was left with a bunch of unclaimed weed to burn, and an extremely irritated DA's office."

"Hernandez is smarter than that."

"He was young then, an ambitious bastard. And his superiors were as much at fault. Been after me ever since, though."

"Highly encouraging since he seems to be involved in Mattie's case."

"We don't know he's involved."

"Works for Gardner, took us to Mattie. He's involved."

She grunted. "Damn! You can't smoke in here anymore."

The door opened and a homicide sergeant escorted Mattie in. I bit my cheek. She looked sallow and weak. Her eyes were a puffy pink. The sergeant guided her down opposite us.

"Hernandez said you could be here," he told me. "Don't know if the lieutenant will like it."

"Gardner and I go way back," I replied.

"I expect total privacy," Alice said vehemently.

The sergeant didn't even justify her comment with a response. He merely left the room and closed the door behind him.

"Nothing like a little aggravation to get the blood pumping," Alice told me, and winked.

"Mattie," I began, "this is Alice Tarkenton. She's a lawyer who will help you."

"You get Joey?" she asked.

"We picked him up first, dear, and dropped him off at a friend's house," Alice said, her rough voice amazingly soft.

"I want to see my baby." And she began to sob.

"In due time," Alice continued.

"Don't worry," I said, "J.J.'s at Mama's, not too far away. He's fine and being well cared for."

For the first time Mattie looked at me. "Thanks. They found gunpowder marks on me."

Alice tensed. "What have you told the police?"

"Nothing."

"Good. Why don't you tell me what happened."

Mattie rubbed her black hair from her eyes.

"Did you take my gun?" I asked.

Alice could have slapped me. But I had to explain: "If you hadn't been so caught up in the Oakley case, I'd have told you it was the murder weapon."

"Yes," Mattie answered in a weak voice. "I took your gun. I'm sorry."

A dreadful knot twisted my stomach and I started to speak, but I interpreted Alice's glare with crystal clarity: *shut the fuck up*.

"Why did you take Neil's gun?" she asked.

"To protect myself from Lamar," she said. "But I didn't kill him."

Alice adjusted her notepad. "Okay, dear, take it from the top and tell the whole story straight through." She caught my eye. "Straight through," she repeated.

I crossed my arms and leaned back against the wall. In my mind, though, I made a note to tell Mattie about the supposed car trouble and that she *hadn't* spent the night.

Then what will you do when J.J. spills the beans, Neil? a voice resembling my father's stern honesty rumbled in my mind. *Surely you won't indicate the child isn't telling the truth.*

Never, I replied to myself. I'll just deal with the situation if it arises.

Mattie was sketching her history with Lamar and describing having seen him at Chip Gunn's party. I cringed at hearing his name pulled into the scenario. Even Alice Tarkenton's expression shifted from routine indifference to oh-shit-how-can-this-get-worse?

"After Neil left I decided to go to my apartment," Mattie continued. "That's when I slipped the gun in my purse. I'd seen Neil stash it so I knew where the piece was."

Alice interrupted the narrative. "Why'd you go to your apartment?"

"What?" Mattie was caught off guard by the intrusion as much as I was.

"I want you to tell me why you decided to slip off to your apartment after Neil left. He didn't know you were leaving, did he?"

"Uh, no."

"So, simply state why you went to your place when you felt you needed to carry a gun in order to feel safe."

"I, ah, forgot something." Mattie was staring into her lap.

"What?" Alice asked.

I broke my vow of silence. "Tell her, Mattie," I said.

"A key," she peeped.

"To what?" Alice asked.

"A safety-deposit box."

Alice lifted her pen from the paper and turned to me. "My ulcer's acting up again, and I'm not even getting paid for this."

"I'll get you some money somehow," I comforted.

"Oh, shut up," she told me, then redirected her attention to Mattie. "What's in the safety-deposit box, dear?"

Mattie took a deep, quivering breath. "Money."

Alice tossed her pen to the pad, leaned back, and crossed her arms. "Let's not play twenty questions. Explain."

"It was money from Lamar when he was stealing cars. You got to believe I didn't know he was stealing cars, then." Her focus darted from Alice to me, then back. "I thought he was a repo man like he said. Until he got busted, anyway. Well, he told me to hold on to this key until he got out of prison. I didn't want to, but he said he'd make life real bad for me and Joey when he got out if I didn't."

"Why didn't he just open a savings account?" I asked.

"Lamar dealt in cash only. He was scared the feds would take his money if it was in a bank," Mattie explained. "He hadn't paid any income tax in years."

"Did you know there was money in the box when he gave you the key?" Alice asked.

"No."

"When did you look in the box?"

"About a year ago. I got curious. And I was real broke. I thought maybe there was something I could pawn, then pay it off after I got a job, put it back, and Lamar would never know."

"How much money?" Alice asked.

"Fifty thousand dollars," Mattie answered. "There were five envelopes each with tightly bound stacks of crisp one-hundred-dollar bills."

My heart skipped a beat. "Fifty thousand dollars!" Now I understood Lamar's remarks on what was owed him.

"Sounds like lots, don't it?" Mattie asked. "But put it together and it wasn't as thick as, say, *The Joy of Cooking*."

"Still sounds pretty thick to me," Alice proclaimed. "Keep explaining."

"Well, I took one envelope. Joey and I were hurting bad. The bakery I worked at had closed down, and I couldn't find another job that'd pay enough so I could make the bills. Suddenly life got easier. We moved from the apartment Lamar had shared with me, and I bought us new outfits, nice furniture, and stuff that normal people have. Then I got the job at Perry Stevens Catering. Kitchen pay still wasn't great, but it was better than most places. And the extra money for parties really makes up for it."

Alice glanced at me for clarification.

"The clients pay for labor on parties," I said. "Mattie gets fifteen dollars an hour when she works a function. I get twenty because I'm one of the chefs and usually in charge. Kitchen pay is lower."

"So did you begin to replace the money?" Alice asked.

"I tried, but then my car died."

"Oh, hell," Alice muttered.

"I went back to the bank and took two more envelopes," she said. "I swore I'd pay it back. Only bought a Geo and used the leftover money for emergencies like when Joey got sick and had to be rushed to the hospital for pneumonia. I don't have insurance."

Alice made no judgments. As if fighting weariness, she waved her hand and said, "Continue."

"Well, I knew Lamar would kill me when he got out, so I moved again, told everyone he knew I was moving to Austin, and began to use my maiden name. Kept my phone number unlisted, too."

"You said you weren't married to him," I spoke up.

"I wasn't, but he made me take his last name. Said that way everybody would know I was his."

"You just might rival Oakley," Alice piped up. "Go on."

"I didn't know Lamar was out until the Gunn party," Mattie said.

"Did you stab him?" Alice asked.

"No, ma'am. I was so scared. Then today I decided I'd get the last two envelopes, take Joey, and leave."

"Leave?" I squeaked, and pulled myself from the wall. My hands fell to my sides. Leave me holding the bag, I thought. Gardner would've eaten me for lunch.

"I knew you could take care of yourself," she explained. "And if I wasn't around, then Lamar wouldn't be bothering you."

"But?" Alice prompted.

"Lamar surprised me and Joey at my apartment," she said.

"This isn't boding well," Alice commented. "I want a damn cigarette."

"He wanted the key, and Joey. So I pulled the gun on him. But he just laughed. He grabbed me and tried to take the gun out of my hand. Joey was in the car and didn't hear me screaming. Lamar was getting real mad, so he backhanded me. I held on with all my might. That was when the gun went off. Lamar dropped to his knees. He was moaning, and I ran out the door. That was the last time I saw Lamar."

"Where'd you go?" Alice asked.

"To the bank. I got the last two envelopes of money."

"Where are they now?"

"A safe place."

Alice sighed. "And so you got picked up outside of Champs."

"Joey was hungry!" Her head dipped and the sobs returned. "I want my boy."

"In due time," Alice repeated with amazing patience. And then like a thunderbolt: "Did you kill Lamar?"

"No! I didn't kill no one! I want my boy."

"Now what?" I asked.

Alice began packing her briefcase. "Get the sergeant," she directed me. "Dear," she said, addressing Mattie, "we've got to go now. Don't you fret about your child. He is in good hands. Only other thing I want you to do is not talk to the police. I'll try to put off your transfer to the Harris County jail by saying you're almost ready to give a statement. That'll buy a day, maybe even two."

"Yes, ma'am," Mattie said, barely audible.

"And keep the faith."

Before fetching the sergeant, however, I informed them both of my discussions with Lieutenant Gardner concerning the malfunctioning car and that I'd told him Mattie hadn't been at my place. Alice was no longer ready to slap me. She was ready to string me up.

Without another word, I opened the door and signaled for the sergeant. The rough-looking detective entered and escorted a silent Mattie back out. Hernandez was nowhere in sight. He really didn't want to deal with Alice, I thought.

Once they were gone, Alice stared me straight in the eye. "Believe she didn't kill him?"

"Yes."

"There will be a trial. No doubt there's enough evidence against her."

"No doubt."

"Believe the rest of her story?"

"Kind of hard not to," I said. "Mattie fell under the spell of that money, but she cares foremost for Joey."

"Maybe. You have any idea where the rest of the dough is?" she asked.

"None."

"Or who might have killed Lamar Fowler with your gun—which she admitted taking—in her apartment after she struggled with the man, then tried to flee the city?" Alice's voice grew increasingly angry.

"You sure have a talent at setting things in perspective," I responded.

"Well, do you?"

"Since you put it that way," I said. "How could I?"

13

"Come on, Alice," I implored, following her as she firmly marched out of the building. "The police report said Lamar was killed execution style, hands bound behind his back. You think a sliver of a girl like Mattie could've done that?"

"The man was weak from blood loss. She admitted to shooting him during their struggle. What's to say she didn't coax him to bed, then finish the job?"

"I don't buy it. As antagonistic as Lamar was toward her, he wouldn't have allowed her near him."

"I'm not ruling anything out at this point," Alice stated emphatically.

"Fine. You'll have to be convinced your way."

We stepped into the September heat. In another month the weather might break and be bearable.

"Is there anything at all you've neglected to tell me?" she asked, coming to a dead stop. "Reassure me, Neil. Right now."

"Do you know about Lamar being stabbed at Gunn's house?"

"Yes."

"That Gunn covered it up so there's no evidence?"

"Yes."

"That Mattie and her son spent the night with me?"

"Yes."

"That Lamar visited me at the apartment, but didn't know Mattie was there?"

"Yes."

"That he collapsed in my driveway, too, then disappeared again?"

"Yes."

"That Gardner came up into my apartment and Mattie and J.J. hid?"

"Yes."

"That I lied to the lieutenant?"

"Oh, *damn*, yes."

"That I talked to C. J. McDaniels and he's looking for a field of waving skeletons?"

"No," she answered sourly.

I told her what Lamar had overheard and C.J.'s quest.

"Anything else?"

"Did I tell you that a friend of mine who is, ah, kind of on the radical side witnessed the cover-up and is trying to bring it to light? He wants to destroy Gunn's political career," I added.

"No," her voice even more curt.

I explained Dean Shriver's mission and how his father did business years ago with Gunn and Gunter.

"So Karl Gunter's involved, too?" she asked.

"That's who Lamar was walking out when he was attacked."

"Neil, honey, you may be right about the girl's innocence, but it'll take an act of God to prove it."

"That's why I called you."

"Don't go shucking me, boy," she said, and opened the door to her new Cadillac.

"I mean it."

"You know, I think you do. But this whole mess is going to require some deft handling. I'll talk to C.J. You stay the hell away from Gunn."

"I'm not worried about Chip Gunn."

"Chip Gunn? You mean the same man who almost killed you a spell back, and did land you a record of justified homicide? That Chip Gunn?"

"All right. I'll stay clear."

"And Gunter. You stay a country mile from that bastard. He'd as soon turn you to compost as to shake your hand."

Before she closed her door I asked, "Anybody else you want me to avoid?"

"Yeah, me. I'll be in touch." And she was off.

I needed a break.

As I putted away in my mighty VW I was grateful we hadn't run into Lieutenant Gardner one more time. First duty now was to run by The Kitchen. I wasn't scheduled to work tonight, for which I thanked God. Perhaps I could convince Robbie to take in an Astros game with me. They were winding down a decent season with a fair shot at the playoffs. I wasn't sure I liked the relatively new division break with the wild-card spot—I was a traditionalist and still, after all these years, lamented that the American League had adopted the designated-hitter rule—but it made for an interesting homestretch. And I loved the 'Stros. I was at Mike Scott's no-hitter against the Giants in '86. About cried when Nolan Ryan left for the Rangers. Thought Larry Dierker was a hell of a pitcher and one of the most underrated guys who ever played the game. And I believed that, with perhaps the exception of Jeff Bagwell, José Cruz had one of the prettiest home-run swings I'd ever seen.

Only the Rockets gave me as much pleasure. Oilers used to. Now they were off to Nashville. Never did forgive their fair-weather owner for firing Bum Phillips.

Managing to successfully keep my mind preoccupied, I coasted to a stop in front of my place of employment. I remembered as I disengaged myself from the Bug that I had to begin serious work on my manuscript. Besides the writing class this semester, I was taking an independent study. Mentored by Professor Keely Cohen. It was a year-long assignment with the projected end result a book-length collection of poems. I had quite a few to work with, though I was dissatisfied with too many of them.

Maybe I'd write a lyric on José Cruz's swing, I thought

as I opened the front door. I recalled then that I had Dean's new batch of poems in my car. Needed to get them to Keely. Good excuse to call her.

Robbie wasn't around, but Perry was. He was busy working on a lunch.

"What's going on?" I asked. "Where's Claudia?"

"She won't be in until later," he replied as he carved out tomato roses for garnish. "Grab an apron."

"Sure." It was unusual that Perry, especially in a dress shirt and bow tie, dug into the food prep anymore. I tied on a full white apron with our logo—an embroidered PSC within the image of a wineglass and hugged by a knife and fork—across the front.

"Mrs. Beauchamp wanted a light lunch for twelve," Perry explained. "She phoned in her order at the last possible second."

"So what are we fixing?"

"For the entrée, cold shrimp on a bed of arugula, Belgian endive, and romaine lettuce with a remoulade sauce. Served with cheese toasts."

"A starter?" I asked.

"Southwestern gazpacho. It's made and chilling."

Southwestern meant we added a little jalapeño pepper and cilantro to a basically traditional recipe. Tangy and delicious.

"Dessert?" I asked.

"Chocolate-chip-pecan pie with a hot chocolate sauce."

"That blows the healthy lunch."

"Oh, these ladies had to have chocolate. Richer the better. That's why they eat light meals." He was in a damn good mood considering his status of emergency chef. For the most part he now preferred the role of quality manager, not preparer.

"I didn't know that," I replied. "Thanks for setting me straight."

He smiled broadly. "Next lesson will be on the psychology of a men's-club breakfast."

"I'll grab my crayons and take notes," I said, and glanced at the clock. "It's eleven. Who's serving the lunch?"

"Robbie and Booker Atwell. They're at the warehouse picking up a few serving pieces."

"Shouldn't they be at the senator's house?"

"Doesn't start until one. All I need help with," he told me, "is the chocolate sauce. And packing everything up for them."

"No problem." I proceeded to whip up a rich ganache with bittersweet chocolate, heavy cream, and a touch of kirsch. We often used a concoction like this as filling, but slightly thinned down, it was a great dessert sauce if you were careful not to allow it to separate.

"What's the story with Mattie?" Perry asked as we containerized the food and collected utensils for the luncheon.

For the time being I gave Perry the short version of the situation. I included Chip Gunn's party, sans the stabbing, because he'd have heard something about it from Booker, but omitted my apartment and the encounter with Lamar while I had Perry's car. I was beginning to need a scorecard to keep all these accounts separate.

"Unbelievable," he said.

"Alice expects quite an uphill fight."

"I'm sure she does."

"But she does expect to win," I told him, wondering how could he believe that when I wasn't sure I did myself. Black-and-white convictions were beginning to tarnish gray, especially after Mattie disclosed the money factor. Then again, the money factor might never come to light, as the last two envelopes were missing. The police were unaware of a cash connection between Mattie and Lamar and had no reason to suspect one. I was pretty sure.

Pretty sure, Neil? I asked myself. Wasn't that like being pretty sure you took the bullets out of the gun before you started to clean it?

Damn.

"I know Alice will swing to the last breath," Perry finally said, trying to sound upbeat.

The front door opened and Robbie and Booker sauntered in.

"Food ready?" Robbie asked.

"Packed and stacked in the coolers," I responded. "Some assembly required." This was a seated affair, the lunch to be plated and served on Mrs. Beauchamp's Wedgwood, far from the to-go deal the doctors received the day before.

Perry and Robbie went down the checklist as Booker and I loaded the food and equipment on the van. Once everything was ready and accounted for, the two young men in their black-and-whites were off.

I realized then I hadn't asked Robbie if he wanted to take in the game tonight. What a knucklehead, Neil. It'll be too late by the time they return from the job—and I'll be long gone.

"I have a meeting myself," Perry said, pulled off his apron, and tossed it on the counter.

I surveyed the kitchen. Perry was a great cook, but he sure could leave a mess. Pots, pans, knives, spoons, cutting boards—you name a utensil, it was lying on one of the counters or in the sink. Dirty.

"Where's Conrad?" I asked of our trusty dishwasher.

"He had to meet with his parole officer today."

"Parole officer?" I asked.

"You didn't know."

"No, and I don't want to hear it."

Perry rubbed his red beard and noticed my twisted face. "I hate to leave you a user-unfriendly kitchen."

"Forget it. This kind of menial mindlessness will be good for me."

"Glad to hear it, child." He adjusted his bow tie while staring at the window of the reach-in cooler up front. Perry, who stood tall as my chin, gave me a short punch on the arm, a big grin, then he grabbed his suit coat and left.

Just call me Cinderfella, I thought.

Before digging into the aftermath of Hurricane Perry, I grabbed the phone and tracked down Keely Cohen.

Maybe she and Mark would want to go to the game. I managed to catch her at her office on campus.

"Good timing, Neil, I just got in."

"You mean just got in to work? My mother's spoiled house cat doesn't have it as good as you professors do," I teased.

"Couldn't avoid it. I have a meeting with Peter this afternoon."

"Professor Winford? He still want me to jot food poems?"

"Don't get nasty, Neil."

"Hey, you read the snotty note he wrote me—"

"Which you still haven't let go. Uncalled for, yes, but I figure you're above that."

"And he did a stint at Harvard. Bet it didn't humanize him a whole lot."

"Jealous?"

The dirty pots and pans were beginning to whisper my name. *Cinderfella, Cinderfella.* "Absolutely," I told Keely.

"So what's up besides your dander?"

"Two things. First, Dean, in his esoteric, Kerouac way, dropped off some poems for you to look at."

"Why didn't he bring them to me?" she asked, confused.

"I'm finished trying to second-guess people today. He gave them to me to give to you. That's all I know."

"And second?"

"Would you and Mark like to take in an Astros game with me tonight?"

"Oh, Neil, Mark's out of town."

"I'll settle for your company."

"Thanks, bud. Shoot, it's been a long time since I've been to a baseball game."

"Be my first this season, sadly enough," I said. "Used to go all the time."

"All right," she said, tone perky. "That'll be fun."

"Great. Where do you want to meet? There's a great Mexican restaurant not far from the Dome. Near Kirby."

"Why don't you just swing by my house," Keely

said. "It's kind of on the way, and then we only have one car to deal with."

"Fine with me. How about around six?"

"This will be fun," she said, and we hung up.

Fun? How about wonderful?

The prospect of going out with Keely made overhauling the kitchen easier. I locked the front door, just to be on the safe side. I didn't want any surprise visits from Chip Gunn or anyone to detain me this afternoon. I also lowered the blinds so no one could peer in, and turned off the front lights for good measure. Then I rolled up my sleeves and attacked.

If it had been ages since Perry had gotten his hands wet on shrimp remoulade, it'd been just as long since I'd had to clean up after a chef. Gave me a new appreciation for Conrad and his toils. Chefs were slobs. Even organized ones like myself, who cleaned an area before moving on to another project. My idea of cleaning up these days was handing Conrad the pots and maybe taking a rag and wiping down the table. About an hour into it, I decided I owed Conrad a drink. Or two.

As I finished putting up the knives Perry had soiled, there came a loud and heavy pounding on the door. In my joy to be going out with Keely tonight, I almost jerked the door wide open. Until a voice snagged my ear like an errant fisherman's hook.

"There ain't no one here," Cracker growled. "Want for me to break the door?"

"No," big Jimmy huffed. "Boss wouldn't like for us to get busted for breaking into this dump when he's running for Congress."

Dump? I thought. Boy, would Perry be pissed off. I eased to the French doors in the storage room and peeked out the side of the blind. Standing there tall as T-rex was Jimmy. Hovering close, Cracker.

"Where you think he is?" Cracker asked. "His shitty car's here."

"Probably on one of them jobs like he does for the boss."

"So what do we do?"

"Wait in the car."

They started to walk away. "How long?" Cracker asked.

"Long."

Oh, shit, I thought. What about the game with Keely? I sank to the floor. God, what did I do to deserve this?

Got your dumb ass involved in something you should've let the cops deal with, came the immediate response.

Fine.

I stood and slipped to the back of The Kitchen. Now what? I could simply hole up here until they left. Could, but Robbie and Booker would be back later. Perhaps mean and meaner would be gone. Not likely, I reasoned. Well, they wouldn't harass my coworkers. Like hell they wouldn't.

I was getting tired of that little voice in the back of my mind raining on my parade.

I put the knives on the rack. Then spotted the back door. Hey, it was worth a shot. I let myself out with my keys. There was a small alleyway, and if caught, I was dead meat.

I eased toward the gate and unlocked it. So far so good. Next door was our produce man. I spied left to the corner where the thugs waited, then, assured the coast was clear, quickly rounded right and ducked into his warehouse. Free, I thought, but now what?

"Mr. Neil," the stalky Greek said. "What can I do for you?"

"Mr. Nick," I responded, "I'm not quite sure."

"You need some lettuce or something?"

"Or something," I muttered. Realizing I still wore my apron, I untied it and tossed the fabric on top of a stack of boxed potatoes. I couldn't get to my Bug, I thought, with the thugs around front. And I couldn't leave Robbie and Booker hanging like fresh meat for a couple of mangy polecats. Best I could consider was walking around and taking the direct approach to find out what they wanted.

Most likely to take me to Gunn for a meeting. Oh, joy.

But what if it was something else? What if they were here on behalf of Gunter? Time to call Gardner.

And then what? Fess up to withholding evidence? Obstructing justice? Not to mention another encounter of the police kind would put a kink in my evening with Keely.

"Mr. Neil," Nick said. "What's wrong?"

Oscar, a tall and lean Hispanic man walked from the office. "My car, she ain't going to be ready, so I called a cab."

"A cab?" I asked.

"*Sí,* Señor Neil."

Back to wonderful, I thought. Perhaps I could delay this little summit with Gunn. Or even better, get the jump on him by pointing out how he backed me into a corner where I almost had to call the police. And if the predicament arose again, I would call the cops, bring Gunn into the fold, and take my lumps from the good guys. Trick was gauging how badly this would piss off Gunn. Would he read my seriousness and allow me some space? Or would he tenderize me like I was an old piece of meat? Maybe I'd phone my statement in to him.

"Oscar, could you call me a cab, too?"

"*Sí.* You want to come with me, share?"

"No, I want to ask you a favor. I'll pay for your cab as well as mine."

Nick said, "Mr. Neil, I can give you a ride if you need one."

"Thanks, but there's a couple of people I need to lose and I need Oscar's help."

"Whatever you want, señor." He went off to call another cab.

"You want me to call the police, Mr. Neil?" Nick asked, guardedly eyeing me.

"No, thanks. And please don't ask, Mr. Nick."

"You're a good man, Mr. Neil. I will help any way I can. Are you hungry? Would you like an apple?"

"No, thanks."

When Oscar returned I handed him a ten—money for my ticket tonight—and asked if he'd help. I told him my plan.

"That's all, Señor Neil? Too much money."

"They might follow you."

"They won't catch up, and if they do, they have the wrong cab."

"Thank you, amigo."

"No problema."

The cabs arrived at the same time. Oscar dropped into his and they eased out down the road to the feeder for the freeway. I gave him a minute before jumping into mine. Then handed the driver my other ten.

"See that little intersection?" I asked, pointing to the corner of The Kitchen property. "I want you to drive up to it very slowly. There are a couple of guys on the front side over there whose attention I need to get. After I do, you slam the gas to the feeder and head north. But don't get on the freeway. There's a narrow street that cuts back to the east. I want you to take it."

"What is it that you are telling me to do?" the driver asked.

"I just explained. Understand?"

"I do not know if I like this."

"Just do it."

I thanked Mr. Nick for his hospitality and slammed the cab's door. "Slowly, now," I told the driver.

He carried through perfectly. Jimmy and Cracker were parked facing away from the feeder route. So when I rolled down my window and shouted, "Hey, boys, you looking for me?" they were caught totally off guard. Cracker fired up their car but had to screech into The Kitchen driveway to turn around in order to chase us.

"Hit it," I ordered, and the man flew. Tires ripped on

the street and squealed as we tore onto the feeder. I about flew out of the window I'd opened.

"Wait," I shouted, "don't go on the freeway. Take this right."

As we did I was able to tumble and roll and see Oscar's cab burn up onto the freeway. A few seconds later Jimmy and Cracker were blazing after them, freeway-bound themselves.

"Okay, you can slow down!" I hollered.

"What?"

"Slow down. You're on a residential street."

The cabbie slammed to a stop.

"First you tell me hit it then slow down—I do not know what it is you want."

"To take the block and drop me off where you found me," I said.

"But that does not make any sense. Why would you pay me ten dollars to drive you around the block?"

"Because I'm a fool who has no sense."

"That is for sure."

That *is* for sure, I agreed. Jimmy and Cracker wanted something. And they were not going to be very amicable the next time we met.

In fact, they'd be downright ugly.

The things a man does for a woman, I thought. And an attached woman at that.

14

I took the long way home, opposite the freeway. It'd be my luck the goons would have figured they were chasing the wrong cab and be lying in ambush. Better hope that wasn't so, I told myself—they'd be on their way back here. Or to my apartment.

No, they wouldn't catch on until I was watching the first pitch of the ball game. I was sure of it. Sure of it.

I hooked a left at North Main, deciding to avoid the apartment. After all, I was dressed *GQ* appropriate. It'd probably shock Keely I wasn't in jeans and a brush popper. And I could pulse money out of my checking account from the nearby Randall's supermarket. I didn't need to go into the hundred dollars I kept stashed in my apartment for emergencies. I thought I still had some cash in my account I could access.

As I sped toward West University Place I thought, for a man who didn't care much for confrontation, I sure found myself in the throes of it all too frequently. I must have done some serious avoidance in a past life.

It was too early to cruise by Keely's, so I decided to take a quick detour and stop by C. J. McDaniels's office. Probably too soon for him to have uncovered any dirt on Gunn, but if he was there, he'd be game for a beer.

I bounced into the driveway where he officed next to a new-and-used record store and cut the power on my Bug. C.J.'s Mustang was not in sight and it took me a minute to realize that a couple of spaces away was Linda Garcia's truck. And she was just getting out of it.

My insides contracted much the same way they did when I confronted my ex-wife. There it was again, the C-word—confrontation. But this was of the hard kind. I was glad to see Linda.

"I thought you were out of town," I said, closing the door to my VW.

"Was halfway to Amarillo when they called to say they broke the case and didn't need me," she said, irritated. "Turned right around."

"So you drove to Dallas and back but kept your retainer?"

"I was beyond Dallas, honey, and retainer or not, it still chafes my butt. How'd you know I was out of town?"

"C.J. and I had a beer the other day. He mentioned it."

Linda leaned against the front of her truck and crossed her arms. "Why are you here, Neil? And don't tell me it's to have another beer with my father."

"C.J.'s doing me a favor, and I wanted to check in with him. A friend of mine's in trouble," I offered. There was a red cap from a Coke bottle on the gravel driveway. I toed and ground it into the dirt, watching a thin film of dust layer my boot.

"You nervous?" Linda asked.

"A bit uncomfortable."

"Why do you think that is?" Linda asked.

"I don't know," I said dumbly. It was a conditioned response left over from my broken marriage.

"Really? Well, I don't know whether to claw your eyes out or tear your clothes off."

I had to give Linda credit. She didn't take the long way around the barn on anything. "I suspect that's the way our relationship would always be," I replied, and met her stare.

"Because you love someone else," she said pointedly.

A "sorry" stumbled off my lips—another conditioned response.

"So am I, Neil. You're missing out on a good thing."

Linda, I thought, there's too much of my ex-wife in

you. As you directed this conversation, you'd also direct my life, and I couldn't go through that again.

"I know," was all I said.

Her cheek twitched.

"Tell C.J. I came by."

"You can wait in the office," she told me, her tone as hard as her nerves. Talk about a steel magnolia, I thought.

"Appreciate the hospitality—"

"You're a client of C.J.'s, aren't you?"

"But I have to run," I finished. "Please tell C.J. I stopped by."

"Goodbye, Neil."

"Bye, Linda."

In a minute I was edging my VW back into traffic. Funny how seeing a person could bring on a twinge of hurt, even when you knew that person wasn't right for you. Linda was a good woman, though she was as married to her work as C.J. was. And though she might bitch about her job, she loved it and would want anyone with her to love it, too. My other worlds, cooking and writing, didn't interest her. The situation was just too similar to the one I'd broken from, I again reasoned. Call me gunshy or foolhardy or plain stupid, but I couldn't help it. The same as I couldn't help the hard fingers of hurt that nonetheless gripped my insides.

I rode the crest of traffic from Westheimer and Montrose to West University, knowing I'd arrive at Keely's house early but not wanting to stop anywhere else for fear of another chance meeting. First Jimmy and Cracker, then Linda. The way my afternoon was going I was apt to bump into Karl Gunter or my former wife if given half the opportunity.

Keely answered the door, reading glasses on, a stack of papers in her hand. "Is it six already?" she asked, and glanced at a wrist that bore no watch. "Wonder where I left it?" she said more to herself than to me.

"It's a few minutes after five," I said, suddenly feeling self-conscious. My early arrival could easily be construed as a touch overeager. "I—you just—oh, I can't explain. I'm just here early."

"You're a man who looks like he needs a drink."

"A beer would be nice."

"Come on in."

I followed Keely into her modest contemporary with its cathedral ceiling, white walls of modern art, and wooden floors.

"Peter asked me to read a complete draft of his new book of poems," she said, waving them in the air. "I decided to come home and do it after I got ready for the game. Boy, you're sure dressed conservatively."

She was appropriately attired in an Astros jersey tucked into blue jeans, and she glided around on a pair of white Nikes. I felt like one of those saps whose boss gave him a free ticket just to get a warm body at the ballpark—the kind who were ignorant in the ways of baseball.

"I was visiting Mattie this morning and had to look presentable. You heard she was arrested for killing Lamar, didn't you?"

"Yes, and I've been anxious to learn what you're doing about it." She pushed through the swinging saloon-type doors that led to the kitchen. "All I have is Newcastle Brown Ale," she called. "Mark doesn't like domestic."

All you have? I thought. Mark not only had good taste in women but also in beer.

"That'd be fine," I said, and plopped down on a large, plush white chair.

Keely returned with the open bottle and a mug. "So tell me," she said.

"For starters, I got Alice Tarkenton to represent her," I responded, and accepted the drink. I sat on the edge of the chair and carefully poured the ale into the mug, avoiding a huge, foamy head.

Keely dropped Peter Winford's poems onto the glass coffee table then sat on the couch with a cup of tea. "Don't you think it may be time to bring up that other incident?"

"At Gunn's house?"

Keely smirked as she dipped the tea bag in and out of the hot water. Her light brown eyes widened as in *well*?

"I almost had to a little while ago," I replied. "A couple of Gunn's thugs cornered me and I came a cat's whisker from calling the police. But I was able to slip away, which is a big reason why I'm early."

"I don't care about you being early. I don't understand what's holding you back from calling the cops?"

"I've labored over this, Keely. But I don't believe that Chip Gunn testifying in court would help Mattie at all. No matter what really happened, if by fluke Gunn didn't thoroughly dispose of all evidence and was forced to testify, he'd state that what occurred at his house was a case of misplaced domestic violence. And to carry the scenario further, Gunn would be admitting to covering up a crime, an event that would end his congressional race. And probably my life.

"Now let's paint a different picture," I said, and sipped the ale. "Let's suppose the cops find no evidence of a cover-up. Now it's my word and that of an accused murderer against that of a popular, rising politician."

"And Dean Shriver," Keely piped in. "You said he was there."

"Keely, he's a radical pothead who's been sleeping beneath a bail-bondsman billboard."

"What?" She set her saucer and cup on the edge of the table then ran her hands through her short dark hair.

"Oh, he's on some berserk mission," I said. "Or binge. Maybe the pressure of that night at Gunn's was too much." The image of him fleeing my apartment, crying, *The bastard!* replayed in my mind. It gave me an uneasy feeling—perhaps Dean really was cracking up. "By the way," I told her, "I've got his poems in my car."

"There's got to be something we can do," she said.

We, I thought. Love it. "Like I said, I convinced Alice to help Mattie. And I'm hoping C. J. McDaniels can come up with something." I explained about the private investigator's search into Gunn's past because of a tip by Lamar before he died. "All I want is to free Mattie," I said, then added, "and enroll Dean in a rehab center."

"I agree. But there also has to be a way to keep Chip Gunn from waltzing into a dangerously powerful position."

"Gunn's karma will catch up with him someday."

"When he's Senator Gunn?" Keely asked, leaning forward. "Or even President Gunn? And how many other Matties and Neils will he have steamrolled by then?"

"Keely, you're driving me nuts. First you want me to call the cops."

"Well, you convinced me that's not a good idea right now."

I took a large gulp of ale. "So a better one is to mount a charge against Candidate Gunn? How? I don't have the answers. All I can figure is to work on one thing at a time and see what else unravels as we pluck at the threads."

"It's frustrating," Keely muttered, and picked up her tea. "But a nice metaphor."

"Thanks." I finished the ale.

"Want another?" she asked.

"One more, then let's go. I really want a break from all this."

While Keely grabbed me another Newcastle I used the phone to check my messages. There was a rather irate one from Gunn, who demanded that we talk—sooner rather than later. I skipped the next communiqué from Perry, asking if I could bartend for a client who'd called for last-minute help—that was the problem with the catering business, a lot of eleventh-hour scrambling. When Perry didn't hear from me, he'd assume I hadn't gotten the message in time and that would be that. No word from C.J.

"Here you go, bud," Keely said, handing me the ale. "I decided to join you this time." She held up a glass of white wine.

"Changing the subject, how are Winford's new poems?"

A glint of mischief danced in her eyes. "I knew you'd ask. Read this one." She shuffled through the papers.

I glanced at the single sheet. The poem was entitled "The Chains on My Soul Are from the Spider in My Heart." It was an honest piece exploring how he bound his morals by actions he knew were wrong. The nesting spider in his heart had to be fed, though each time it was satisfied it spun another link on the iron chain wrapping his soul. Grudgingly, and even with the allusion to Dickens, I had to admit it was good.

The poem ended:

> I fed the student
>   to my ego—
> waved goodbye for points
>   north, the ghostly
> clawing of my hand
>   reflected like a spider
> crippled against the window
>   pane.

"Not bad," I told Keely, handing the paper back to her.

"I say. Does it remind you of anything?"

"Should it?"

"Come on, Neil. Recall the conference you had with him right before he left for Harvard?"

"What is he saying?" I asked. "That because he has the ego of a spider, it's okay to tell students like me to write food poems?"

"Don't work yourself into a tizzy," she told me. "I think it's his way of trying to atone for his actions."

"You really believe that?" Even if he's a good poet, the man's a pompous idiot, I thought.

"These poems are stuffed with new, confessional images. It's a break from his usual work." Keely kicked off her sneakers and swung her legs onto the couch, knees drawn up. As she thumbed through the poems I noticed the curve of her breast against the jersey. She handed me a couple more. "Don't you dare let on to Peter that you saw these," she said. "He's particular about who reads his manuscripts."

"Why show me?"

"I think it might help you in your relationship with him. He's talented, Neil. It would be a shame to shut him out because of one incident."

"He's the one who closed the door, Keely."

"Well, seems to me he's knocking on it now."

"Why should I open myself to more abuse?"

Keely lowered the papers and pushed her reading glasses up onto her bangs. "First," she stated, "every writer's going to have a day when he gets knocked around. The great Peter Winford's even experienced that. Rather recently, for that matter."

"What do you mean?"

"Let's just say his Ivy League sojourn wasn't the high life he thought it was going to be."

"Really? What happened?" I asked.

"Not now. Let's stay on my point."

"Okay, say he's had an awakening. That still doesn't excuse a bashing by the person you're trying to learn from. You don't knock me around."

"I'm beginning to believe I should."

"Funny. But I was going to add you offer constructive criticism."

"As it should be," she continued. "Thank you. However, Neil, you should let go of last fall and see what happens now. You know, I've discovered that you're slow to anger, but also very slow to forgive."

"I've heard that before," I mumbled. Both Mother and Susan, my ex-wife, used to point out that characteristic.

"I hope you work on it." Keely lowered her glasses back to the bridge of her nose and returned her attention to the text.

Instead of responding, I read the pieces she'd given me. They were smooth. Crisp. Powerful. They passed the jealousy test—I wished I'd written them.

Keely and I combed through every line of every poem.

Lost in this cycle, it wasn't until the phone rang that we realized how late it had gotten.

"Hello, dear," I heard Keely say. "Been poring over Peter's manuscript with Neil." Pause. "No, we're going to the Astros game tonight. He invited you, too, but since—" Another pause. "What do you mean it's eight o'clock?"

"Eight o'clock?" I asked, looking around the room. I didn't see a clock, but I did notice light still filtering in. However, the illumination did bear the gray of dusk.

"What time does the game start?" she called to me.

"An hour ago."

"Oh, damn." Pause. "I did not do it on purpose, Mark," she said. "I really wanted to go to the game. Oh, stop it." Again a pause, this one long. "Don't be foolish." Silence. "No, no, *no*. Listen, just because you had a crappy day, don't take it out on me. Well, fine. Bye."

The phone went down hard.

"Maybe I should leave," I said, rising.

"Why?"

"I don't figure Mark's hot on the idea of me being here."

"He claimed I kept you from the game because I never want to go. But that's not true."

"I know," I replied, but thought, He's claiming more than that, Keely.

"Do you?"

"I was as wrapped up in what we were doing as you," I said. "I wanted to relax tonight, and I am."

"Or were until Mark called," she said, and folded her arms.

"That didn't upset me," I replied, half lying. His call did make me feel a little uncomfortable. Or was it guilty? I was glad to spend time with her alone. But I added, "I don't want to cause trouble for you."

"Don't you start. Mark's a big boy who's always trusted me and has no reason not to now. I don't know what's given him this little-boy fit."

Yes, you do, I thought. A person standing too close

could get burned by the sparks that at times flew between us. And Mark wasn't blind, unless it was to the fact that he could trust Keely. Or to the respect I held to our friendship. I let it be.

"Since I made you miss the game, what if I buy you a pizza and we finish going over Peter's poems?" she asked.

"Deal. But only if I can have another beer."

"I can work with that," she said, and picked up my empty bottle.

I made for the door, announcing, "I'm going to grab Dean's poems from the back of the Bug before I forget."

"Okay. We can take look at them, too."

I should've known better. I should've let the beatnik's poems slip from my mind as easily as the ball game had.

But the river of life was twisted by should-haves, and the angel of death lurked around each bend like a hungry alligator.

15

The soft curve of body. Warm breast pressing against skin. Oval mouths and full lips compressing fast and hungry. Hips grinding together and tongue running the long length of neck. Fingers digging into back. The moans—

And then the image of Susan standing before me. A twisted smile. Anger. The gun drawn.

"Son of a bitch," she whispers.

And I shield Keely, facing Susan. Words catch in my throat. No, I think I say. No.

The gunshot. I prepare for the burning I'd felt the last time a bullet ripped through me. The shock. The numbness and then black.

It doesn't happen. Deafening sound, but it's Susan whose face contorts. Arms drop. Gun falls. Then she collapses.

Standing beside the bed is Linda. I stare. She faces me, sadly shakes her head. Walks . . .

I jolted awake. Sheets clung to me from sweat. I swung my feet over the side of my bed, ran my hands over my greasy hair, and rubbed my beard. My breathing was thick. I was in my apartment, alone. Late.

It had been a long time since I'd had a Susan-ready-to-shoot-me dream. Fantasizing about Keely must have done it. But why was Linda there? And as the savior?

I slipped my blue robe on and stumbled to the kitchen. The apartment was as lonely and still as any bachelor's at three in the morning. I peeked out the window. Nothing. Even that knuckleheaded dog, Samson, was asleep.

The tequila was tempting, but I opted for a glass of ice water as I calmed the revving of my heart and my shaking hands. Keely and I had had a wonderful evening of poetry, pizza, and Mozart. Good talk kept me there until almost midnight. The only strange twist happened after we took a quick look at Dean's poems.

His work was a confused grab bag. If he was creating recipes, he'd be using crepes to make burritos. For one, Dean had declared it open season on form. Seventeen-syllable haikus, usually savored for nature and beauty, described the carnage left by exploding bombs. A rhyming sonnet told of the beating of a street person. He called people *wheat*, politicians *scythes*, and special-interest groups the *farmers that held the scythes*. Not bad, I thought, but then Dean went into some tirade about the Irish Republican Army and whether what was going on in the United Kingdom was senseless killing or killing for cents. There were apocalyptic images of hunter and prey. The universe was a tank, time was its fuel, and human frailty had no chance. What hit Keely and me the hardest, however, were the references to suicide. I'd taken one poem with me and reached for it now, clicked on the lamp, and sat on the couch. I took my glasses from the coffee table and slipped them on.

Outlaw

Soldier return
to the ranch—
Soldier scarred
as barbed wire—
Soldier return
to the worm—
Everything died
when Crazy Horse died
by the hand
of his own people—
his own people

like mercenaries
think like my people
I have seen
the mercenaries
and given up the ranch
wear a crown of barbed wire
and return to the worm—
like a soldier—
with mercenaries—
by my own hand

   The poem gave me the willies, pure and simple. The
"by my own hand" line was what did it. I could handle
his soldierlike mission and Christ complex with the
"crown of barbed wire"—though I had no idea what
people were "his people," what the ranch symbolized, or
why exactly drop Crazy Horse's name—but implying he
was going to turn off his own light for the big sleep bothered the hell out of me. I'd been going along thinking his
head was sadly stuck in a cloud of smoke, but that eventually there'd be a break, a clearing, where intelligent
conversation and perhaps help could slip in. Suicidal
thoughts falling from his haze, though, showed me how
badly I'd misjudged the situation. It could be a bunch of
clatter. Or literary claptrap. But the lousy feeling I had
wouldn't buy into that.
   I figured C.J. could locate Dean in a day or two, so I'd
go ahead and redirect his energies. Then I recalled Dean's
signal through the classified section of the newspaper.
What was it? Say I was looking for a rare Kerouac book
and he'd get in touch with me. Yes, that would work.
Save me from interpreting Dean's poems for C.J.'s sake.
   When a respectable hour rolled around, I'd let Keely in
on my plan and solicit her help. I had to do something to
ease her nerves. Last night Dean's work had blown away
the thoughtful mood we'd acquired through Winford's
introspection.
   "This is Kerouac meets Rambo," she'd said when we'd

read "Outlaw." "I know he wants to forge his own space, but isn't this a bit much?"

"I think he's playing the crazy poet."

"Well, it's working. He's flirted with the self-destructive path too long. Sounds like he's dangerously close."

"Have no fear, we'll slap some sense into him," I'd said, wondering seriously if Dean would even recognize a good knock to the head.

"Fight fire with fire?" she'd asked. "Wonderful."

And that pretty much had brought our evening to a crunching halt. A short time later I was on my way home.

I tossed the poem on my coffee table and finished my water. Feeling jittery, I knew I wouldn't be able to get back to sleep. Without Mattie or J.J. to worry about, though, I opted for a dead-of-the-night run.

That jogging at this time could be dangerous had never really bothered me before. Contrary to relaxing me, I found myself staring hard into the blackness as I rounded every corner. The air was so stationary I felt I announced my presence with every scuff of my Nikes and every breath I puffed out. Occasionally a dog behind someone's fence would erupt in hackle-raising barks, spurring me into high gear. The temperature had dropped into the low seventies, but the moisture staining my glasses and drenching my Clint Black T-shirt was the same that coated my lungs like a basting sauce.

The muscles in my lower back strained under the pace I was keeping. Even a mile down the shadowy roads and in and out of the harsh streetlight, I was still hitting the pavement in long, forceful strides. As to exactly why I was almost fearful, I could only imagine. Dean's flaky image came to mind, as did Mattie's scared appearance. Lamar wouldn't be out here. Of course, Jimmy and Cracker could be. Or Gunn or Gunter. The cops would almost be a welcome sight. Almost.

Another growling dog sent my heart to palpitations. It was the same racing I'd felt in my dream when Susan had pointed the gun at me. Whenever I dreamed like that I knew I was trying to tell myself something. But this time I had no idea what it could be. I knew I was enamored of Keely. Susan's anger had abated. Come down to the nitty-gritty, however, she'd as soon take a potshot at me than see me with someone else. As for Linda, she might have the controlling attitude of Susan, but she also possessed the passion, and fairness, of Keely.

I ran harder. At the two-mile point I realized I was only good for one more and so began to plot a straighter course home. When I finally hit the driveway, Samson worked himself into a frenzy. I was of the temper to huff over to him and take a healthy bite out of his ear. And I had to restrain myself not to. Samson must've picked up on my vibes because he quieted down before Jerry Jacoma woke up to bellow at him from his house.

My gut crept to my throat. I couldn't remember the last time I'd run so hard. Sweet Jesus, I thought, and sat on the bumper of the VW. I tilted my head back. There were a few distant stars up there, nothing like what I'd grown up with, or what you could see out at Candace's stables. When my breathing finally slowed, I hiked back up to my apartment. No Jimmy, no Cracker, nobody in tow.

A few hours later, sun intruding in the living room, I awoke on the couch. To my delight, I reasoned that I'd fallen asleep after the run. I was still in my running shorts and the T-shirt was clammy against my chest. My insides were back where they were supposed to be, and a fresh breeze blew through my veins. I felt great.

I showered, trimmed my beard—ignoring the scar—and was out the door before nine. The first order of business was structuring my day at Perry Stevens. Next was touching base with Keely about my plan to raise Dean from the dead. After that, I didn't even want to try to guess.

Jerry Jacoma stopped me outside. "Hey, partner," he said, grinning. His Fu Manchu mustache ran the length of his round face. "The postman delivered some of your mail to me."

He slapped a large manila envelope in my hands.

"At first I thought it was sex films and almost opened it. But after I felt it, I figured it was just books. And knowing you, they ain't sex books."

A chill ran down my spine as I felt the envelope. "You'll never know what you lost," I quipped.

"Right," he said, and walked around front to his truck.

Once Jerry was out of sight, I tore the top of the envelope open and peered in.

Two white envelopes inside.

I eased one to the top and broke its seal.

Sure enough. Money. Mattie's. Now I knew the safe place she'd chosen.

But what to do with it? I wondered, and tucked it under the front seat of my car.

It was after Jerry's truck had rumbled down the street that I heard a set of car doors banging closed.

Frantically, I scrambled in the Bug, cranked the engine, and began backing out of the driveway. Sure enough, blocking the entrance was the mammoth Jimmy and ornery Cracker. I kept backing, but they stood as placid as gravestones.

Quickly it became apparent they weren't going to move. I kept coming. They waited. Jump, idiots, I thought. Jump!

Like gargoyles, they guarded the street until finally I hit the brakes and skidded to a stop before them.

What the hell, I thought. Take me to your leader. I rested my head on the steering wheel.

I should have run them over.

16

Before Jimmy cracked my Bug like it was an egg, I came out on my own accord.

"Gentlemen," I said.

Neither man smiled or returned my greeting. The stony gaze from Cracker told me how mad he was for yesterday's wild-goose chase.

"Boss wants to see you," Jimmy ordered.

"Why doesn't that surprise me?" I said.

"Let's go."

"Don't suppose I can follow you in my car?" I asked. "Promise I won't ditch you this time."

Cracker took a step toward me. Jimmy swung out one of his lumbering arms and caught him. "Boss said no rough stuff."

Clearly, he spoke to the both of us. "That's all right, I'll ride with you," I said, using my politically correct tone.

"Unless we had to," Jimmy added.

I put my hands up. "You don't have to."

"Yet," Cracker spat. And that was all he said the whole drive over there. Of course, Jimmy wasn't much of a conversationalist, either. Not that I was up for small talk. I wasn't a babbler when I became nervous, and I was nervous. In fact I tended to close up tighter than an oyster holding a pearl.

Cracker pulled the Cadillac into Gunn's driveway and swung around to the servants' entrance. First good sign, I thought, we were actually at Gunn's house and not some remote section of the bayou. When we jerked to a stop, Jimmy simply jabbed a thumb at me and got out. I followed.

In spite of the sultry morning, it was actually pleasant on Gunn's small veranda. Shade from a large live oak took away the harshness from the sun and a pair of ceiling fans kept the air moving. A lavish array of plants brought a heavy dose of green into an otherwise simple space. Chip Gunn was seated at a round, white table, a newspaper folded tightly to the article he was reading. A plate of half-eaten eggs and toast was in front of him, and on his left rested a cordless phone. A familiar-looking man was talking to Gunn as we approached. It took a minute to place his face.

"You've got to talk to him," the man implored, then immediately shut up once he noticed our presence.

Gunn rested the paper and looked at us. He faced the French doors that led into the house.

"We'll talk later, John," Gunn said.

"It's not me you need to talk to," John managed to say, voice low.

"Later," Gunn firmly reiterated.

John sighed, glanced at me, and hesitated. Then I knew where I'd seen him. He was the gray-haired man at the doctors' office arguing with Karl Gunter the day I dropped off the lunches. A flash of recognition sparked in his eyes also.

"You two know each other?" Gunn asked.

"No," I replied with a shrug.

"John?"

"He works for the caterer, right?" John asked.

"Yes. Actually, Neil is an exquisite chef."

"That's where I recognize him from," John said.

"I see. Forgive my lax manners. John Taft, campaign manager, meet Neil Marshall. A chef, among other things." The last comment was added with more than a hint of disdain.

I accepted Taft's hand. Campaign manager? I thought.

What the hell was he doing meeting with Gunter at the doctors' compound?

After assuring me it was a pleasure, Taft told Gunn he'd talk to him later and left.

"Sit," Gunn directed me, and sipped on a cup of coffee. I faced Gunn. Behind Gunn, outside the veranda, was a short hedge. Behind the hedge was a swimming pool. Jimmy stood off to the side.

"I wanted to talk to you yesterday," Gunn said. He tapped his cup against the saucer.

"I'm sorry, but I just couldn't make it."

Gunn coiled all his attention on me, pausing, eyes piercing, cup still. And then he leaped to his feet, smashing the cup and saucer against the table.

"Don't you ever ignore me again!" he bellowed, finger pointing. "I'm sick of your attitude. I'm sick of your antics. I'll be damned if I'll sit around and let you get away with these things. You think Lieutenant Gardner can protect you all your life? He can't! He can't! And it's getting to the point where I don't even care if Gardner's around, and that places you in a very vulnerable position, Mr. Marshall."

"What the hell are you talking about?"

Gunn grabbed the newspaper and read. " 'A rumor that the congressional campaign for businessman Chip Gunn is being harassed by a member of a radical underground organization is being investigated by special agents of the Houston Police Department in cooperation with the FBI. Complaints from the Gunn campaign apparently initiated the investigation, a source within HPD stated. The source spoke only on terms of remaining anonymous.' " Gunn slammed the paper on the table. "Complaints by my campaign? To HPD and the fucking FBI! I wouldn't go to them if someone was trying to kill me." The veins in his neck were ready to burst. "A radical underground organization! Shit, a drugged-out hippie wannabe."

Or a genius, I thought. Dean was out to get Gunn, and

if I was right, he had him on the ropes. I'd never seen Gunn lose his cool like this.

"An anonymous source?" Gunn repeated.

"You don't think I'd—"

Gunn pounded his hand on the table, then swiped his breakfast dishes into the wall. "Have you talked to Gardner?"

"Only about Lamar Fowler." I remained seated. If I stood, the action could very well invite Gunn to physically come after me, which would also bring in Jimmy the brick outhouse.

"Only about Lamar Fowler," he mocked. "Oh, is that all? What about Lamar Fowler?"

"He's dead."

"Don't I know it!" he snapped. "Dead as that goddamn son of a drug addict's going to be once I get my hands on him."

"Drug addict?"

"Like father like son, stupid."

"But you're not a killer, remember?" I said.

"I've changed my mind."

I drew in a deep breath. "Listen, Mr. Gunn, I've worked hard to keep your name out of this. I've danced around Gardner, withheld evidence—oh, hell, plain lied. I've been concentrating on Mattie Johnson and her predicament and how not to mention you."

"So you bring in Alice Tarkenton," Gunn said, his voice closing in on normal tones, though far from pleased. "How much does she know?"

"Not enough to hurt you," I said, hoping he'd buy it. Instead of waiting, however, I changed the subject back to what I was saying. "When you sent your thugs after me you almost forced what would've been an act of final irony—me to call the police. Of course, if you're convinced I've already sung to the police, then this is all a vicious circle that is slowly tightening around my neck. And what I'm saying has no bearing on what you're thinking. With my history, I'd be a fool to use the law against you."

"What about that girl?" he asked, ran a hand through his hair, and tucked in the tail of his shirt.

"Mattie? She has her own problems. You wouldn't know anything about Lamar's death, would you?"

"No." He paced to the broken dishes. "Jimmy, go tell the maid to clean this up," he said, waving at it.

Jimmy hesitated.

"I'll be okay with Neil," he said. "After all, I can trust Neil."

Jimmy's bulldog face weighed its strength on me as he walked by. The man could cast a shadow across Brazil.

"I want Shriver," he said. "You hear me?"

"How could Dean leak any information to the cops?" I asked. "They'd lock him up before listening to him."

"I want Shriver," he repeated. "You know where he is?"

"No. Last he told me he was going into hiding. I thought he was riding out a bad trip."

"You contact me when he contacts you."

I wasn't going to even try to stand up to Gunn, at this point. Grin, Neil, I told myself. And lie.

"I don't expect to hear from him," I said. "I laid into him pretty bad recently over his drug problem."

"He'll communicate with you. A sleaze like that doesn't have many friends."

Words from experience? I wondered. "I still can't figure how Dean would—"

"Just call," Gunn said. "You can go now."

"I need a ride. Your associates wouldn't allow me to take my own car."

"Call a cab," he said calmly.

"What?"

"Call a cab. You appear to like cabs."

"Thanks." I started off the veranda.

"You can use my phone, Neil. I mean, what are friends for?"

"No thanks." Suddenly Gunter crossed my mind. Back to his appearance with John Taft, campaign manager.

"Chip," I called, deliberately using his first name.

"Yes."

"How well do you get along with your brother?" I asked.

His face whitened. "What?"

"Karl Gunter, your brother. I heard you two don't exactly see eye to eye. You don't think he'd be out to get you, do you?"

Gunn shook, the cordless phone in hand. For a second I thought the anger might return, and he'd throw the phone at me.

Instead, it was worse.

Gunn recaptured his composure and walked to the end of the veranda. "Mr. Marshall," he stated coldly. "With your growing knowledge, you are quickly becoming a liability. Don't forget how I feel about Lieutenant Gardner and his role in the scheme of things. Good day."

I couldn't get off Gunn's property fast enough. So much for not standing up to him, though. Had to open my big mouth, raise the doubt again. Oh, hell, the doubt would've been there regardless.

Might not be bad I threw Gunter's name into the ring. Keep the confusion up. Or the anger. Gunn's strength was from his coolness, and his ability to control his emotions.

But something bothered me. If Dean was causing Gunn all this anxiety, how the hell was he doing it? Was he a genius? Lucky? Or was someone helping him?

I swabbed the sweat off my forehead. Most likely they'd be following me, so I needed to reevaluate my plan to contact Dean. I didn't want him waltzing smack into a trap.

Now what? Guess I'd walk over to the Museum of Fine Arts. It was the closest place I could think of with a public phone. I had to call a cab.

17

My denim shirt was quickly stained with sweat as I strode through the museum district. I was thinking I sure hoped I locked the VW, since Mattie's money was stashed under the front seat. Normally no one gave that vehicle a second look. Be my luck today for some lunatic to be drawn to the Bug like a barn cat to buttermilk.

I crossed Montrose to the museum. First I'd try phoning C.J.'s office as he wasn't too far away—by car. Then I'd call work to let them know I'd been inadvertently detained. I entered the cool structure and immediately felt a wave of relief.

The last time I'd been to the Houston Museum of Fine Arts was during the Pompeii exhibit. This and the Menil Museum were favorite spots of mine to visit, unwind, and stimulate what intellect I could muster. So many people thought of Houston as a cow town—or a hellhole, seeing the city was built on a steamy swamp—but didn't recognize that culture rubbed elbows with good ol' boys. Perhaps Houston was an adolescent spreading his shoulders, had a bit of an attitude, but the city was ready to play with the big boys. And the diversity was why I loved Houston. We had a strong fine-arts community, led by the symphony and supported by outstanding opera, ballet, and theatre companies. But there were also plenty of places to two-step across a sawdust floor on a Saturday night, listening to the country sounds of George Strait and Mark Chesnutt. Diversity. A large rap community.

Tejano. Underground Bohemia. Jazz. Aboveground oil pumps lazily cranking out cash day after day.

And no one knew Houston better than C. J. McDaniels, but he wasn't at the office to talk about it. I left a quick message inquiring on his search for the supposed field of skeletons then debated what to do.

Soft voices and heavy footsteps echoed throughout the halls. A group of young school kids on a field trip squealed and bounced next to harried teachers and parents. I dropped another quarter into the phone and dialed The Kitchen. The machine answered. Again I left a message, explaining I wasn't in yet because of circumstances beyond my control. I dug in my pocket. Two more quarters.

It occurred to me that if Perry Stevens wasn't at The Kitchen, then he could still be at his town house. His town house wasn't too far from here, either. Perry was a late riser who often meandered into work close to lunchtime or even early afternoon. I gave him a try, though wondered how I was going to explain being stranded at the museum.

"Perry," I said as he answered. "It's Neil."

"I recognize the voice. What's up?"

"I'm at the Museum of Fine Arts, ah—"

"Why aren't you at The Kitchen?"

"Circumstances beyond my control," I replied sheepishly. "Ah, listen, I need a ride."

"A what?"

"A ride. Could you swing by and pick me up?"

"How—? Never mind. I've got to meet a client," he stated. "I guess you can come with me."

"I appreciate it," I offered.

"Are you dressed appropriately?"

"Yes."

"Look for me in ten minutes."

"You got it, boss."

He hung up. I believed he was irritated with me.

I pushed through the front doors in the large lobby when I spied Perry's Lexus coast to a stop out front.

Traffic wasn't particularly heavy and Perry wasn't particularly friendly.

"I don't want to hear why you're so far from the Heights without your car," he said. "I imagine it has to do with your former wife, or current relationship, or Mattie. That's your business, though I think you should leave Mattie's case to the police and Alice Tarkenton."

"You've covered about everything," I said, and closed the door. His car felt delightfully cool and comfortable despite his aggravated fatherly attitude. And I didn't blame him for that considering the messes I'd found myself in the last year or so. Perry could be a curmudgeon, but he was a faithful curmudgeon.

Also, he was probably nervous about the client he was about to meet. I noticed he wore his pale gray business suit and maroon paisley bow tie, an outfit saved for important first impressions. A Bartók piano concerto chimed from his CD player. I was more in a Tom Waits mood.

"So who's your appointment with?" I asked, grabbed a tissue from his console, and cleaned my glasses.

"Karl Gunter," he replied. "Chip Gunn's brother."

A kick to the backside would've been less of a shock. And more pleasant. I put my glasses back on.

"Really," I managed to say. "Is it a dinner party?"

"Something to do with Gunn's candidacy. The message wasn't clear." We twisted out of the museum district and headed southwest. "Apparently, he was impressed with your performance at the last Gunn function," Perry added.

"What performance was that?" I asked, my voice on the verge of quivering.

"You're a damn good chef and you know it," he said, risking a glare from the steering wheel. "If you didn't spread yourself so thin, you'd be great."

"I can't give up my writing. You're a musician, too. You understand." Perry had, in fact, played piano at Carnegie Hall. He was a Fulbright scholar. I knew he understood. I thought.

"It's not necessarily your writing," he told me. "Your

personal asides are distracting you, too. But I don't know if that's exactly it, either."

"What are you saying?"

"You don't have the passion for food," he stated. "When I was teaching music I had students like you. Brilliant musicians, but the passion wasn't there. I could never comprehend it. How can one go so far in a field and lack such a crucial ingredient?"

I do love food, I thought. But, Neil, you eat, sleep, and dream letters, my nagging conscience echoed.

"That's not fair," I told him, ignoring the incessant voice in my mind, and shuffled in the seat. "I love my job."

"I agree you love your position, and you've done a wonderful job."

"But?"

"I wish you had the passion," he replied. "You could be as good as anybody."

"Not obsessing on one part of your life doesn't mean you lack the interest—the passion, as you say. You're right I have a lot happening, but you told me a minute ago you didn't want to hear about it. By cutting off a major part of my life, you're getting a biased picture." I paused. Perry only stared over his tight grip on the steering wheel.

"The passion's there," I added, "but at the moment a huge chunk of it is directed at helping Mattie."

Perry, in heavy thought, finally said, "You wouldn't clue me in on everything even if I begged you to."

"Probably not. But I'd give you an indication of what the situation was without endangering you."

"Endangering?" he repeated.

"It's turning downright harrowing."

"Your life has certainly taken a turn to the dark side."

"No, Perry, not a turn to the dark side," I said. "I'm just not ignoring it, anymore. The blinders of apathy are off." Though I wondered if Dean Shriver would agree. Of course, with his attitude, there was no middle ground between apathy and fanaticism.

"Maybe I worry about you," Perry finally scolded. "And if you're in The Kitchen cooking, then I don't have to fear you getting knifed or shot."

Perry's concern was heartfelt, though his tone was terse. "Don't worry," I muttered, and smiled to myself, "I'll be careful." Then I redirected the conversation. "Where does Gunter live?" We cruised down the Southwest Freeway then headed south on Loop 610.

"Meyerland."

"As big a shot as he is, that's surprising." Not that Meyerland was the slums—more like the Marvin Gardens of Houston—but a man with Gunter's money signified Park Place. In other words, River Oaks material.

"From what I gather he's very low-key."

"You haven't talked to him?"

"No. Robbie took the message from Gunter's secretary."

Secretary? I thought. I was sure the caller was as much a secretary as Jimmy and Cracker were for Chip Gunn.

"Robbie also indicated the man was rather rude in that he told him the time I was to meet Gunter, not asked," Perry added.

"Gunter sounds kind of particular," I said. "You sure you want me along?"

"No, I'm not, but I didn't have much choice in the matter. It was either leave you to wander the halls of the museum the rest of the morning or tote you with me and put you to work."

Damn my big mouth.

Perry sighed. "Besides, as I told you, your name came up when the secretary called. I figure your being there can't hurt."

If you only knew, I thought, but kept the words to myself the rest of the drive.

Surprisingly, the man who answered the door wasn't a four-hundred-pound gorilla but a slim Vietnamese dressed in a three-piece black suit.

Perry introduced us.

"Of course," the man replied, eyed me carefully, and

nodded. Obviously, he had his doubts about my presence. After all, Perry, though he carried his weight well, looked like a traditional man of the kitchen. But me, with my bearded face and partially hidden scar, might actually have fit in better answering doors for thugs. A frightening thought.

"You are expected," he finally added, and led us into a small foyer.

The modest ranch-style house was nestled in a quiet suburban neighborhood, and the inside was as unassuming and silent—with the exception of a clock knocking out seconds from the fireplace mantel—as the outside. A small formal dining room was to the right and a sitting room to the left. Ahead of us was the living room. There was something odd about its appearance, and I needed a minute to put my finger on it. The oddness wasn't really the flowery green-and-white furniture, even though it looked like a perfectly preserved set from the late Sixties or early Seventies. Nor was it the strange mix of paintings on the wall. Some nature scenes appeared as though they'd been unscrewed and stolen from cheap hotel rooms. Others were stark representations of the Holocaust. No, a great part of the oddness was the clear plastic runners on the floor, and the plastic covers over the couch and chair cushions. The last person I knew who sterilized an atmosphere while protecting items whose worth were of sentimental nature at best was my paranoid, neat-freak grandmother. The uneasy feeling that had started in the car grew to almost paralyzing proportions. Karl Gunter lived here? I didn't get where he was coming from.

"Sit, please," the Vietnamese said, and motioned to the couch. Perry rolled his eyes as the man turned his back.

"You sure Gunter is Chip Gunn's brother?" I whispered.

"Maybe one of them was adopted," Perry replied.

Heavy curtains were drawn over the windows, trapping the coolness of the AC, and a standing lamp glowed in the corner by the bookshelf. For all intents and purposes, it was hard to tell whether it was day or night. Perfect place for a compulsive, color-blind vampire.

Karl Gunter entered from the back of the house. He was wearing his trademark white suit. After seeing the interior of his house, I'd have bet my paycheck that the white suit was so he fit in at his brother's place. Then again, it could be the only suit he had.

Perry rose and offered his hand. "Good to see you again, sir." I also stood.

He shook both our hands, his grip firm.

"This is convenient," he said to me, his voice surprisingly high, though hoarse, as though he was suffering from a cold. "I didn't think you'd be with Mr. Stevens."

"Quirk of fate."

"Sit down," he ordered, rested his cane on a chair's arm, and sat. A coffee table separated us.

Perry took a notepad from his attaché case and opened his pen. "Oh, no," he explained. "I heard how highly you thought of Neil and decided he should help plan your function."

One of the Holocaust paintings caught my eye. Black lines, the image of a face in pain. Star of David transposed over a red swastika. Smoke in the background. I felt awful.

"You appreciate the pictures," Gunter said, catching my gaze and ignoring Perry. "I'll tell you about them someday. Soon."

Soon? What the hell did he have in mind? Common sense, however, forbade me to ask him.

The Vietnamese stood behind Gunter. Perry put on his game face.

"Well, what kind of party are you considering?" my boss asked.

"Small."

"I see. Does that mean dinner?" Perry followed up.

"Or lunch. Which one's cheaper?"

Perry was taken aback. "Generally lunch," he replied

coolly. "But it depends on what you'd like to serve, whether you'd prefer a sit-down affair or buffet—"

"Nothing wasteful like my brother does." He turned to me. "What did you bring to the shrinks' building the other day?" he asked.

"What?" Perry also faced me.

"The doctors' bourbon chicken," I informed Perry. "I saw Mr. Gunter there talking to John Taft, Gunn's campaign manager."

"Yes, you did. Makes me want to know what else you see," Gunter stated.

Perry tried to step in. "Well, I hate to say it—"

"Then don't," Gunter cracked.

I could sense Perry's patience ebbing. He prided himself on remaining professional in every circumstance, and I'd never seen him lose his composure. Yet. That Gunter was Gunn's brother helped. Perry wouldn't want to risk alienating an important client such as Gunn. As for myself, I felt like a piece of raw meat in a lion's den and would just as soon appease the beast then get the hell away.

"My brother has always been distracted by his image," Gunter tossed out. "That's why the extravagance. And stupid decision making."

"Different styles," Perry offered, growing uncomfortable.

Gunter smirked. "His run for office is too soon. It'd be even better if he'd get married and groom his kids for politics."

"What can we do for you, Mr. Gunter?" I asked, pulling him back to the purpose of our visit.

"I think I want a lunch. It will be a strategy meeting. Let's say six people. No, five. Serve that chicken stuff. I want you to cook it here," he told me, "and Dean Shriver to serve it."

My breath caught. "I don't believe I can get hold of Dean," I told him.

"Then have your private-investigator friend do it instead of digging into my business." He leaned forward. "Understand?"

I stood. "Yes."

Perry was in left field and didn't attempt to hide it.

"Two days," he said. "I want lunch, yes, a Sunday lunch in two days, with you and Shriver serving."

C.J.'s words of warning sprang back to mind. "I understand," I heard myself say. Had Perry not been with me, I might have taken a different course. Like what? I asked myself. And be glad Perry is here. If not, Gunter and his sidekick might have taken a different course.

"But why Shriver?" I risked asking.

"Don't foolishly bring your employer into something he may not want any knowledge of. Let's leave it as a family feud."

My eyes widened.

"So you've learned something," he said, and shook his head. "Hoang, show them out."

But I was way ahead of them.

"Lunch in two days," he called, voice sharp and very much in control.

I hit the muggy air never having welcomed it as strongly as I did now. Perry certainly wouldn't ask me to explain, and he might not listen even if I took the initiative. I wasn't going to. Instead, I was going to call C.J., and if not him then Linda. He'd been made, and I hoped he was all right.

Two days.

Where was C.J.?

What should I do about Dean?

And why was I still reluctant to call Lieutenant Gardner?

18

As I hugged the curb with my VW I noticed Claudia's old silver Lincoln parked prominently in front of The Kitchen. When he dropped me off at my apartment, Perry had said he was running out to the bank and then indicated he had other errands to attend to and he didn't know when he'd be in. I suspected Gunter shook Perry up and he needed some time to clear his head and calm his nerves. The only thing he'd said during the drive back was, "Gunter seems to want you to handle his luncheon. So you handle it. I don't want to be involved whatsoever."

Neither did I, I'd thought. There was no sense in protesting, though. I was involved and had to deal with it.

I double-checked that the envelope of money was still beneath the seat. It was. The idea of leaving the greenbacks at my apartment worried me. For any reason, should Gunn or Gunter or even someone Lamar blabbed to ransack my place, they would almost certainly find the stash. Shaking down my car was less likely. And searching The Kitchen even more remote.

I slipped inside and into the front room where we kept the dry goods. The metal-wire racks were full of number-ten cans of tomatoes, artichoke hearts, and baby corns, of odds and ends like small cans of salmon, jalapeños, and cornichons, and of gallon-sized containers of mayonnaise, mustard, and olives. A couple of racks were full of liquor and mixers, and in the very back was a top shelf covered with paper goods. A stack of unmade cake boxes lay flat in the corner. I counted three from the bottom, lifted the others up and tucked the envelope of money as far back as I could reach. As I stepped back and examined the stack I noticed there were no gaps and that the bulge was barely perceptible.

The money taken care of, I went out to meet Claudia. She was sautéing a case of ground mushrooms mixed with onion, garlic, oregano, sage, thyme, salt, and pepper for what would eventually be mushroom strudel. Whenever I caught the odor of this mixture cooking down, I was reminded of Thanksgiving. In part it was the smell of the sage, reminiscent of turkey dressing. Mostly it was because many holidays ago was the first time I'd made the recipe. Now, regardless what time of year it was, for a split second the feel of Thanksgiving wrapped my senses, securing me like a favorite blanket on a cold night. The effect was very calming.

"Hey, Claudia," I greeted.

"What you been doing up front?" she asked.

"Checking our supply of capers for a lunch in a couple of days," I replied.

She barely nodded. "I wish Mattie was here," she mumbled. "Could use her help today."

"She'll be back soon," I said, mustering an upbeat tone. Claudia, though, was worrying me. The large woman was moving slowly. Her usual dominant attitude was almost nonexistent. I glanced at Conrad, who was carefully drying the blade for the Cuisinart. He shrugged.

"Suppose you're right," she told me. "Didn't know if you'd be in. That's why I be here."

"What's wrong?" I asked.

"Don't know." A thick sadness tugged at her eyes. "Doctor thinks it might be cancer."

A cold dose of reality bathed me, washing out the feel of Thanksgiving. "What does he mean, thinks it might be?"

"That's what he say!" she snapped.

"Sorry." I raised my hands. I could kick Robbie for not informing me that Claudia's situation was serious. Then a wave of regret followed the wash of reality and I felt miserable for having fought with Claudia earlier in the week.

"You want to go home?" I asked. "I can cover."

"No," she replied firmly. "I been sitting on my couch feeling sorry for myself too long. Why, look at Mattie. She's in big trouble and she be young. Least if the doctor says the worst, I'm old."

"You aren't old."

"Older than you and Mattie put together. And if the Lord calls me home, then it be fine."

"What can I do for you?"

"Help pull tonight's job together."

"Planned to. Fact is, I'm on the crew to work it."

"I got to see the doctor this afternoon."

"I'll be here," I said. "I'm looking forward to the quiet."

We worked in relative silence. After cooking the mushroom strudel filling dry then adding some cream cheese, Claudia set it aside to cool. I rolled and filled mini-*empañadas* with a cilantro, jalapeño, spicy onion, and beef filling. Then I finished prepping the black olive purée for the *bruschetta*. We would top the Italian-style toasts with the purée and fresh mozzarella cheese at the client's house and warm them there. Claudia completed the prosciutto-wrapped asparagus then left for her appointment. Tonight's function was strictly hors d'oeuvres and promised to be short and sweet. The clients were using it as a starter before heading to a private performance by the Houston Symphony's concertmaster and a visiting pianist I wasn't familiar with. Afterward there was a late dinner, but we weren't involved in that.

With Claudia gone and things under control, I went into the office and made a few phone calls. Perry still wasn't back, so I had the privacy I desired. First, I called C.J., and by a stroke of luck caught him.

"Glad you're all right," I said.

"Why wouldn't I be? Granted, this has been like looking for an honest politician right before election day, but I think I got a bite."

"I'm sure you do."

"I've got to track down a guy named Oakley," he continued. "Word is he used to do some work for the Gunn-Gunter brothers."

Oakley? Why did that name sound familiar?

"Well, watch your back," I said, "especially now that you've been made."

Dead silence. "What?"

"You didn't know?"

"No. Are you sure?"

"Positive," I told him, and relayed my meeting with Karl Gunter.

"Son of a bitch," he grumbled. "Hope I can find Oakley before they do."

Then it clicked. "Oakley," I said. "Alice Tarkenton defended him. She was using that case to explain her relationship to Sergeant Hernandez."

"I don't recall Vic talking about that one."

"He wouldn't. He was left literally holding the bag after Alice got Oakley off for running marijuana. I guess Oakley's not exactly a genius and didn't know what he was doing."

"Well, well, I find that highly interesting," he said. "Who was his contact?"

"It never came out; besides, she was vague with details. Talk to Alice. There's something else." I then regaled him with my early-morning conversation with Chip Gunn and asked if he'd seen the newspaper article.

"Son of a bitch," he repeated. "That hippie friend of yours is marked. Stay away from him."

Marked? I thought, and remembered Dean's Outlaw poem. Or marked himself. And I wasn't going to stay away from him, though I saw no point in arguing with C.J. over my stand.

"But how, after Gunn squelched the first story, would Dean be able to conjure up an investigation that not only brings in the police but the FBI?" I asked.

"Could be as simple as phoning in a threat against

Gunn, claiming he was with some radical underground group."

"That sounds too easy. Something's missing."

"Or you're overanalyzing." There was a pause. "The winds are blowing hot and angry," he said.

"I know that tone. If I run to Gardner I'm knee-deep in horseshit for lying and covering up, and also out comes Lamar's stabbing, implicating Mattie."

"Better than being knocked into the next world. Gunter's not fooling around."

I said nothing.

"Okay," C.J. told me. "I'll track this Oakley character and we'll go from there."

"There's a reason Lamar was murdered," I offered.

"Still could be as simple as his ex-girlfriend blowing him away."

"Keep in touch, C.J."

"If there's ever a next time, kid, it's going to cost you."

"No doubt."

After we hung up I called the *Chronicle* and placed an ad in the classified section looking for the Kerouac book as the signal for Dean to contact me. It was too late to get the message in the next day's paper, but there was enough time for it to make Sunday's. I hoped I could convince Gunter I'd done all possible. As I checked my message machine Conrad popped his head into the room and mouthed that he was going to run out and buy some cigarettes. I flashed him the okay sign.

The voice of Sondra Anderson scolded me for inviting her out for a beer Thursday evening and then standing her up. I slapped my forehead, having completely forgotten. That was the night I was lost in Keely's world. Speaking of, there was a message from the young professor also, informing me she'd received new poems from Dean in the mail and would look them over with me when I had a chance. With the beeping that signaled the end of the tape, I hung up and placed a quick call to Sondra. No one picked up, so I pleaded to her machine for forgiveness.

I leaned back in the office chair and took a deep breath. Where was I? I thought, when I heard the front door open and close.

"Robbie?" I called.

No answer.

"Claudia?"

Again, no answer.

"Conrad, you back?"

A nervous twitch knotted my stomach. Funny how I was getting used to it. I rose and eased to the door.

Standing by the pastry table and looking shell-shocked as a gun-shy horse was Mattie Johnson.

I felt a grin overtake me. "You didn't bust out of jail, did you?"

The joke made little impression. "You have my money?" she squeaked.

"It's safe." I pulled up a stool and she collapsed onto it, leaning against the stainless table.

Puffing through the door next came that tough old bird Alice Tarkenton. "Damn, the girl runs like a jackrabbit," she huffed, and pulled out a cigarette.

"What's going on?" I asked.

"The police still ain't convinced she didn't do it," Alice declared in her gravelly voice. "But, by Jesus, I am."

19

Alice Tarkenton took a stool next to Mattie and caught her breath. I fetched a pitcher of iced tea from one of the coolers and poured them each a glass. Mattie didn't move.

"You okay?" I asked.

A small nod.

I caught Alice's eye. She motioned with her hand for me to relax. "Tell me about it," I told the old lawyer.

"The autopsy report was the ticket," Alice responded, enthusiasm jumping into her voice. "It showed that Lamar had been clubbed in the head before he was shot the second time."

"Is that what killed him?"

"No, but the blow that fractured his skull had to have knocked the poor bastard cold."

"So what are you saying?" I asked.

"Someone had to lift him over to the bed in order to put the last slug into his head. No way could little Mattie have carried a man as huge as Lamar across the room. I don't figure she could even have dragged him across the room—never mind picking him up and dropping him on the bed. The DA agreed."

"Ed Krieger?" I cried.

"No, not that warthog. He'd send his neighbor's dog to the pound if it crapped in his front yard. I'm talking about the big guy, Langly Barnes." She paused and fished out a cigarette. "At least for now Mattie has a reprieve. There's still the matter of the first gunshot, but I think I can get that dismissed as self-defense."

155

Mattie's head was back down on her arms.

"She's exhausted," Alice offered, and lit up a cigarette. "That old goat would scalp me if he walked in right now, wouldn't he?"

"Perry? Absolutely." Perry despised cigarette smoke.

Alice grinned. "Hope he walks in."

Smoke billowed and a disturbing thought came to me. I rounded the table and whispered to Alice. "You think she had help?"

"It occurred to me," she replied. "But now I'm going with her story."

"And it ain't changed none," Mattie said, and raised her head. I felt foolish.

"It's something the police will think of," I explained. "Best to know now if someone helped you."

"And who would that be?" she asked. "Only person I'd trust is you, and you didn't heft Lamar across the room."

"No, I didn't. Sorry."

"Don't apologize. You trying to help. I left that big dog kneeling on the floor, blood running from his leg where I done shot him. That the last I saw him."

"And you didn't notice anyone outside waiting for you, or watching—anyone familiar?"

"I told you, I was scared from the sound of the shot and drove J.J. away quick as I could."

"We don't need to get into it now," Alice said, and searched for a place to flick her cigarette ashes.

I rounded up a saucer from the back and placed it on the table.

"Where are you going to stay tonight, dear?" Alice asked Mattie.

"Don't know." She glanced at me.

"I'm sure Mattie wants to go to Mama's," I said, "and see her son."

That thought gave Mattie a little perk, though her voice shook when she said, "I was so worried about him. I didn't know what I'd do if they incarcerated me."

"Told you Alice would do you right," I said.

"I want the address and number," Alice said, not even trying to hide her grin. "And you stay put," she directed to Mattie. "We've come a long way, but we ain't out of the woods yet."

As the young woman absorbed what her lawyer said, I could see the weariness again wash over her. She laid her head back into her arms on the table.

I jotted down the number and address for Alice. "Thought you got this when J.J. was dropped off."

"Meant to. Didn't."

"If for some unforeseen reason she's unable to stay at Mama's, I'll leave word on your machine."

"Good enough," Alice replied, and crushed her cigarette in the saucer.

The door then popped open and in glided Robbie Persons. He set down a case of Kendall-Jackson Chardonnay. "Mattie!" he exclaimed.

A gentle snoring rose from where she sat.

"Hush, boy," Alice ordered. "Let the girl rest until Neil's ready to hit the road."

"I'll fill you in," I told Robbie in response to his confused look.

"Got to run," Alice said. "I'll be in touch."

"Thanks," I called as she cruised out the door. I picked up the saucer and Robbie trailed me to the sink while I gave him a quick rundown on Mattie's release. When I drew to the end I asked if he could cover the hors d'oeuvres party for me tonight.

"I'd like to get Mattie settled with J.J.," I added. Sooner or later missing these jobs was going to take an economic toll not to mention further irritate Perry. I recalled his "lack of passion" speech from earlier in the day.

Robbie simply said, "No problem. Candace is going to be disappointed, though."

"She's working it?"

"Mattie was originally scheduled. I thought it wise to replace her," he said dryly.

"Oh. Good call. Thanks for tossing her some work."

"It'll be me, Candace, and Booker—the A-team." He grinned.

I rolled my eyes. "As you say."

Robbie cruised into the office. I opted to use the phone in the prep area and called Mama.

"Great, honey," she told me. "You bring that girl to my house. Her baby's missing her something awful. And they can stay just as long as they want."

"Thanks, Mama."

I woke Mattie up.

"Can't I just sleep here?" she asked groggily.

"No, and we're not going to my apartment. We're going to see your baby at Mama's. Remember, she's the woman who took care of my private-investigator friend, C. J. McDaniels, when he was growing up. You'll be safe there."

"I need to get my car."

"No, I'll drive you."

"But—"

"You're too tired," I said, and I don't want you running off, I thought.

She pouted. I didn't care.

"Where's my money?" she asked.

"In a safe place. When the time comes, you'll get it. All of it."

Mattie flashed what I thought was an angry look, then I realized she showed more hurt.

"I'm sorry, Neil. I know you been doing a lot for me."

I rapped the stainless-steel table. "Don't worry about it. You've been through quite an ordeal."

A smile finally raised the corners of her mouth. "Thanks."

As we left, Conrad returned. "Good of you to join us for the remainder of the afternoon," I commented, slightly irked.

"Had personal business."

"I'll remember that the next time you want to run out for just a second."

"Why, did I miss anything?"

"No," I said. "But you might."

"Why are you being a hard-ass?"

Conrad was thin as a rehabbed drug addict, complete with the tattoos on his forearm. I usually cut him slack because I knew Perry didn't pay the man much. Right now, though, I had a funny feeling about him being gone so long—and the way he was eyeing Mattie.

"Just do it," I told him, and accompanied Mattie and her son out.

I had the willies as I opened the doors of my Bug. Mattie fell into the front seat. Paranoia, I thought, and started the VW up. But images of Jimmy and Cracker waiting, of Gunn throwing his temper tantrum, and of Gunter with his subtle threat ticker-taped through my mind. We needed to head southeast, but I began by heading straight north. That was when I knew someone was following me.

An unobtrusive brown sedan with tinted glass fell in and out of lanes with us on the freeway, exited when I hit Tidwell and U-turned south, and zipped back on the freeway with us. Now, I wasn't a Rockford when it came to car chases, especially since my car was no Camaro, but I'd been followed a few times and the intrusion didn't rattle me as it had before.

Mattie snored. I picked up speed when I hit the Nolan Ryan Expressway. My pattern toward Mama's remained erratic. At Loop 610 I chose south and hit heavy traffic by the Astrodome. The sedan stayed back, but it was with me. I exited at Buffalo Speedway. With traffic, I was held for a couple of turns by a red light. When it began to look like I could make it, I hesitated as the light went yellow then hooked a hard left at the last second. I shot under the freeway and ran a red as I took another left and headed back the way I'd traveled. A quick glance in the rearview mirror told me that the sedan hadn't been able to hop over to the U-turn lane to stay on our trail. I returned to the freeway sure the car was pinned in traffic behind a red light.

I kicked the Bug into high. Well, as high as it would go. Unless I exited quickly, the tracker would be able to catch me on the open highway. Soon. Once I spun to the east, I slipped off the freeway. We were exits from where we were supposed to be, but I suffered through the standing traffic and lights. No sign of the sedan. By the time I hit Mama's turnoff, I was over an hour into this flight. But from all appearances, I had lost my tail. Sadly, I had no one to share my small victory with as Mattie remained oblivious to my remarkable driving.

As I rolled to a stop in front of Mama's small house, I realized I was covered with sweat and that my heart was racing faster than the damn Bug. A series of deep breaths and slow releases were all I could do to control my shaking as I rose from the driver's seat. I guessed I was more rattled by the intrusion than I'd let myself believe.

I paused a moment before I awakened Mattie. As usual, I was asking questions.

Who had put a tail on me?

Was the sedan the only one, or a decoy?

Who was I going to talk to about it? C.J.? Perhaps. As he'd been made, he might have a thought on the subject.

Or should I call Gardner? Wouldn't be the first time the cops had followed me. I released one last deep breath as if I had a cloud of smoke in my lungs.

Damn if I wasn't getting sick of asking questions.

20

As a child, Saturday mornings had been my favorite time of the weekend. I was an early riser. For a while I had a paper route, and I'd peddle through the quiet neighborhood, visions of someday seeing my byline beneath the headline story. Then I'd spend the rest of the morning watching television or reading *Boy's Life* and *Ellery Queen's Mystery Magazine*. By afternoon, however, my parents had compiled a list of chores that would take me until supper to finish.

Now Saturday morning was one of my least favorite times. I was usually working or catching up on errands I had neglected to do over the course of the week. Rarely did I sleep in—I saved that for Sunday mornings. My journalistic ambition having fallen by the wayside once I fell into the company of Frost, Hemingway, Faulkner, and Eliot, the lure of the newspaper had even diminished. And that I had been the subject of articles instead of the author certainly didn't help. No, Saturday mornings had tumbled from grace, and this one was no different.

After a dreadful night's sleep, I awoke early. The scenario of Mattie and Lamar struggling played over and over in my head. The gun going off. Lamar discovered on the bed, bound, and shot in the head. Something was bothering me, but I couldn't put my finger on it. Could be the thought of dealing with Gunter was distracting me. Or the source of my uneasiness.

Tired as I felt, I took a light run to clear my head. A couple of miles were all I cared to do, and though it pumped a little energy into my system, my head remained as clogged as ever. At least I had peace of mind in knowing that Mattie and J.J. were under the caring eye of Mama.

The phone was ringing as I stumbled into my apartment. I let the machine screen the call for me.

"Neil, it's Perry. Karl Gunter called to ask how his lunch plans were coming along. I informed him that you were handling it and I'd have you call him back. The number and message are here on my desk. I want you to take care of it this morning. Bye."

I eyed my window and wondered if answering machines could fly.

As soon as the fool mechanism completed its various clicks and spins, I deleted the message. Saturday morning, true to form. I hoped I didn't drown while taking a shower.

The evil red eye flashed that someone else had called while I was in the shower. It was tempting not to check it, but I did.

Keely needed to talk. She was heading to the university now. If I missed her there, she'd be home by late afternoon.

I tried to quick call back, but she was already gone. What did she need to discuss? Dean's work? Surely wouldn't be my work. As of late I was stagnant as heavy air on a windless afternoon. Perhaps she heard from Dean. Or maybe she was going to fess up that her marriage wasn't all that happy. Right, Neil, I told myself. Put your money on contact from Dean.

Robbie was straightening the wine and liquor when I arrived at The Kitchen.

"How'd the job go last night?" I asked.

"Great. But Candace had a thing or two to say about you not working it."

"I bet she did. The food come out okay?"

"The *bruschetta* were to die for, child. Undoubtedly the food's success was a result of the person who placed the finishing touches." He noted on his clipboard how many bottles of white wine he had left.

"You handled the food?" I asked.

"Naturally."

"You're getting to be a regular hash slinger, Robbie. I'll have to watch my back or you'll be after my job."

"No way." Robbie smiled. Honesty shone so brightly from those gray eyes he couldn't lie if he wanted to. "You work too hard."

"Like you don't."

"But I don't have to answer to Claudia." Robbie counted the Cabernets, Burgundies, and Bordeaux.

He's got a point, I thought, then switched gears. "You heard from Claudia?" I asked.

"Not today."

"Yesterday after I left?"

"No."

"She went to the doctor's," I said, and leaned my hands down on the stainless table. "She told me she thinks she has cancer."

Robbie glanced up, pen behind his ear as he shifted a few bottles in the wine rack. "Maybe you'll be more understanding."

I bit my tongue. For someone who was always spatting with Claudia himself, he was sure protective of her. "Maybe," I eventually said, then drifted into the office to retrieve Perry's message.

"Bossman's gone?" I called as I read the note. It was exactly what Perry had said over the phone.

"He ran to La Grange to see his aunt Loretta."

"She up from her hip operation yet?" I wandered back into the storage room.

"Apparently not."

"Guess I'm going to have to deal with Mr. Karl Gunter," I lamented.

"Was there ever any doubt?" Robbie was inventorying the hard stuff now.

"Don't suppose you'd consider—"

"Don't even ask. But if you can't scrounge up Dean Shriver, I'll cover the job with you."

"Thanks," I said, "I'll keep it in mind." If I don't scrounge up Dean, I thought, or at minimum, scrounge up word from him, then I'd better hire C. J. McDaniels to accompany me.

I returned to the office and punched in Gunter's phone number. His Vietnamese sidekick answered.

"This is Neil Marshall at Perry Stevens Catering," I stated, "I'm returning Mr. Gunter's call." Please, I prayed, let him be unavailable.

"Yes, sir. One moment." And I was on hold.

Damn.

As I waited in the void of communication I tossed around how I was going to make Gunter understand that in all probability I would not be able to raise Dean Shriver until Sunday afternoon. Before any brilliant idea hit me, Gunter's high-pitched voice slid across the telephone wire.

"Marshall, are you and Shriver ready to serve my lunch tomorrow? Fix enough for six, though there might be only four."

"Right. But, ah, I might be winging it solo." I decided I wasn't going to drag Robbie into this mess.

"What the hell do you mean?" he asked, so low and scratchy I shivered.

"I don't know where he is." I spoke strongly, commanding the quiver out of my voice. "There's a decent chance I can catch him tomorrow, but most likely it'll be late afternoon."

"Not good."

"I was afraid of that."

"I have to talk to Shriver."

"Just talk?" I didn't know why I said that—the question popped out.

"Are you holding back, Marshall?"

"No, sir. I'm playing my hand—no cards up the sleeve."

"I certainly hope so." He paused. I heard ice clinking against the side of a glass and a quiet gulp. "And, yeah, I just want to talk. This time."

"I'll do my best."

"Do better."

Go to hell, I thought. Prudently, however, I said, "Would you consider changing your meeting to the evening? We could serve dinner and there's half a chance I could get Dean to come." Damn I could. So why did I say that? Buy a little more time. For what? I was treading water.

"No, I want lunch. Besides, my brother's giving a speech outside the downtown library in the afternoon. He feels a need to explain this investigation issue." He groaned.

"No problem. I'll be over around eleven."

"I want to eat at high noon."

"Make that ten-thirty, then."

He hung up without another word. The man had the personality of a water moccasin.

I flicked on the light to the back of The Kitchen and rummaged through the coolers to see if we had everything necessary for Gunter's lunch.

"Get everything worked out with Karl Gunter?" Robbie asked.

"Piece of cake." Speaking of which, I needed to whip up something for dessert. Also, we didn't have salad fixings.

"Do you have time to run to the market for me?" I asked. "Then I could begin prepping for tomorrow."

"Sure, soon as I finish counting the booze."

I listed the greens I wanted. Watercress, arugula, Boston lettuce, spinach, endive, and a little radicchio for color. Once I added some roasted pine nuts and edible blossoms for garnish, Gunter was going to feel like he was grazing. I decided to go with a tangy honey-Dijon vinaigrette with crumbled blue cheese, though I suspected Gunter was a Thousand Island man.

Robbie completed his chore, grabbed the list, and left. Unless we had a huge function going on, Conrad was usually off on weekends, so I was alone. I locked the front door, noting that the hookers were already walking the street. Early bird catches the worm, I thought.

I was halfway through the almond crust for the Linzer

torte, my favorite dessert, when someone pounded on the front door. Like Pavlov's dogs salivating at the sound of bells, I broke out in a sweat these days at any sudden disruption.

Methodically, I wiped my hands on a kitchen towel and eased to the door. The pounding continued. Rather than flinging the door open, I edged up to the mini-blinds in the storage room and lifted the corner of one. Last time this happened I stared at the massiveness of Jimmy and the mean visage of Cracker. But today the good Lord reassured me that surprises could also be good. Standing just beyond the locked door was Keely Cohen.

"Well, I'll be damned," I announced as I invited her in. "What brings you to my humble place of employment."

"Are those prostitutes on the corner?"

"I prefer the term working girls," I replied, then closed and locked the door.

She turned to me quickly, eyes wide, mouth slightly open, though no words were slipping between her lips.

"They aren't associated with the catering company," I added.

"I know that, dummy," she said, and laughed nervously. "I just don't come across this, um, environment very often. You even locked the door."

"I tend to do that when I'm left alone or don't want to be needlessly interrupted—no sense inviting trouble. It's grown to be a rough neighborhood. We've had street people walk in and ask for food and money, though the girls simply add a little color to the area."

"Do you ever call the cops?"

"Why? They don't bother us. And the cops know they're here. Every once in a while they clear them out. Doesn't last long."

"How do the *working girls* get away with it?"

"Keely, you've been in the ivory tower too long," I told her. "Speaking of, why aren't you there now?"

"Oh, hush. I came to show you the new poems Dean mailed me."

"This must be serious," I said, and finished cleaning my hands on the towel. Keely had never ventured to The Kitchen before.

She opened a folder and thumbed to one piece in particular. "I'm afraid it might be," she replied, "but since you know Dean as well as anybody, I wanted to get your reaction before I jumped to conclusions."

I accepted the poem she held out and read it slowly. It was eerily titled "Skeletons." It began:

> My father is the skeleton in the field.
> His scythe creates bales of smoke
> that rain money
> for my enemies.

I dropped to the stool Mattie had occupied yesterday and lowered the paper. "What the hell?" I asked.

"Read on," Keely said, brushing back her short, dark hair. "It gets better." She poked around like a child exploring her grandparents' attic. I'd have to give her the grand tour in a couple of minutes.

For now I concentrated on Dean's disjointed cursive. A few lines down came:

> Perception is the root of power,
> the hallucinogenic of the masses
> that keeps them high in the closet
> and righteous on the street.

I paused. "This is weird, even for Dean," I said.

"I think he's lost his grip on reality," Keely responded, nudging the cloth kitchen witch that hung for good luck from an air-conditioning duct.

"Maybe. Let me finish." The poem concluded:

> And in that graveyard,
> leaves of grass produce
> power that will turn

to smoke beneath the righteous
scythe of a new generation.
My father is the skeleton in the field.

I set the poem down. "What do you make of it?" I asked.

"Look at the drug references," she said. " 'Bales of smoke,' 'hallucinogenic,' 'high in the closet,' and 'leaves of grass'—may Walt Whitman forgive him."

"Dean is drug crazy," I said. "That's the reason he's running around half-cocked."

"No, I think it's a symptom. I don't think you and C.J. are looking for a field of bodies, as Lamar Fowler indicated. It sounds to me like it's a field of pipe dreams."

"Marijuana?"

"Be my guess."

"Dean said his father worked in produce," I stated. "But he died some years back."

"The 'skeleton in the field,' " she offered.

"The enemies—Gunn and Gunter?"

"We knew that without reading the poem."

"So how does it all tie together?" I asked. "What is Dean trying to tell us?"

"I don't know, that's why I trotted this folder right out to you." Keely wandered to the front window and picked up a glass bottle from the butcher-block table. Inside the bottle were red and green jalapeño peppers marinating in vinegar.

"Why the game?" I asked. "Why doesn't he speak, or write, plainly?"

"Again, Dean's not in his right mind. And I believe he believes he *is* communicating plainly."

"This saga keeps getting better and better."

Keely placed the pepper-sauce bottle back on the table then sat on the stool opposite me. "How'd his father die?" she asked.

"By his own hand."

"Oh, God, that's awful. Well, that explains part of Dean's craziness, and also confirms our fears."

"Fears?"

"Children of suicides often follow the same path."

The tiny hairs on the back of my neck stiffened. I was back to being glad I'd placed the ad to signal Dean.

Keely stuck the poem into the folder. "You might want to show these to C.J.," she said.

"If it ain't Hank Williams or Ernest Tubb, he has no interest."

"You could point out the images."

"I suppose I could try. Somehow this ties into Lamar's death," I added.

"Think Lamar knew more about the field than he was letting on?"

"Looks that way. I don't know."

Keely glanced at her watch. "I need to dash."

"How about a tour of The Kitchen?"

"It's fascinating, seeing this side of you, but I'm late. Mark and I are going to the opera tonight. *Tosca.*"

"How tragic."

"Of course. Yet, so beautiful." She flashed her lovely smile. I unlocked the door.

"Do be careful," she said, gave me a peck on the cheek, and hustled down the driveway. A final wave of her hand and Keely disappeared into her car. She zipped quickly by the hookers and down the road.

Yes, I thought, how tragic. And yet so beautiful.

Living love vicariously.

I guessed Dean wasn't the only screwed-up poet in this city.

21

I completed the prep work for Gunter's party then collected the food together for tonight's function. It was a slow Saturday, with only a little dinner party scheduled. Claudia had signed herself on the job but so far was a no-show. As I missed last night's job, I had resigned myself to cover for her when she traipsed through the door.

"How are you?" I asked as I boxed up the raspberry *génoise*, the French sponge cake that was for dessert.

Robbie appeared from the office.

"Yes, how are you?" he asked.

"Doctor said he going to operate on me then do chemo or something. Said I should be okay in time."

"Operate?" I asked.

"I don't want to talk no more," she stated. "Doctor said most women in my condition beat it and I going to beat it, too."

"That's great," said Robbie, mustering enthusiasm.

"I'm so glad," I said.

"Is you?" Claudia put her fists on her hips.

"I is," I replied, and mocked her stance.

"Good to see nothing ever changes," Robbie piped in, shook his head, and returned to the office.

"Want me to take your shift tonight?" I asked.

"No, sir. You can't have my money."

"I just thought—"

"I needs the money, Neil. I be out of work for a while."

"You have insurance," I stated.

"Yes, but Perry can't afford to give me no sick pay. I

might be able to collect some from the government. Ain't going to be much."

I thought of Mattie's money. She'd kill me. I resolved to talk to her, though.

"I'm in a bind, that's all. Now, what's on the menu tonight?"

I explained that the cilantro-and-saffron rice, ribs, chicken, and smoked sausage for the *paella* were cooked and simply had to be warmed. What remained were the shrimp, scallops, mussels, and crab legs. And, for topping, steamed fresh peas. There was no doubt the Perry Stevens version of the Spanish dish pulled out all the stops, and the presentation was no less subtle. A large white platter sat in the middle of an even larger flat basket. Around the perimeter of the basket, resting on banana leaves, were whole *poblano* peppers, jalapeños, and bulbs of garlic as garnish. A mountain of rice covered the white platter with the meats and seafood running throughout. The peas added color on top and the peppery-garlic aroma was enough to make a dead man's mouth water.

There was also a green salad similar to the one I had gathered for Karl Gunter—and bread twists. Claudia seemed pleased at the production and announced she'd take it from there. That was fine with me.

Late afternoon and it threatened rain. Working while it rained outside wasn't so bad, as dark skies added a cozy atmosphere to a small dinner party. Toting food and equipment in and out of torrents wasn't fun, however. I wiped sweat off my forehead and chugged away in the VW.

I figured I ought to call Mama to see how Mattie and J.J. were holding up. Or rather, how Mama was holding up under J.J.'s energy. Before I touched base with C.J., I reconciled myself to giving her a ring.

With little sleep the last couple of days and as frayed as I felt, I got sloppy. It wasn't until I was pulling into my driveway that I noticed the sedan with the tinted glass coasting to a stop up the street. I acted like I hadn't seen it, and didn't panic. Whoever was inside the car was keeping a distance. Casually, I opened the hall door and hiked up the stairs.

I locked my apartment door and punched a familiar number into the phone. First call instead of Mama was Lieutenant Gardner. Being Saturday, I hardly expected him in. I reckoned I'd leave a message and tell him to take his cowboy off my tail. Surprisingly, I reached Sergeant Hernandez.

"Hey, it's the boy wonder. What do you need? Guess that bitch of a lawyer got another one off."

"Alice is my friend," I said with exaggerated politeness. "And you know how I feel about Mattie." He wasn't going to set my ass on fire. I'd kill him with kindness.

"Right."

"What are you doing at the station this late on a Saturday?"

"Pulling overtime. You didn't call to shoot the shit."

"Maybe I did. What can you tell me about the Oakley case?" I asked.

"How do you know about that?"

"Think, Vic."

"All right, that—I mean, Tarkenton took us for a ride on that one, too."

"How?"

"I can't talk about the case to you, little gringo."

"Oh, it's a closed case. Give me a break. Who was Oakley working for?"

"Don't know."

"Come on, Vic. Linda says you're great at figuring out who done it, but that the legal system sometimes straps your hands. I bet that was one such case."

"Linda says that?"

"Absolutely." Well, she said he was a good cop.

"Son of a bitch," he said to himself. "What do you know about the Oakley case?"

"The basics. Oakley was caught running pot. The truck was in his name. But he's a simpleton and couldn't have pulled any complicated scam."

"You're right. Trouble is, he knew who the contact was. He wouldn't talk," Hernandez added.

"I heard he spilled his guts."

"Naming your boss Big Mac and calling yourself Little Fry is not spilling your guts."

"Scared?"

"Too stupid to be scared."

"Then what was it?" I asked.

"I don't know. I know he was tied to Karl Gunter."

"But you couldn't prove it."

"There was a missing link, and without a statement by Oakley or nailing his contact, we had nothing."

"Still do," I said. But a thought concerning the contact finally smacked me directly over the head.

"Okay, smart-ass, anything else?"

"Actually, I called to tell Gardner to get the cop off my tail," I stated, trying to sound like an irritated citizen.

"What?"

"You've got someone watching me."

"Man, you've seen too many episodes of *NYPD Blue*. We don't have anyone on you. We don't have the manpower for that. And if there's anything we need, we know where to find you."

"You aren't shadowing me?" I asked, beginning to feel nervous. Again.

"No."

"You're sure."

"Goddamn it, *muchacho*, no! I ain't got no more time for this."

"Bye," I said as he hung up. My first reaction was to call Keely and tip her off that I'd been followed. Whoever was watching me had surely caught her trip to The Kitchen. I wanted to alert her to be on guard.

I reached her infernal answering machine. Not wanting to send Mark into spasms or frighten Keely, I left an innocuous message asking Keely to return my call at her convenience.

Brown sedan. Not cops. Who, then? I carefully replaced

the receiver. Unlikely it was Gunter. Had to be Chip Gunn's baboons. Suppose he figured I'd lead them to Dean. In that case, he'd figure Keely could lead him to Dean, also. I fought a flash of panic. Keely was with Mark. She was at the opera, not exactly Dean's, Jimmy's, or Cracker's hangout. And I'd hear from her later tonight or tomorrow.

So it was down to me. Well, I wasn't going to screw with them, at least not directly. The last time we'd crossed unfriendly paths I found myself nursing busted ribs. But I might tantalize them a bit.

Linda answered the phone at C.J.'s office.

"The old man there?" I asked.

"No, and he better not hear you calling him that."

"I really need to talk to him. Has he checked in?"

"Not a word. All I know is he ran out in the direction of Orange this morning."

"He say why?" Orange was a small East Texas town out Beaumont way.

"Come on, Neil, you know C.J."

"Yes, I do." I thought for a minute. "If you have a free minute or two, could you help me?"

"Not sure I want to," she replied.

"Don't blame you, but I've got a brown sedan tailing me and I'd like to lose it for a while."

"Know who it is?"

"Could be Gunn's goons, but I'm not certain."

"Vic Hernandez just called and asked me out for a drink tonight," Linda said.

Why that old rooster, I thought. Guess rubbing his ego had an effect.

"He's going to meet me here a little later," she added.

"This won't take long."

"I'm sure." There was a stretch of silence like she was turning over FM 100's daily trivia question, weighing her answers so she could collect the hundred-buck jackpot. Buzz, I thought. Time's up.

"What do you have in mind?" Linda finally asked.

"Meet me at The Black Lab," I said.

"By the Montrose library?"

"Yes, only park in the lot behind the restaurant. I'll find a spot right in front then cut through to the back. I know the manager, he'll let me out."

"What if the sedan circles around back?"

"Then it won't work. But I'll bet the farm they won't let my Bug out of sight because they don't want to enter a small pub. Fastest way for them to get made."

"What if they don't care?"

"Stop with the what-ifs. If they're with Gunn and want me to guide them to Dean, then they care."

"All right," Linda said. "The place isn't that far away. I can do that. But after I pick you up, then what?"

"I'll wait for C.J. at the office."

"What if he doesn't come back?"

There she went with the what-ifs again. I slowly said, "I'll take a cab to get my car and take my chances."

"Fine. See you at The Black Lab," she responded, and hung up.

"Fine," I said aloud. "You deserve Vic Hernandez." I put on a clean shirt then cleared out.

I didn't look at the sedan as I drove away from it down the street. The car remained a respectable length behind me all the way to the restaurant. I found a place up front and took my time collecting myself before ambling in. The sedan squeezed into a small spot by the library. In front, as I'd expected.

Once inside I winked at the hostess and asked her to direct me to Jack O'Conner, the headwaiter and assistant manager. Many moons ago, when he'd first arrived from the Emerald Isle, he'd done some work for Perry Stevens Catering.

"Last I saw him, Neil, he was sitting in the smoking section behind the bar having a cig and pint with Mrs. Gibson."

"The English consul general's wife?"

"Mr. Gibson's out of town."

"I see. Life's rough in management."

The hostess leaned close. "I think he's baiting the old gal again with his talk of treason."

"IRA?"

She nodded.

I laughed. "Jack best be careful. She'll take him seriously."

Sure enough, Jack was at one of the small two-tops jabbering about the plight of Northern Ireland. Mrs. Gibson, who was large enough to take up both of those chairs, puffed on a cigarette so forcefully I thought that at any minute she'd dump the rest of her brew on his head.

"Jack," I called. "I'm sorry to interrupt, but can I see you a moment?"

"Neil, my friend. You know Anita Gibson, of course."

"Good evening, ma'am."

She recognized me, but I could tell she wasn't sure from where. "Good evening," she replied.

"Jack, please." I didn't want to become involved in chitchat just in case the tail decided to curl up in the pub.

Jack caught my expression. "Yes. Excuse me a moment," he told Anita Gibson.

"Yes, go, before I order my husband to have you shot."

Jack grinned, and I pulled him aside. "I need to get out the back way," I whispered.

"You trying to duck the tab?"

"That's why I'm asking the headwaiter for an escape route," I said, and rolled my eyes.

"And assistant manager," he added.

"Heaven forbid I should neglect your full title."

"Seriously," he asked, "what kind of trouble are you in?"

"Not as bad as that time you-know-who's husband had you followed."

"The dirty bastard never found anything."

"Like the Donovan party?" I asked. "Bedroom window? Hiding in the catering van?"

"I see."

"No more questions, please."

"If I can talk treason, I can commit a tad of it."

"Not a question of treason," I said. "Only survival."

A couple of minutes later Jack had me through the restaurant and into the waning day. A light rain began to fall. I heard Linda's truck fire up.

"Thanks, Jack."

He flashed me the okay sign and closed and locked the door. Linda swung around and I hopped in.

"Appreciate it," I told her.

"You dumping them to be irritating?"

"No, I want to meet with C.J. without them knowing I'm meeting with the big guy."

"Oh."

I hunched down as Linda rumbled around the front and onto Montrose. The brown sedan rested patiently. My Bug kept guard. The rain picked up.

Small talk apparently wasn't on the menu, as neither Linda nor I spoke as we sped back to the office. Once there, I noticed C.J.'s Mustang parked next to Hernandez's truck.

One big happy family.

Linda's large dark eyes engulfed me. "Looks like you get your date, and I get mine," she said.

Oh, boy, I thought.

22

"Just for the hell of it I ran a check on Oakley," Hernandez was saying as we entered the office. C.J. was planted in the chair behind Linda's desk, a smoldering cigarette in hand. The sergeant half sat on a corner of the desk. A wall-unit air conditioner hummed. The austere office was tidy, at least in front. C.J.'s area, beyond the second closed door, was sorely in need of federal funds for cleanup. As usual.

C.J. said nothing. Vic Hernandez eyed us carefully.

"Hey, Vic," was all Linda said.

He nodded. "Anyway," Hernandez continued, "according to Oakley's social-security number, he's working for a bakery in Orange. I tried calling but they were closed."

"Why would you run a check on Oakley?" C.J. asked.

Hernandez turned to me. "Someone got my curiosity up."

I forced a smile.

C.J. blew out a large puff of smoke. "Well, don't let your curiosity get too damn high," he stated, and snubbed the cig out in a large ashtray.

"You going to explain that?" the sergeant asked.

"I found Oakley this morning," he announced.

"The bakery?"

"The morgue," C.J. said.

"Oh, my God," I muttered.

"Find out what happened?" Hernandez asked.

"Overdose. Heroin."

"Goddamn," said Hernandez, and shook his head. He pushed himself up and began to pace.

Linda sat in one of the chairs in front of the desk. She was being unusually quiet.

"You busted him," C.J. said to Hernandez. "Was he a user?"

"No."

"People change."

"Goddamn coincidental," Hernandez responded. "What were you doing in Orange?"

"Personal business," he replied.

"Well, you better unpersonalize it."

"Unpersonalize?" I asked.

"Shove it, boy wonder," Hernandez snapped.

C.J. lit another cigarette. Forcefully he clicked the lighter shut and tossed it on the desk.

Hernandez tried a different tack. "Now, what kind of business would be so personal you couldn't tell me about it?"

"Looking for a piece of land," he replied.

My heart shifted from second to third. Why would he tell the cop that?

"For what?" Hernandez asked.

"Build a retirement home."

"You telling me you traveled to Orange to look for land to build a retirement house on and just happened to run into Oakley at the morgue?"

"Kind of funny, huh?"

"Not even a fucking chuckle."

In the churning silence, Linda finally stood. "Let's go, Vic," she said. "You promised me a drink."

"You better play clean, McDaniels," the sergeant told him.

C.J. nodded.

Hernandez marched out the door.

"Looks like you two are going to have a grand time," C.J. told his daughter.

Linda scowled at both of us. "I don't know what you guys are up to, but you'd better bring it to a close fast.

I've got a bad feeling." She wheeled around and took off after Hernandez.

"So do I," I said in the wake of her leaving. I closed the door behind them then dropped into the chair Linda had occupied.

"I'm being followed," I told the detective. "That's why I arrived with Linda. I ditched my car, and my tail, at The Black Lab."

"I wasn't able to find out anything more about Oakley," C.J. said. "They're pretty tight-lipped out there. His place was off-limits to me."

"Not very cooperative."

"Not at all."

"Nothing on the field?" I asked, then remembered Dean's poems.

"No." He shifted his weight in the creaking chair. "Your friend's out of jail. There's no reason to go on."

"Don't you care who killed Lamar?"

"No."

"What if the police come back after Mattie?" I asked.

"If the cops still wanted her, she'd have been transferred to the Harris County jail by now."

"I don't believe Gunn or Gunter would just let me walk away from this mess."

"They might," C.J. said.

"What about Dean Shriver?"

"What about him?" C.J. ground out another cigarette. I could use a puff at the moment.

"He's a friend, too," I said. "And he's hitting warp speed away from reality."

"Warp speed from reality, huh?" He leaned back in his chair, hands behind his head.

"Think it partly has to do with his father's suicide," I continued, ready to test the revelation I'd had while talking to Hernandez.

"Yeah?"

"MacArthur Shriver. Heard of him?"

"Nope."

"Used to work in fresh produce. Dean recollects seeing the G brothers when he was little. Wonder if they called him Big Mac like Oakley did?"

I caught C.J.'s attention. "The contact?" he asked warily, and leaned forward.

"Appears to point that way."

"Son of a bitch," C.J. muttered. "Hearsay, but damn good hearsay."

"There is written documentation, of sorts." I had forgotten the folder of poems in my car but paraphrased some of them for C.J., especially the drug images I could remember.

"He's sending you and your professor messages through his poetry?" C.J. asked, and shook his head. "You've just shot your theory back into the ozone."

"I told you he's losing his grip, and I placed an ad to see him. I need to reach Dean, though I'm afraid I might be leading him into a trap."

"You placed a what?"

"Never mind. But I'm not backing down."

"Then Monday morning we go to Lieutenant Gardner and begin straightening out this hogwash. Gardner can dig into this Big Mac crap, and if your hippie friend needs help, we'll let the cops provide it. Remember, behind all this smoke, Mattie still has an assault charge against her for shooting Lamar in the leg."

"Alice swears she can take care of that as self-defense."

"Probably so," he replied, and leaned forward, "considering the only person, as far as we know, who could dispute her story is dead."

"So what are you going to do?" I asked.

"Eat. I ain't put nothing in this big belly since breakfast."

"Eat?"

"You need a lift to The Black Lab, don't you?"

"Yes." I ran a hand across my beard. "Are you thinking—"

"Might as well find out who's shadowing you, too," he said. "Given he's still waiting."

C.J. stood, opened the top desk drawer, and took out his .38. He tucked it in a shoulder holster and put on a black, lightweight vinyl jacket. Only someone knowing what to look for would recognize the slight bulge. He also slipped a Notre Dame baseball cap on his head.

On the way out I said, "Did I mention that I'm supposed to cook lunch for Karl Gunter tomorrow?"

The door rattled closed.

"Could you repeat that?" C.J. asked above me as he jiggled the key and locked up his office. "I sure as hell don't think I heard you right."

"Lunch for Karl Gunter. He wanted Dean, too, but I've warned him that he might not get the beatnik."

I shoved open the downstairs door and, followed by C.J., headed for his Mustang. A light rain still fell.

"Son, you got yourself a death wish?"

"Perry knows I'm going there. Robbie knows I'm going there. You know I'm going there. What's Gunter going to do?"

"Cut you up in little pieces and mail you all over America," C.J. replied. "The man has no fear."

"You saying I should ditch the job?" I asked, and got into the Mustang.

"Pretty smart for a college boy." C.J. revved the engine as the windshield wipers slapped against the glass.

"Can't understand how you got made driving around in this overzealous advertisement," I commented.

C.J. spewed gravel as we pounded into traffic.

"If my tail's not gone yet, he sure as hell will be when you get us there," I called. "Might as well call him on the car phone."

All my talking only made him scream faster through traffic. Wisely, I shut up.

By the time we reached The Black Lab, C.J.'s tantrum had evidently subsided and he eased down the street.

"It's hard to see through the rain," I told him, "but the

brown sedan was by the library. Might want to swing around back so—" I closed my eyes.

Without hesitation, C.J. cut into the entrance by the library and came to a screeching stop in front of the sedan. He unzipped his jacket but didn't draw the gun. I was still bouncing around the seat when I saw C.J. rap his knuckles against the hood of the sedan.

God, don't let it be Jimmy and Cracker, I thought. They won't understand.

There was only one person in the car, a man in his late forties or early fifties. Slowly, he exited the vehicle. The man was trim, had silver hair, and knew C.J.

"McDaniels, I ought to plug you one."

"You ain't never hit me before. What makes you think you're going to begin now?"

"Guess you're here because of the kid, huh?"

"Get out, Neil," C.J. ordered, "and meet Dexter Young, private investigator."

"Why are you following me?" I asked. Rain quickly spotted my glasses. I squinted to see Young's face.

He shrugged.

"Dex, out of professional courtesy, I'm not going to beat your brains in this time."

"How noble. And confident."

"But I know who you're working for," C.J. added.

"That won't fly, McDaniels."

C.J. put his hands in his jacket pockets.

Gunn would've used Jimmy and Cracker, I thought. Or someone like them. I couldn't see Gunter going to a private investigator. Unless he thought I'd make contact with Dean tonight to tip him off not to show his face tomorrow. Still, a PI? Who else would want me followed. Obviously, the cops wouldn't go that route. Who else was there? My ex-wife? Hardly. Then I had an idea. Two in one day. Damn if I wasn't on a roll.

While C.J. played his bluff I asked, "Why would John Taft want me followed?"

Only a tightness to his smile and a slight widening of the eyes gave him away.

C.J. let me play it.

"Yes, Chip Gunn's campaign manager. What could I have that he wants?"

"Don't know the man," Dexter replied.

"The obvious response is that Taft wants Dean's whereabouts," I thought aloud. "But why would Taft get involved? Gunn and Gunter are already onto that project. Of course, one hand might not know what the other hand is doing. What do you think?" I asked Dexter Young.

"I have no idea what you're babbling about."

"Then stick this in your craw," I told him. "Tell Taft I'm fixing lunch for Gunter tomorrow. Noon, sharp. He has any questions, he can reach me then." I began to turn, then hesitated, recollecting he tailed me from The Kitchen. "By the way, you get any juicy information from Conrad?"

"Who?"

"The former drug addict turned dishwasher."

He shrugged. "It was worth a shot for the price of a carton of cigarettes."

"Night, Dex," C.J. announced. We dropped into the Mustang and C.J. popped the car into gear. Dexter stared in our direction a minute, then climbed into the sedan and left. C.J. parked close to my Bug.

"Well, we know who he works for," I said.

"You sure?"

"Pretty sure. And he'll be off my back, tonight."

"Maybe. You still hungry?" C.J. asked.

"Not really. But I'm finding The Lab hard to resist," I said. "Some of the best fish and chips in the city."

"Okay."

"Got any money?"

"You want me to pay?" he asked, brushing at the rain on his jacket. "I'm already digging around for you for free."

"Could be my last meal," I tried to joke.

C.J. paused. "Son, don't get my hopes up," he said.

"Your concern is overwhelming."

"You started it." He slapped his hat against his knee to shake off the excess rain. "You started all of it."

What choice did I have? I thought, though chose to say nothing more as we entered the pub together.

23

Colors twist and turn. Red, yellow, a hint of orange and blue. Charcoal everywhere. They spring from white walls holding images of fear and pain, power and hate—death. A hand comes into view, limp, and pinned to an iron cross. Faces gather like storm clouds. Air still. Then a ringing and I hear myself talking before a voice rumbles, "And thunder will roar from the hand of the righteous."

I shot up in bed, rubbed my temples.

"Sounds downright scary, doesn't it, dude?" I heard from my answering machine. "Got your message in the paper. Have visions for today, hipster, but will definitely click tonight."

I hopped to the floor, slipped once as I dashed into the living room.

"Keely said you feared I was out to off myself," he continued. "Not gonna happen to me! Peace, love, dope."

"Dean," I yelped into the phone.

He hung up.

Shit. I slammed the receiver in its place. Again I rubbed my temples and groaned. Strange dream, then superimposed by our voices. If I hadn't been so groggy from last night's beer with C.J., I'd have caught the beatnik. Bad, Neil, my poor head scolded. Bad, stupid, dumb, Neil.

I straightened myself, stumbled into the kitchen, and choked when I saw that it was a few minutes after seven. Damn Dean, I was going to beat the crap out of him the next time I saw him. Reluctantly, I made a pot of coffee.

Sleep beckoned me back to the bedroom, but I resisted. I had to get into work soon, anyway, to collect Gunter's food. With a mug of steaming java in hand, I peered out my little window. The sky had cleared and there was a gentle sway to the trees. No sign of the sedan, or anyone else for that matter. Samson was baring his teeth at a mean old tomcat. Judging from recent events, if the animals ever got into it, I'd lay my money on the cat.

After wrapping myself in a blue cotton bathrobe, I crept downstairs to retrieve my Sunday paper from the driveway. Guess I didn't need to check to see that my ad made the paper. As picturesque as the day appeared from my window, the heat factor melted any pleasant pastoral image away. A good run, I thought, would certainly sweat last night's beer out. But I was feeling too lazy and chose to give the exercise routine a rest.

Sipping my coffee, I trudged back upstairs, kicked my door shut behind me, and tossed the two plastic-wrapped bundles on the coffee table. I placed my cup next to them then stretched out on the couch.

As I ripped open the first bundle I thought of Dean's reference to Keely. Odd. How did he put it? Keely said I was afraid Dean was going to off himself. I swung myself from the couch and listened to the message again, hearing my desperate call at the very end as he disconnected the line. But I'd caught the reference right. Dean must have already talked to Keely.

I pulled the phone over to the coffee table and returned to the couch. Could be he caught her yesterday. Surprising, though, Keely hadn't phoned. I refused to bother her and Mark this early on a Sunday morning. I had some time. I'd wait.

The first part of the paper I dove into was the book section. There staring back at me was a large photograph of Professor Peter Winford. Incredible. The article that accompanied the picture was mostly about the professor's sabbatical back east last semester. A lot of name-dropping and anecdotes rolled across the page, including mention of a rather unflattering review of his work by a well-known New York critic. Must be the knock Keely was alluding to, I thought.

Near the article's end, Winford plugged the university's creative writing program, citing Keely Cohen's work and Sondra Anderson as a rising star. I was pleased for Keely's and Sondra's deserved recognition. With that exception, however, the article was *People* magazine publicity for Winford and an advance push for his new book due out next spring. The book Keely and I had read. I found it amazing how someone so starved for fame alongside the literary lions could write so sensitively and sincerely. I folded the article carefully to save it—for Keely and Sondra.

I was about to subject myself to another piece on the Oilers' move to Nashville—cursing their owner the whole time—when a jolting chime from the phone about sent me through the roof. Someone should've shot Alexander Graham Bell.

"Keely, I heard from him—"

"Who?" the deep, gruff voice responded.

"C.J.?"

"Get your sorry ass out of bed," he barked. "You're dreaming."

"Through no help of yours and no fault of my own, my sorry ass has been out of bed for almost an hour," I retorted.

"You lie well."

"Did you call simply to insult me?"

"Not this time. I've got an idea, and I'm riding back to Orange this morning."

"What idea?" I asked.

"Shout at you later."

"You most certainly can be aggravating."

"Watch your back around Gunter," he cautioned.

"Intend to." I thumped the phone down then tossed the sports section on the table. I couldn't handle the Oilers' fiasco now.

As I rose to procure another mug of coffee, a headline in the Metropolitan section of the paper caught my eye:

GUNN DENIES NEED FOR INVESTIGATION
by Katherine-Erin DePaul
Staff Writer

Congressional candidate Chip Gunn denied that he was the target of harassment by a radical underground organization and declared any law-enforcement investigation "fruitless."

"Some crackpot making absurd charges does not constitute a radical organization," Gunn stated. "After all, no group has claimed responsibility for attempting to disrupt my campaign."

"Furthermore," he added, "it is a waste of the taxpayers' money to involve either the Houston Police Department or the FBI in a fruitless investigation."

Gunn refused to elaborate on what charges had been made against him or how his campaign has been disrupted. He has scheduled a rally in front of the downtown library at three P.M. this Sunday afternoon.

I tossed the metro section on top of the story about the Oilers moving. Should've depressed myself with my football team leaving, rather than reading about an idiot people will actually vote for. Waste of the taxpayers' money. Slick, I thought.

It was about that time, so I showered and changed directly into my black-and-whites. I glanced at the phone before leaving but decided not to bother Keely. Maybe she was satisfied with Dean's flaky, though seemingly sincere, pledge not to do himself in. If there was anything bothering her, she'd have called. At any rate, I wasn't going to intrude on her and Mark's Sunday morning like a fox in a henhouse. I stopped. Interesting way to think about it, Neil, I told myself. Get out of here. And I did.

The Kitchen was dim, with only the humming of refrigeration units, the blowing of air conditioner, and the
clattering of ice maker to welcome me. For the time
being I left the lights off after locking the door and
checked to see if there were any notes for me or anything
on the answering machine. None. No news could be good
news, and I began rounding up the necessaries for Karl
Gunter's little fete.

Nervous as I was, I could've prepared a six-course meal
complete with sorbet between the fish and the meat. That
reminded me of the time I was readying a meal for one of
the Texas senators and Elizabeth Dole was the guest of
honor. I was fixing a raspberry sorbet. It was the night
after a huge job when all the wait staff helped put up the
food and kitchen utensils. As I was allowing the sorbet to
set, my little voice told me to taste-test the concoction.
After having worked with a recipe so long, I often didn't
check it until the culinary delight was complete—and
many times we were at the job site. This time I ran my
finger through the raspberry sorbet in Perry Stevens
fashion, and came up with a mouthful of salt. After spit-
ting the mixture into the sink, I ran to the sugar and tested
the top layer—salt. Someone had inadvertently dumped
the canister of salt into the sugar bin thinking the travel
container held just that—sugar. Angry as I was, I was
grateful I'd come across the faux pas at The Kitchen and
not shortly before we were to serve it to the good senator
and the honored secretary of transportation.

For whatever reason, that was how I felt now. I was
living litmus paper in need of running my finger through
some composite in order to avoid a disaster.

Or, by God, all hell was going to break loose.

24

Entering Karl Gunter's house again felt like parading into the wolf's den on the way to grandmother's. Hoang directed me to the modest kitchen. A table for four was set up, complete with white tablecloth, silverware, crystal, and an orchid centerpiece, in the small formal dining room. So it was a well-groomed wolf's den.

The range was electric, stove small, and there was no island to work off of. Primitive conditions. I couldn't even crack a smile at my own attempt to stay loose. Then I noticed how cold it was in the house. If the AC was any lower I'd have had frost on my nose hairs.

I unpacked the food and utensils. The salad fit easily into the refrigerator, which was mostly empty, with the exception of a couple of bottles of Dourthe, a relatively inexpensive French table wine.

"Serve that with the meal," Gunter said behind me.

I almost dropped the bottle I was examining.

"You came alone?" he asked.

"I couldn't touch base with Dean Shriver," I offered.

"Such a surprise." Regaled in his white suit, Gunter tapped his cane on the floor and entered the kitchen.

I pulled a chef's knife from the travel box and laid it on the counter.

"Are you afraid of me?" he asked.

"Should I be?" I replied, and unloaded the capers, bourbon, cream, and tenderized chicken breasts from another container.

"Yes."

191

This was getting old. I stared at the plump, balding old man. "Why? Am I to be the main course instead of the chicken?"

"You have balls, Marshall. Or should I say Mr. Marshall, as my brother would?"

"What do you want from me?"

"You'll join us for lunch," he ordered. "Put all the food down at once—salad, chicken, and dessert."

"What?" I knocked a serving spoon onto the tile floor.

"My brother's scheduled appearance downtown doesn't give me a hell of a lot of time."

"Join you? Mr. Gunter, we never dine with the guests."

"I'm aware of that."

"It is very improper."

"Improper." He spat the word out. "You will sit at my table. You will listen to what I have to say."

"Perry Stevens doesn't allow—"

"I'm paying for the food, goddamn it. You do as I say. "Hoang will be the fourth, as your radical friend was a no-show." With that, he rapped his cane on the floor, turned, and walked away.

Perhaps I should dive out the living-room window like the Cowardly Lion leaving Oz, I thought.

Insanity getting the best of me, I organized my space so I could fix lunch. For all of us. A nagging question, though—with Gunter, Hoang, and me, who was the fourth lucky party?

Aroma of garlic, onions, and chicken that was usually so comforting did nothing to ease my anxiety. In preparing the sauce I added so much bourbon the pan shot a flame that scorched the ceiling. Hoang, who had stuck his head in, jerked back at the sight. Small consolation. By noon, I was ready.

I set the salad first and identified the mystery guest. John Taft, Gunn's campaign manager, arrived as tentatively as I had. Hoang let him in then unscrewed the wine to present him a glass. Taft acknowledged my presence with blank eyes.

Next I placed the Linzer torte by the coffee cups. By this time Gunter was making small talk with Taft.

"A better atmosphere than last time," Gunter said.

"Colder, anyway," Taft replied.

"It's the one luxury I allow myself," he explained.

I disappeared into the kitchen, wondering if Taft's response to their last meeting outside the doctors' office was an intentional double entendre. Probably so, I thought, and plated the steaming chicken dish. Taking two at a time, I questioned Gunter's seriousness about me eating with them, not to mention my feelings about the idea—I'd rather chew glass.

After placing the remaining plates, however, Gunter commanded me to sit down. I questioned my judgment and obeyed. Hoang stood ready with the wine bottle, which was loosely wrapped in a white cloth napkin.

"Pour some for our young friend, too," his boss said, motioning his cane at my glass.

Hoang obeyed, then set the bottle on the table and sat down. Never in all my years at Perry Stevens had a client so blatantly crossed the employer-employee line. I unbuttoned the top of my chef's coat and tugged at my collar. The bourbon chicken should have tempted me, its rich fragrance curling into the chilly air. But I was tiring of the recipe—a problem in the food business, repetition. And the furthest thing from my mind was eating. I sipped the wine.

Gunter dug into his food. "Not bad," he said, swirling a piece of meat around in the heavy sauce.

Taft picked at his lunch. "Yes," he absently agreed. "Good stuff."

Hoang ate slowly, steadily, and without comment.

On the wall behind Gunter, I noted another Holocaust sketch. It brought back my dream that Dean had called and awakened me from. *And thunder will roar from the hand of the righteous.* I stiffened. I knew now what bothered me about the events surrounding Lamar's death.

"You're not eating, Marshall," Gunter stated. "Are you trying to poison me?" He forced a squeaky laugh.

"I chowed before I came," I answered, though I tucked a portion of the chicken in my mouth to ease his suspicions.

"Those pictures fascinate you," he said.

"How about unnerve?"

"I will tell you about them as I promised."

After I swallowed a mouthful of wine, Hoang topped off my glass. Bells rang in my head, warning me to take it easy with the *vino*.

"You see, the artist, a man very close to me, was a guard in one of the concentration camps during World War Two," Gunter said, eyes boring into me. He wiped his mouth with his napkin, drank from his wine, and continued. "The artist came to despise those people who so passively allowed themselves to be victims. I keep the pictures because of the artist but also to remind me how easily people can be controlled. If a man isn't aggressive, he can be controlled."

Casually as I could, I strained to see the artist's signature while running my eyes over the sketch. Though I could guess what letter the last name began with.

"You think you know," Gunter said.

"Know what?"

"The artist's identity."

"I thought we were going to keep that tidbit of trivia in the family," Taft spoke up. "The press would blow it all out of proportion."

"Family," Gunter scoffed. "You are not family."

Taft drank.

"My brother wants this election so bad he hires himself a so-called expert," Gunter told me.

"Most campaigns are not as complicated as your brother's," Taft retorted in a tight voice.

"And if you had checked with me before acting, I would have made sure you understood the soft underbelly."

"I was supposed to be running the show," Taft stated. He finished his glass and signaled for the bottle. Hoang handed it to me. I gave it to Taft, contemplating how I could change the direction of the conversation. I wasn't sure I wanted to hear any *family* secrets.

"Taft, we ironed that out at the shrinks' office. My brother is more of a dandy than a businessman, always has been and always will be. Talks fancy, dresses fancy, and surrounds himself with those meatheads to make himself feel important. But he listens to me. Without me, he's lost."

He was selling Gunn miles short. If anyone was lost, I thought, it was Gunter. Lost in his own delusions.

"Lost, yes, maybe the election," Taft said.

"You know I don't approve of my brother's run for office," Gunter pronounced. "The attention it's bringing." He glowered at Taft. "More because of your bungling."

So Lamar was on target about Gunter not being supportive, I thought. Gave me cause to speculate how close to the bull's-eye he was on the field, too.

"I never intended the press to catch wind of the investigation," Taft defended, and ran his hand through his hair.

"Don't ever do anything without clearing it with me first."

My jaw dropped. Taft brought the investigation on, himself? And here I'd given Dean credit for being a genius.

"I'm a professional," Taft informed him.

The icy room was heating up, and I didn't know where I stood. For the sake of stoking the fire, I tossed a curveball. "I venture that this has something to do with the private investigator," I commented, and chewed on another piece of meat. I hoped I didn't throw up.

Taft paled. Gunter flushed.

"Dexter Young," I explained, filling in the silence. "He drives a brown sedan and has been on my tail the last couple of days. I kind of ran into him last night at a pub off Montrose."

"I was just thinking if I could find Dean Shriver," Taft began.

"Shut up, that is family business."

"Having to do with the Oakley case?" I pushed Gunter.

He set his silverware gently down on his plate, rested his left elbow on the table, and leaned his head against his hand. "What do you know about Oakley?" He stroked his cheek with his forefinger.

"He's dead."

Gunter shot upright. "What did you say?"

"He's dead," I repeated, but lacking the same confidence. Gunter's surprise wasn't the reaction I'd expected.

"How do you know?"

"He overdosed on heroin in Orange a couple of days ago."

"Impossible," Gunter muttered to himself. "That idiot wouldn't touch a beer, never mind heroin."

"People change," I said, echoing an earlier conversation.

"Not simpleminded diabetics."

"Oakley was diabetic?" I asked.

"Yes." Gunter turned to Hoang. "Check on Marshall's information," he ordered.

The Vietnamese man nodded, and left.

If Gunter's response was as genuine as it appeared, then he sure as hell didn't have anything to do with Oakley's death. What now? Press on.

"Why am I here?" I asked Gunter.

He leaned forward. "I want Dean Shriver."

Big news flash, I thought. "I'm not hiding him."

"He will contact you or the teacher."

The teacher? Keely? Stay away from her, exploded in my mind. However, I said, "He'll communicate with the teacher through me."

Gunter folded his hands together and stretched back. "Soft underbelly," he muttered, and chuckled. His eyes glimmered like flames stretching to scorch the sky.

I refused to feed into his prodding at Keely. "What has Dean Shriver done to get both you and your brother on this manhunt?" I asked, glanced at Taft. No expression on his face, though buckets of sweat gave away his fear.

"Tried to kill me," Gunter told me.

I laughed. "That's the biggest pile of buffalo chips I've ever heard of."

"My brother's driveway. The fund-raiser you worked. Dean came at me with the knife. I saw his face. He was after me, not the black man, but couldn't get through him."

"You're incredible. If Dean tried to kill anyone, it would be himself."

Gunter bent forward. "Explain yourself," he ordered.

Time to regroup, I thought. Hit a sensitive nerve, though the shiver ran through me.

I fumbled with my wineglass, took a sip. "Death's throughout Dean's writing," I rationalized, "and he lives on the edge."

"Like a fox on the run?"

"I suppose so."

"But there's more," Gunter said, bearing down on me.

"What I know comes from reading his thoughts on paper and observing his lifestyle."

"His work ever get into family history, or he talk to you about it?"

"Never," I lied.

"Don't take me for a fool, Marshall."

"All I know is what everyone knows about him. Dean's a native Texan. He was raised by his mother because his father died when Dean was young."

Gunter pondered my words then slowly rose, a quiver across his cheeks, mouth pinched closed. "Lunch is over," he announced, and tossed his napkin onto his plate.

I remained seated.

"You know more than you're letting on," Gunter told me. "And now I must decide what to do about it."

Taft also stood. "Another potential public-relations problem?" he asked Gunter, though he anxiously looked at me.

The rotund host rapped his cane on the floor and narrowed his eyes. "Nothing I can't handle. Let's go to my brother's and advise him on what to say this afternoon."

Hoang reappeared and whispered something to his

boss. Gunter nodded. "Seems you're telling the truth about Oakley. The private dick find that out for you?"

I didn't respond.

"Of course," Gunter continued. "Now clean this shit up, Marshall, and get out. And if you don't help me land Dean Shriver pretty damn quick, I'm coming after your ass. Might pay a visit to the teacher, too."

I clenched my fists, ground my teeth, and slowly pushed myself to my feet. The point of not giving a damn was quickly approaching. If I was going to go to Gardner, anyway, I was determined to stop pussyfooting around these bandits.

"Just remember, Mr. Gunter," I began, "people in glass houses—"

"Shoot to kill," he interrupted.

My anger stalled as Hoang stepped in front of Gunter, a .38 Smith & Wesson drawn and pointed at me.

"Mark my words," Gunter added, jabbing a finger at me. He then jerked his head and he and Taft went out the front door.

I cleaned under Hoang's watchful eye, though he'd considerately tucked the gun away. Before leaving, I caught the name on one of the sketches. Bruno Gunter. Father? Grandfather? Uncle? Did it matter?

It was quite obvious the family attitude had been carefully preserved. Even inflated.

After all, why in hell would Dean Shriver want to knife Karl Gunter? A question I would surely put to Dean when he contacted me later in the day.

25

I dumped the cooking utensils and bourbon on the front table at The Kitchen, put up the leftover butter, cream, and spices, and hit the trail. I didn't even go into the office to see if there was a note for me or a message on the answering machine.

I decided that when Dean called I'd tell him to make like a bear and hibernate. Only I'd be sure to learn where he was hibernating so I could reach him when I needed to. Then I'd double-lock my apartment door, curl up on the couch with my .45, and wait for C.J. to return from his crusade. Fine time he picked to go waltzing across Texas.

My Bug sputtered and growled like an overloaded electric mixer. Could run down to the stables and hole up with Candace and the Winchester, I thought. I didn't notice anyone following me. Of course, an ounce of discretion could throw me off. Besides, was it worth endangering Candace? It was bad enough that Gunter would involve Keely. I balked at putting Candace at risk, too.

So it was the apartment, I reconciled. Barricade myself in. Wait for the calvary. Oh, the best-laid . . .

Sitting on the back porch of Jerry Jacoma's house was Keely Cohen. She was petting Samson, scratching him behind the ears and across the belly.

"Some guard dog," she said, and stood.

"So I've heard," I replied as I got out of the VW. "First you show up at work and now here. People are going to talk."

"Give drab lives some color."

The folder with Dean's poems caught my eye. I picked it up before swinging the door closed.

She waited on the porch. Evidently, Jerry wasn't home. I smiled and pointed above the garage.

"My castle in the clouds," I said.

Keely cocked her head, motioned toward the house. "This isn't your house?"

"Landlord's. I have the bachelor flat."

"Oh."

"Keely, why are you here?" I held the poems across my chest.

"I think I've figured out what Dean is up to," she said, the color suddenly falling from her face. "Can we talk upstairs? The revelation frightens me. I mean, I don't know, maybe I'm reading too much into this. Maybe I've got it all screwed up. I needed to talk about it."

"What about Mark?"

"He's at the club halfway through eighteen holes—or eighteen martinis."

I didn't touch her last comment. "Let's talk," I replied. "There's a thing or two I need to let you in on."

My humble abode never seemed so ratty as when the elegant professor entered it. At least there wasn't dirty underwear on the living-room floor and only a couple empty beer cans on the kitchen table.

"Nice place."

"You're kind," I responded.

Keely began to sit on the couch.

"Hold on," I said, and reached under the cushion for the .45. I had to break my habit of stashing that damn piece in odd places. Her eyes grew the size of silver dollars as I placed the gun on the coffee table.

"Roach problems," I offered.

"Cute. Dean's not the only one who's frightening."

"You know how to make a margarita?" I asked.

"Frozen or on the rocks?"

"Rocks with lime and salt."

"I can do that. Where?"

"Booze and salt in the bottom-right kitchen cabinet. Mixture and lime in the fridge. Crushed ice and frosted mugs in the freezer."

"You chefs know how to live," Keely replied.

Right. That's why we find ourselves caught between gangsters and the law, have psychotic friends running around, and are in a small apartment with a beautiful woman but have no intention of making a pass, I thought. Yes, live it up.

I closed my bedroom door and changed from my black-and-whites to black jeans, black boots, and a GO TO HELL, I'M READING T-shirt from Murder by the Book. Once Keely left, I'd throw on shorts and go barefoot. For the time being, though, I opted for presentable.

"Going somewhere?" Keely asked.

"Maybe an Astros game with Robbie," I heard come out of my mouth.

"I did screw that up for us, didn't I?" She handed me a margarita. I sipped. Salt, lime, kick—perfect.

"You didn't screw anything up," I replied. "Reading the poems was fun. And this is good." I gestured as if we were toasting.

"Speaking of poems," Keely quickly rattled, "that's what I figured out." She sat on the couch, set her drink down, and rifled through the file.

I took the chair and waited.

"Have you gone over these poems?" she asked.

"Not since you gave them to me." I slugged a healthy portion of the drink.

"Rough day?" she asked.

"You don't know the half of it."

"Tell me while I find what I'm looking for," she said, and continued to shuffle.

"Lunch for Karl Gunter. First he had me join in as a guest. Then he chewed out his brother's campaign manager for putting a private investigator on me and Gunn. John Taft was the leak."

She looked up. "Not Dean?"

"Nope. But he wants Dean for another reason, and if he doesn't find him, then Gunter's coming after me, or you."

"Me!" Keely jumped up.

"He believes you can ferret out Dean."

"That's crazy."

"Gunter's crazy. Relax." I guided her down. "I'm going to Lieutenant Gardner tomorrow."

"Might be too late," she said with a tremor. She drew out a sheet of paper and gave it the once-over. A slight shiver accompanied her hand, too.

"What do you mean?" My heart threatened to do an end run by speeding up and sprinting out my throat. I swigged more margarita to cut it off, then had to brush the salt crystals out of my beard.

"Consider this poem," she said, handing me a sheet of the manuscript. " 'The Hand of the Righteous.' "

I began to see where she was going. "As in, 'And thunder will roar from the hand of the righteous'?" I asked.

"I thought you said you hadn't looked at these?"

"I haven't. Dean enlightened my answering machine with that line."

Keely took my mug and made me another margarita.

I examined each word carefully. The piece was, for the most part, more of the same. Drug images. The ghost of his father. And then, at the end, I caught what Keely was referring to.

> The dust of the skeleton
> blows into this hipster's
> brain—and thunder will roar
> from the hand of the righteous.
> Vengeance lives in America
> You're coming back America
> America
> I fight for you.

"What's your understanding?" I asked Keely.

" 'Vengeance lives in America,' " she quoted. "And Dean's heart."

"For what?"

"Something that sent his father to suicide," she replied.

"He blames Gunter and Gunn," I said. "And Oakley," I absently added.

"Who?"

"The connection," I told her. "An unwitting drug runner. What if MacArthur Shriver's produce was the drugs Oakley was carrying? What if Oakley could've named Shriver. What if Shriver killed himself to avoid jail?"

"Or it was made to look like suicide?" Keely asked. "But wasn't."

"Vengeance."

" 'America, I fight for you.' "

" 'Thunder will roar from the hand of the righteous,' " I said.

"Do you see what I see?" she asked.

Have visions for today, hipster, Dean said into my machine.

"You think he's going to pull a minor-league Lee Harvey Oswald?"

"I think he's going to try to kill Chip Gunn," Keely stated guardedly.

"I don't believe it."

She shrugged. "Neither did I."

We stared at each other in disbelief.

I tossed the poem down and rested the chilled mug against my forehead. Well, the G brothers wanted Dean. Guessed they were going to get him.

I had to call Gardner a sight sooner than expected.

26

I paged Lieutenant Gardner using the number on the business card he'd given me a lifetime ago. With a prefix that indicated a Heights number, I suspected he'd have a pretty good idea who was trying to reach him.

"Something's been bothering me about Lamar's murder," I said as I waited for him to return the page, "and I couldn't zero in on the problem. Until this morning when I was at Gunter's house."

"Okay," Keely replied. Absently, she picked salt crystals off the rim of her mug and ate them. "Speak to me."

"While Gunter isn't as refined as Gunn, he definitely isn't stupid." I began to pace around the small living room, pausing periodically for a sip from my margarita. "With that in mind, think of how Lamar was found."

"Facedown on the bed, hands tied behind his back, shot in the head execution style."

"Exactly."

"What's your point, Sherlock?"

"Someone went to a hell of a lot of effort to imply a gangland murder," I explained. "Now, suppose you're a man like Gunter. You've just come across the man you've been tracking. He's wounded, shot by his ex-girlfriend. For one reason or another, you want the man dead. Would you point the finger at yourself by staging a moblike murder, or simply finish the man off and leave the murder to look like domestic violence?"

"Leave it to look like domestic violence, of course,"

Keely replied. "But you've said Gunter thinks a lot of himself. Maybe he couldn't resist his signature as a warning."

"He lives in a small house, keeps a low profile. I think his business sense keeps his ego in check."

"So you don't think Gunter murdered Lamar."

I shook my head.

"Chip Gunn, then?"

"I cite the same argument, along with the fact that I believe Gunn leaves all the bloody work to his brother."

"So we're back to Mattie?" Keely asked.

"I believe Alice's argument," I said. "No way could that wisp of a girl have lifted that huge man onto the bed. Not alone." I put my hand out before Keely started speaking so I could finish. "I think the gun went off. Lamar was wounded. Mattie freaked, and ran."

"And someone else did the deed," she added, stopped her mug halfway to her mouth. "You don't think?"

"Who else?"

"Why?"

"Protect Mattie. Direct guilt toward Gunn and Gunter."

"He left the gun," Keely said.

"Presumably it was by Lamar. He could've thought it was the wounded man's," I reasoned.

"You're going pretty far with this scenario."

"I know I can't prove it," I said. "But the police may be able to. Or get Dean Shriver to confess."

"I can't believe this," Keely said, more to herself than me, and finished her drink.

Finally, the phone rang.

"This is Lieutenant Gardner of the Houston Police Department. Did someone at this number page me?"

"Lieutenant Gardner, Neil Marshall."

"I wondered."

I took a deep breath. "Lieutenant, I've got reason to believe someone is going to try to kill Chip Gunn."

A long silence. "What makes you say that?"

I froze. How was I going to answer that? *Well, you see, there's these poems. . . .*

"Mr. Marshall?"

"It's hard to explain, Lieutenant Gardner. We've been piecing together a puzzle and—"

"We? McDaniels with you?"

"Ah, no. Professor Keely Cohen has been helping me."

"Neil, do you realize that today is Sunday? I'm with my family. Understand?"

"His name's Dean Shriver," I told him. "It appears he has a vendetta against Gunn and Gunter." I hesitated then took a chance. "I think he was also involved in Lamar Fowler's murder."

Another long pause. I glanced at my watch.

"Gunn's holding a rally down in front of the library in about forty-five minutes. If I'm wrong, we waste a Sunday afternoon listening to a bad speech. But if I'm right and nothing's done . . ." I left my argument there.

"You stay away," he ordered. "I'll check it out."

"But I know Dean," I retorted. "I know what he looks like."

"Then give me a description."

I complied, being as specific as possible.

"That'll do," Gardener said. "Now hear me out. You come within a mile of the library, I'll have you arrested."

"For what?"

"For being a pain in the ass," he snapped, and hung up.

The man needs to eat more prunes, I thought, and replaced the receiver.

"Well?" Keely asked.

"He's going to look into it."

"Good." She set her empty mug on the table. "Poor Dean. What set him off like this?"

"I don't know."

"Could we be wrong?" she asked.

"Wouldn't be unusual for me," I responded. "I mean, I felt a little foolish trying to convince Gardner of the danger. It's one thing to sit here with you and decipher

Dean's actions and work, but it's a different ball game taking the case to the law."

"I hear you. So what do we do?" From her tight-lipped expression and the reticence in her light brown eyes, I gathered she was sorry she asked the question.

"What every red-blooded American does on a Sunday afternoon," I replied. "Listen to some good old political bullcrap."

"Does Gardner want you at the rally?"

"Said he'd throw me in jail if I came within a mile," I told her.

"Have those margaritas impaired your judgment?" she inquired.

"My judgment has been at question long before this. Just ask my ex-wife."

"You ought to consider the lieutenant's forceful advice."

"I have," I replied, and again glanced at my watch. "And I'm going down to the library. You coming?"

"I wish I'd never foolishly promised your mother I'd look after you," she said, and grabbed her handbag.

"Foolishly?" I repeated. I snatched the .45 off the coffee table.

"But you leave that thing."

"I'm almost licensed to carry a concealed handgun," I said.

"Almost?"

"Well, I've thought about enrolling in the course to be certified."

"Certified? You're certifiable. And the concealed-handgun law was the stupidest piece of legislation ever passed in Texas," Keely cursed.

I wasn't going to get into a debate over the merits of carrying a handgun. Besides, handguns probably were prohibited from political rallies. Only cops and assassins could tote them.

Reluctantly, I carried the gun into the kitchen and stuffed it in one of the drawers.

"You sure you want to ride along?" I asked.

"Oh, shut up and let's go. We only have half an hour before Gunn is scheduled to speak."

And, I thought, if we were right, about that much time before Dean made his statement, too.

27

Helped by the cultural extravaganza honoring Spain down around city hall, there was a healthy crowd congregating by the library to greet Chip Gunn. Gazing at many of the beer-carrying members of the audience, I wondered if they realized they were about to hear a politician and not the raspy sound of the Gypsy Kings. So far, however, no sign of Dean Shriver.

In the distance I heard a Tejano singer paying tribute to Selena by performing "Dreaming of You." Not exactly a Spanish import, but still nice.

"What now?" Keely asked. I realized she was holding on to my left arm.

"Good question." We hung to the back of the crowd. "I don't see him."

"Neither do I." Sweat dampened the fringes of Keely's dark hair as well as mine. We'd had to park in the underground lot by Jones Hall and walk over beneath a sun the color of a basketball. The activity, the vendors, and the smell of meat grilling helped distract from the heat but not beat it.

Not that we weren't sweating for another reason, too.

"I don't see Gardner, either," I told her.

"Maybe he didn't take you seriously."

"He'll show up just to carry out his threat to arrest me."

Keely twisted my arm to catch the time on my watch. "Almost show time."

"Let's go this way," I suggested, leaning to the right.

Keely resisted. "Might be best if we split up and search the crowd."

"Too dangerous."

"We don't have time to argue," she stated.

"Keely!"

"Neil!" Our eyes locked.

Then the library doors opened and Gardner appeared with Hernandez and a contingent of blues. Gardner signaled for the street cops to spread out then drifted to his right. Hernandez took the left side of the platform Gunn was to speak from.

"There they are," I said, turning my face away from them. "Okay, you win. You go left to Gardner's side. I'll go right. You see Dean, don't screw around. Get one of the cops."

"You do as you say, too," Keely stated.

"Yes, ma'am."

She gave my arm a squeeze then circled wide left and into the crowd. I slowly faded right. What if Dean wasn't here? I wondered. Then Gardner would dismiss the tip as hare-brained information from a flaky artist. And throw me in the slammer for good measure.

Comforting thought.

A uniformed cop crossed my path but didn't give me a second look. Still no Dean. A lot of sunglasses, tank tops, and shorts both long and almost nonexistent. Cowboys caps. Rockets caps. Bulls caps. Astros caps. Some kids rolled down the sidewalk on skateboards. A kikker wearing a straw cowboy hat and faded blue jeans chewed on a turkey leg.

I wondered if Gardner tried to convince Chip Gunn to cancel his appearance. Probably. Of course Gunn would refuse, maybe even hope the threat was real and he was flushing out Dean.

The applause grew loud. The mayor appeared alongside Chip Gunn. Karl Gunter was a step back and to my right. Cracker and Jimmy flanked the three. After a grin and a wave or two, the mayor began Gunn's introduction.

Saying such kind words as a "crusader for the workingman" and "a man who can't be bought by special-interest groups," the mayor welcomed to the podium "future Congressman Chip Gunn, who will fight big government and defend the rights of all God-fearing, gun-bearing Texans."

The gun-bearing part invited a thunderous reaction from the crowd. Then I spied Dean Shriver.

Dean had his hair tied in a ponytail and tucked through the back of a nondescript baseball cap. He was wearing blue-tinted sunglasses, baggy black-and-white shorts, and an oversized black T-shirt. His hands were stuffed in his pockets.

Chip Gunn was beginning his speech when I turned toward Dean and stepped square into a very large man wearing a Harley-Davidson shirt, sleeves cut off, and covered in enough tattoos to give a crocodile nightmares. As if that wasn't bad enough, our chance meeting caused him to dump a full cup of beer on me.

"Goddamn you," he growled from behind his bushy salt-and-pepper beard.

"No shit," I said, flicking foam off my hands. "Sorry about that."

"That was a full beer."

"It feels like one."

"Cost me four fucking dollars." His voice grew loud. We were attracting attention.

"I'll buy you another one."

"I stood in line ten minutes to get it. I'm going to be real thirsty by the time you get back. I want two beers."

"Hey, I'm not happy about this, either."

"Maybe I should whip your ass—"

"Fine," I said, sidestepping him, wanting the commotion to go away. "Two beers."

"You run off, I'll hunt you down."

I motioned with my hands for him to calm down. "Two beers are not worth skipping town over. I'll get them."

I proceeded toward Dean.

"Hey, boy, you're going the wrong way," the biker hollered. "I'm going to kill you."

That did it. Dean glanced back, caught my eye, then pulled a gun from his baggy shorts and aimed at the platform. The police were already rushing the biker and me. Gunn stopped talking and turned to ask the mayor what was going on. Then came the shots.

Slowly, the scenario unwrapped. Karl Gunter was the first to go down, astonishment the last flicker of life to vacate his eyes. The crowd screamed and broke. Gardner and Hernandez each drew their guns. One of the uniformed cops caught me and brought me to the ground.

"No," I yelled, "they'll kill him."

I faced the podium and felt myself being cuffed.

Big Jimmy shielded both Gunn and the mayor from the audience. The bodyguard's head jerked from left to right and back. His gun was drawn. Dean turned on him but never got off another round. Cracker popped my radical friend with two quick shots. Dean spun. His gun clattered to the ground. He then collapsed, wide-eyed, onto his back.

I felt all the tension evaporate from my muscles. A silent cry escaped me. This whole episode with Dean had started off a mess and now ended in tragedy. From the way Gardner and Hernandez were standing over Dean, not helping him, I knew the young beatnik was dead. And Gunter—I felt his icy soul slither into the earth. So where were we? I'd blown Dean's ranting off as a quixotic drug binge, and perhaps it had begun that way, but at some point he'd crossed the line. And I'd caught on too late. My suicide suspicions had been right, though I hadn't realized it'd be an eye for an eye. A rock from my glass house to your glass house. And for what? Where was the clarity in this? The reason? Or would I ever know, with Dean Shriver dead?

The cop jerked me to my feet. Sirens filled the air. The

biker was close by, also subdued, and yelling, "I ain't a part of this. I just spilled a beer. Ask the bearded kid."

I ignored him.

"Tell them, boy," he shouted as two cops cuffed him.

"I don't know that guy," I muttered to the officer who was with me. And shut out the remainder of the biker's pleadings.

Keely ran from the other side of the courtyard.

"Are you all right?" she asked. "Your lip's bleeding."

I nodded.

"Let him go," she ordered the cop. "He didn't do anything."

"Please stay back, ma'am," he responded.

I stared at Dean, then met Lieutenant Gardner's eye. He ran a hand through his hair and shook his head. I turned my attention to the platform. A medical team was examining Gunter. Jimmy had taken Gunn and the mayor away. Cracker waited for official word.

Out of the corner of my eye, I saw Gardner approach, holstering his gun as he walked. A medical team was on Dean, too. I didn't watch.

After Gardner ordered the police officer to release me, I fell into Keely's arms and stayed very still for a very long time.

28

Keely and I presented Dean's poems and our theory to Lieutenant Gardner. He listened patiently. I still omitted the stabbing scene with Lamar at Gunn's, and that I strongly felt Dean was behind the execution-style murder. There was no proof, and the two suspected principals in Lamar's death were both dead themselves.

"Glad you called the right person," Gardner said, after taking our statements. We were in his office, not the interrogation room. "But I wonder why you're protecting Gunn."

"I'm not. I was trying to protect Dean," I replied coldly.

"Of course."

"He was," Keely piped up. "We both were. Dean was a very good student of mine and meant a lot to me."

"Excuse me, Mrs. Cohen," Gardner said. "No matter how good a student he was or what he meant to you, he opened fire on a candidate for the U.S. Congress. Acts such as that tend to affect the way we, in the law-enforcement business, view a person."

Keely held her tongue.

This wasn't over, I thought.

"Three dead," he continued. "Two today, one a few days ago. And then there's that drug overdose in Orange. That makes four. Funny how Oakley's name came up in this, too. Now, if you're right about MacArthur Shriver, I know the connection, but not exactly how it fits."

"Anything else, Lieutenant?"

"No, you two can go. For the time being."

Keely dropped me off at my apartment. For most of the ride we kept to our own thoughts. I noticed Keely had taken to biting her nails. Before I jumped out of her car, though, she spoke up.

"You all right?"

"More numb," I replied, "than anything. I mean, I liked Dean, thought he was kind of off-the-wall, but generally okay. Come to find out, I didn't know him."

"Isn't that the way relationships are, unless they're of the most intimate kind?"

"I suppose that's true."

"You suppose," she said, "but you don't like that idea."

"I guess it comes down to the whole human frailty scene—"

"Now you're sounding like Dean," she jabbed.

"Please, I do have a point. Look, a while back I get shot. Today Dean gets shot. I live. He dies, and he took out the meanest son-of-a-bitch in the Southwest. If anybody deserved to live, Dean did."

"But you were shot trying to protect someone, not harm the person. I think it makes a difference. Karma and all that."

"I don't know," I replied, then changed tracks. "What's Mark going to say? You're going to reek of beer just for holding me."

"Same thing he's been harping on," she said, and sighed.

"What's that?"

"Never you mind, dear." Again Keely pecked me on the cheek. I wanted to take her in full embrace, feel her breasts pressed against my chest, her lips—I pushed the image from my mind. I knew better.

"Thanks for your help," I said.

"*Vaya con Dios,* babe," she told me as I stepped from the car. Then she was gone.

I trekked up to my apartment. As I was about to unlock the door it creaked open a few inches. My heart couldn't take much more shock. Out of anger, and with a touch of stupidity, I shoved the door open. There, sitting on my couch, was C. J. McDaniels. He was the picture of health—in one hand a margarita and in the other a cigarette as he watched the end of *60 Minutes*.

"Did I lock the door or did you simply break in?" I asked.

"Tried waiting outside with the dog," he explained. "By the way, he's—"

"Not much of a guard dog," I finished for him, and swung the door closed. "I've heard."

"I decided to wait where it was cool. For what it's worth, your lock's about as good as that dog."

"Thanks. Heard what happened?"

"From Hernandez."

"Hernandez?" I asked, then remembered he'd left us to Gardner's discretion. "You must have caught him right after the shooting."

C.J. didn't seem to feel the need to respond. So while fixing myself a drink, I elaborated on the gunning.

"Sorry your friend bit it—not sorry Gunter did."

"Popular sentiment, unless you take Gunn's point of view."

"Think he's double glad," he said, and snubbed the cigarette on a dessert plate. When I'd quit smoking I'd thrown away all my ashtrays.

"That his brother's dead?" I asked, and dropped down in the chair.

"You reek of beer," he said, scowling and fanning the air with his hand.

"The biker doused me good," I replied.

"Smells like you spent the afternoon in a cheap Mexican whorehouse," he added.

"I wouldn't know about cheap whorehouses of any nationality. What was that crack about Gunn?"

"Gunter's overbearing hand is now lifted from Gunn's shoulders," C.J. stated. "Allows him to run affairs the way he sees fit."

"What are you getting at?"

"Making observations."

"Why are you here, C.J.? What did you go to Orange for?"

"Something you said." He lit another cigarette.

"I'm sure I spoke with intent. What'd I say?"

"You mentioned Dean Shriver was hitting warp speed away from reality." His words wove through a cloud of smoke like lost ships through fog.

Odd words of wisdom to remember, I thought. "So?"

"Made me think of Gunn. A gangster with a JFK complex. He honestly believes he can ignore his past and sail into a glorious political future."

"Warp speed away from reality?" I questioned.

He blew smoke, rubbed sweat from his bald head, and nodded. "But he had baggage to cut," he added.

"His brother?" I finished my margarita but resisted having another.

"No, that's a load of mixed feelings. I went back to Orange because Oakley appeared to be the baggage."

"Hope to get some cooperation from the officials?" I asked, and rose. Pacing sometimes helped my urge for a cigarette. I thought of black lungs. Oxygen tubes up the nose. The rasping when you breathed. Nothing helped. I still wanted one. Why were people born so intelligent and so obviously self-destructive? Smoking. Alcohol. Drugs. Money. Power. It was all relative.

"Didn't announce my presence, this time," he said. "Took Linda's truck."

"Smart."

"And Linda."

Too bad she's not here to at least corroborate the story, I thought.

"Smarter," I said. "So cut to the chase." I wandered into the kitchen for that second drink after all.

"Fix me one, too."

I reached for his mug. "I found the field," he said, before releasing the glass.

"Of skeletons?"

He nodded. "Guess who was caretaker?"

"Oakley."

Another nod.

"Where did Linda fit in?"

"Patience," he said. "Wouldn't you rather hear who killed Oakley?"

"He overdosed," I said, though I suspected otherwise. I tugged the mug from his hand.

"With a little help from his friend, he sure did," C.J. replied, and ground out his latest cigarette.

29

C.J. stood and pulled back the curtain on the window. "The field was hidden right good," he drawled. "Had to hike through a patch of white pines to reach it. If not for Linda's finesse, I doubt we'd have located the spread."

"What about Oakley's death?" I asked.

He checked his watch then reached into his pocket. "This is what was growing in the field."

I caught the Baggie. "Marijuana," I spouted, squeezing the withering leaves and smelling the sweet odor.

"A hippie's dream," C.J. announced. "Acres of that crap."

"You're up to something." I tossed the Baggie back to him.

"You want to know how we found the stuff? It was good detective work." C.J. paced across the room but didn't sit.

"Of course I want to know," I said.

"Linda and I first broke into Oakley's old shack. It was in great need of paint on the outside and stuffy, dirty, and torn apart on the inside. Someone had rifled through the small house with no shame, and digging through that rubble for some kind of lead would've taken forever. We poked, gave a few token kicks, then went out the back door only to find ourselves staring down the wrong side of a double-barrel shotgun." He returned to the window, lit a cigarette, and stared down at the street.

"You expecting someone?" I asked.

"Now that fella holding the shotgun," C.J. continued, ignoring my question, "was inclined to shoot me on the spot, but he took an instant liking to Linda. Needless to say, a smile and a wink from her was all the distraction necessary for me to jerk the shotgun straight up and stick my gun directly under his chin. I immediately warned the man he didn't want to tangle with us as we represented some powerful people. His response was curious, asking in a nasty way if we were already checking up on him. It'd only been two days since Oakley had died."

"Impressive. But how does that little encounter tie in?"

"You'll see after we parley with Chip Gunn."

I about dropped my mug. "What?"

"I invited him over. Might be best if we wait outside." The cigarette dangled from his lips as he checked the clip in his 9mm.

"We?"

"You got me into this fun," C.J. stated. "We're going to see it through together."

I finished my drink then opened the kitchen drawer and pulled out the .45.

"You won't need that," C.J. announced.

"I've dealt with these goons before."

"Trust me."

"Heard that before, too," I muttered. I set the piece on the counter. When C.J. turned I stuffed the gun under my shirt and into my belt by the small of my back. I hoped I didn't blow my ass off.

"My landlord comes home to this meeting he'll turn into a babbling fool."

"He is a babbling fool."

We stepped into Sunday evening, the time to rest for the upcoming week. "You sit on the porch by the vicious guard dog," C.J. directed.

"You're holding back," I said. "What part of the picture have you left in the dark?"

He crossed over to my Bug and leaned against its rear in order to view the whole driveway. "I'll wait here," he called.

I sat stiffly so the gun wouldn't dig into my back. For a

long ten or fifteen minutes I fended off slobbers from the dog and the urge to throw up from the tightening fist in my stomach. Finally, Gunn's black Cadillac cruised into the driveway.

Jimmy and Cracker appeared first. I nodded as each noticed my presence. Neither one so much as smiled back. Surprisingly, Samson growled.

"Hands up," Jimmy told C.J.

"No can do."

"Listen, smart-ass—"

"No, you listen," C.J. said, and stood straight. "You're not searching me. I'm carrying, you're carrying. There's two of you and one of me."

"You got Marshall," Cracker said, and directed his thumb at me.

"He's clean."

Oh, shit, I thought.

"We search him," Cracker stated.

I wondered if I could slip the gun to Samson. Might improve his stature as protector.

Cracker took a step in my direction. Visions of C.J. shooting me himself after they found the gun flashed before my eyes. Breaking my thoughts, however, was another low growl from the dog. I gave Samson a pat on the back. Perhaps he wasn't chicken but simply a good judge of character.

"No one searches anyone," C.J. said. "Or is that how you get your jollies, shorty?"

Cracker reeled around.

Chip Gunn emerged from the car. "Enough," he ordered, and stared at C.J. "You must understand, Mr. McDaniels, that my staff is a tad on edge after this afternoon's unfortunate altercation."

"Quite theatrical."

"Theatrical? My brother's dead and you call it theatrical?"

"Now you've got all the profits from the field of— what was it of, Neil?"

"Skeletons," I replied. "But I think he wants to unload it, something Gunter wouldn't hear of. Something Lamar Fowler overheard."

"Is there a point either of you are foolishly trying to make?"

"I'm reaching into my top pocket with two fingers," C.J. warned the thugs. "No piece there, only a point of interest."

They watched carefully as C.J. drew the Baggie out.

"I found your grass," he said, and tossed the pouch at Gunn's feet. "And I know you ordered Oakley's murder. I have a witness who put Jimmy and Cracker at the crime scene the day it occurred."

Gunn broke out in laughter. Cracker grinned. Jimmy stood as still as a sculpture designed to honor the Incredible Hulk.

"That's preposterous," Gunn said. "Next you'll accuse me of staging my own brother's death."

"Interesting thought," I commented.

Gunn glared so strongly at me, for a moment I feared he was going to order my execution.

"But why kill Oakley?" C.J. asked, gaining his attention.

"Because he was the connection to Dean Shriver's father," I spoke up. "At first I thought Dean had killed Oakley out of revenge, but now I believe he wanted to use him against you, Chip, and your brother to avenge his father's death."

"You can't hold me responsible for every drug addict's overdose," he said, shaking his head.

"If you'd waited a few more days, though, you wouldn't have had to blemish your record," I added. "Dean died, taking the threat away. You could've quietly dumped the pot operation and relocated Oakley someplace safe instead of killing him. You can't say you're not a murderer any-more, Chip."

The chuckling faded. "All politicians are killers of one sort or another," Gunn stated. "But you can't prove anything."

"I think we can," C.J. replied.

"Even if we can't, your campaign's over," I said. "The publicity from the investigation will kill your candidacy." *Warp speed away from reality.*

"Want me to ice them?" Cracker asked.

"Always knew it was in his blood," I commented.

Chip Gunn looked hard at me. "I can cause a lot of trouble for you."

"A man's got to know when to fold in order to hang in the game for another hand," I reasoned. Shades of Clint Eastwood, I thought. Wondered if I sounded as tough.

"I think this will be your last hand," he told me.

Guess I had to work on the toughness.

"I wouldn't have even been involved if you hadn't brought me in to do the fund-raiser," I pointed out, putting my hands on my hips. Slowly I began untucking my shirt-tail. The nervous sweat in which I was drenched didn't make the process easy.

"Life's not fair, Mr. Marshall."

"Gunn, you're going down for Oakley's murder," C.J. stated.

"No, McDaniels, you and Mr. Marshall are going down."

Cracker started for his gun. Samson barked. I ripped my shirttail out, reached behind my back. C.J. stood calmly, arms folded. Jimmy was almost oblivious to the situation.

"But not here," Gunn quickly added. "Not like this. Too messy. Too goddamn public."

"Wait until our backs are turned," C.J. prodded. "You'll be a hell of a Capitol Hill crusader."

"I think a nice drive-by shooting would be in order for you," Gunn told C.J. "Dramatic, anonymous—could be anyone from your sordid past."

"It's been tried."

"Try, try again." Gunn turned to me. "Drug overdoses appear to be making a comeback."

"Like Oakley?" I asked.

"The same. A healthy shot of heroin instead of insulin and voilà!"

I locked my knees so they wouldn't buckle. The thought of a needle sinking into my vein with that crap in a syringe was enough to put black spots before my eyes.

"Come to the killing game rather naturally," C.J. drawled. "Makes me think you're more experienced than you let on."

"I learned well from my brother," he said. "And once you've committed the act, one or one hundred times don't matter."

"So now that you've aced Oakley, Neil and I don't matter," C.J. clarified.

"Exactly," Gunn responded, eyes burning into C.J.

"Guess that says it all, then," C.J. announced loudly. He stood straight. Cracker stirred, glanced at Gunn.

"Only getting a cigarette, shorty," C.J. said.

"I'm going to do you myself, fat man," Cracker spat.

"Look forward to it." C.J. lit his cigarette.

Then suddenly there were cops everywhere.

"Everybody freeze!" Sergeant Hernandez cried. "Police. Don't move. Hands up where we can see them." He dashed up the driveway, gun outstretched. I caught sight of Linda circling in from behind the garage.

"You son of a bitch," Gunn said. "You were wired."

"See, you're not so stupid, Chip," C.J. responded.

"Hands up," Hernandez called.

Cracker pulled his hands up and brandished his gun. "I ain't going down like this," he said, and swung his gun around.

A wild shot went off in my direction. I dove down. As the gun wound toward C.J., Hernandez hollered for Cracker to drop it. Then suddenly Samson, ace guard dog, who was lunging as I fell, broke the tether. The powerful dog was on Cracker before anyone had half a chance to react.

Cracker's gun flew into the lawn. Screams emerged beneath growls. I bolted over.

"Samson," I commanded, and pulled at his collar. "No, no. Stop. Here, boy. Here." Amazingly, he obeyed, and sat next to me.

Cracker whimpered. The police paused a second in shock. Gunn and Jimmy both held their hands above their heads.

C. J. McDaniels stepped up to me. "Evidently I've misjudged this beast," he said, and scratched Samson on the top of his head.

"Haven't we all," I said, and watched. The officers patted down and cuffed Chip Gunn and big Jimmy. For good measure, I yanked the .45 from my back and slapped it into C.J.'s hand.

30

As I chewed out C. J. McDaniels for not letting me in on the setup ("Wanted you to act natural," was his explanation) and once again hanging me out as bait, the police hauled Gunn and his toughs away. We were to be key witnesses in the Oakley murder trial, then later for the feds when they busted open Gunn's marijuana operation. If Gunter was still alive, I'd have gone into the Witness Protection Program. But with the G brothers now history, we'd simply created an employment opportunity that sooner or later someone would move in to fill.

The police went so far as to make a case that Gunn had ordered the execution of Lamar Fowler. Gunn screamed that it was Mattie's doing, foolishly bringing up the stabbing at his house. The strategy backfired as the police suspected there was more to the story than Gunn was letting on, as he'd covered the incident up to begin with. Building the Fowler case against Gunn might have even worked, too, if I hadn't turned over the letter I received in Tuesday's mail.

Dear Neil,

If you're reading this scratch then I've left Turtle Island to join the great Kerouac in hipsters' heaven and was unable to lift it from your mailbox. Of course, if things went bust I could be in custody. I then leave this confession for you to do with as you wish.

I know you think my action was totally uncool, but

drastic bastards call for drastic visions. My mother told me not too long ago that two men had turned on my father, causing him to hitch the train to God's kingdom. Always knew the old man committed the big sin but never knew why. When I found out, I didn't swear almighty vengeance. I only felt bummed. And then I looked the men in the eyes and saw dark earth. The angel of death was injected into my veins.

Along this twisted path of destruction, I killed Lamar Fowler. He was a bad dude out to break Mattie. I caused her grief by stabbing the son of a bitch to begin with. So I had to finish it, partly to see if I could break the Lord's commandment. My doubt was serious, but my path was right on. I followed him from your pad, figuring he'd track Mattie to you. Big high five you kept her hidden. Waited with him in sight outside Mattie's place. Don't tell me I didn't freak when she showed. But I heard the shot, and watched Mattie split the scene.

I ran in. He was hurt, all right, and moaning. I had to work fast, knowing the blast would bring in the cops. When I knocked him across the head then put the bullet in him, I knew how it felt to kill. And I knew I could ace Gunn and Gunter, too.

If I'd had my way, I'd have taken him out of there to avoid connection with Mattie. I did my railroadin' best to pin the blame on Gunn and his evil brother.

Dig a safe journey through this bitchin' life, man. If I'm locked in the slammer, come see me. If not, I'll hold a chair for you at heaven's jazz bar. Tell Keely she's the hippest friend I had besides you.

Stay cool . . .

And it was signed Dean Shriver. Reading the dead man's words sent a ghostly tremble through my system. The thoughts and energy were so alive. But Dean wasn't. Lieutenant Gardner was partly irritated, as he wanted the double-murder rap against Gunn, and partly glad he could put the Fowler case to rest. After I got over the shock of reading Dean's last earthly message, I simply felt, as Dean would say, bummed.

"So much waste in this world," Keely said. After our weekly writers' circle, she asked me out for a drink. I retreated to an old comfort zone, and coaxed Keely off campus and over to The Ale House.

"I read the note. I feel the thoughts, but I still don't understand how he lost his equilibrium so easily." I rolled a mouthful of Newcastle Brown Ale across my tongue.

Keely delicately sipped a glass of white wine. "It's like the person who drives at breakneck speed down an old country road," she told me. "He knows another car or truck could be facing him around the next bend, but he continues to pick up speed. Part obsession. Part denial that anything bad could happen. A vicious circle that feeds on itself.

"Remember, Dean had an excessive appetite," Keely continued. "He spent half his time stoned. He was also very opinionated. No middle-of-the-road sentiments."

"And to top it off, there was some deep-seated resentment over his father's death," I added.

"All too much to handle, and he exploded."

A moment of silence, and then I said, "Alice thinks the worst Mattie will get is probation for leaving the scene of a crime. Other than that, Mattie's looking for a new apartment. Guess I'll spend this weekend helping her move in."

"What an ordeal."

"True, but Mattie's calmed down. She's in possession of the money from Lamar. I understand she's going to offer some to Alice, who might or might not take it— God knows she earned her keep. And Mattie's pledged to help Claudia while she goes through her ordeal."

"What a nice gesture," Keely commented.

After a strong suggestion, I thought. Life seldom affords

second chances, and I was glad Mattie realized she could help Claudia as well as herself.

I noticed my glass was empty, but didn't recall drinking the brew. The waitress stopped by.

"Want another one?"

"Sure." I glanced sideways at her. "And a bowl of peanuts, sweetheart."

"You're McDaniels's friend, aren't you?"

"Yeah."

"Then you know we don't have peanuts. God," Sweetheart muttered, walking away, "birds of a feather."

I couldn't help but grin.

"You have a nice smile," Keely said. "Whatever that was about."

"Thanks."

"I need to run soon."

"I figured."

"Mark's flying to Dallas tonight."

I nodded. "He travels a lot."

"Yes, he does." She sighed and finished her wine. The waitress set the ale down. "What are you going to do?"

"I've got my notebook in the car. Think I'll sit awhile and write."

"How bohemian." Keely opened her purse.

"I've got it," I said.

"I'm an independent woman." She dropped a five.

"No doubt."

She stood. "Astros in town?"

"Through Sunday."

"I owe you a game," she said. "How about tomorrow night?"

"That'd be nice," I replied, and toasted her with my ale.

Keely flashed a little finger wave, her winning smile, and strolled out of the rustic bar.

The ale tasted good. The jukebox kicked on and the throaty Tom Waits sang, "A sight for sore eyes . . ."

I closed my sore eyes a minute, leaned back. Writing wasn't what I really wanted to do at the moment. A light read might be good. Or take in a movie. The Astros would be fun, with Keely.

There was a thump on the table, and my eyes popped open. A small bowl of honey-roasted peanuts lay before me.

"I was saving them for the big guy," Sweetheart said, and winked. "But I reckon I can share some with you."

I smiled softly. "Thank you."

"Your friend leave?"

"To join her husband."

"Too bad." Sweetheart picked up Keely's wineglass and napkin and wiped the table. "You make a nice couple," she added.

"Thanks again for the peanuts."

"Knock yourself out, honey." And she drifted to another table.

I tossed a couple of peanuts into my mouth, chewed slowly, and chased them down with the brew. Simple pleasures. Enjoy the munchies. Relish the ale. Then it's home for a good night's sleep, I promised myself.

Yes. And when I awakened tomorrow I'd go for a long, long run.

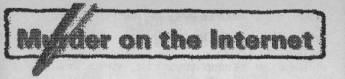
Murder on the Internet

Ballantine mysteries are on the Web!

Read about your favorite Ballantine authors and upcoming books in our monthly electronic newsletter MURDER ON THE INTERNET, at **www.randomhouse.com/BB/MOTI**.

Including:

🦋 What's new in the stores

🦋 Previews of upcoming books for the next three months

🦋 In-depth interviews with mystery authors and publishers

🦋 Calendars of signings and readings for Ballantine mystery authors

🦋 Bibliographies of mystery authors

🦋 Excerpts from new mysteries

To subscribe to MURDER ON THE INTERNET, send an e-mail to **srandol@randomhouse.com** asking to be added to the subscription list. You will receive the next issue as soon as it's available.

Find out more about whodunit! For sample chapters from current and upcoming Ballantine mysteries, visit us at **www.randomhouse.com/BB/mystery**.

TIM HEMLIN

"Tim Hemlin is a welcome new voice
in the mystery field."
—EARL EMERSON